THE CASE OF THE DISGRACED DUKE

A WISE Enquires Agency Mystery

by

Cathy Ace

FOUR TAILS PUBLISHING LTD.

The Case of the Disgraced Duke

ISBN 978-1-990550-03-4 (paperback)
ISBN 978-1-990550-04-1 (electronic book)
ISBN 978-1-990550-05-8 (hardcover)

Other works by the same author

(Information for all works here: **www.cathyace.com**)

The WISE Enquiries Agency Mysteries
The Case of the Dotty Dowager
The Case of the Missing Morris Dancer
The Case of the Curious Cook
The Case of the Unsuitable Suitor

The Cait Morgan Mysteries
The Corpse with the Silver Tongue
The Corpse with the Golden Nose
The Corpse with the Emerald Thumb
The Corpse with the Platinum Hair
The Corpse with the Sapphire Eyes
The Corpse with the Diamond Hand
The Corpse with the Garnet Face
The Corpse with the Ruby Lips
The Corpse with the Crystal Skull
The Corpse with the Iron Will
The Corpse with the Granite Heart
The Corpse with the Turquoise Toes

Standalone novels
The Wrong Boy

Short Stories/Novellas
Murder Keeps No Calendar: a collection of 12 short stories/novellas
Murder Knows No Season: a collection of four novellas
Steve's Story in "The Whole She-Bang 3"
The Trouble with the Turkey in "Cooked to Death Vol. 3: Hell for
the Holidays"

For Mum, with love

THURSDAY 20ᵀᴴ OCTOBER

CHAPTER ONE

Henry Devereaux Twyst, eighteenth Duke of Chellingworth, was terribly worried about his wife. His delight that her pregnancy appeared to be progressing without any real health concerns was profound; however, he was alarmed that his darling Stephanie had become fixated upon the hunt for what seemed to him to be an inordinate number of furnishings to fit out the new nursery she was intent upon planning for their soon-to-arrive offspring. Indeed, there seemed to be an entire outbuilding filled with pieces that were being treated for woodworm, repaired, and French polished.

He couldn't imagine why a 'new' nursery was even necessary; the one that had been his – and which had been used by several generations of his forebears – was in pretty good order, though he'd admitted it could probably do with a lick of paint. And maybe some new wallpaper. He'd said as much to his wife, but his comments hadn't been well received. The words 'lead' and 'arsenic' had been bandied about in relation to paints and inks, and that had been the end of that.

However, bearing in mind that Stephanie had spent a couple of months – or so it seemed – scrabbling around in dozens of dusty, generally-unused rooms at Chellingworth Hall, he was in the process of preparing himself to address her firmly about the matter; the baby might be adversely affected by her activities – after all, who knew how long some of the things she was hailing as 'perfect treasures' had been lurking in various unloved corners of the family pile.

He stood in the Long Gallery, looking out across the estate; the room offered a magnificent view of the lawns and floral beds, and even the walled garden beyond. He enjoyed the way the Capability Brown-designed landscape before him rolled toward the distant hills, and chuckled to himself as he acknowledged that the rain lashing against the windows was what kept those hillsides so green, and the sheep grazing them so well fed. Yes, Powys was, undoubtedly, a magnificent part of Wales; though he wondered if quite as much rain was necessary – it hadn't stopped for days.

Henry sighed. 'Into every life a little rain must fall,' he muttered under his breath. He turned and faced his predecessors' portraits, which lined the oak-panelled walls. 'I dare say I've had it a great deal easier than many of you, but I too feel the weight of the Chellingworth title.'

Stephanie's voice surprised him. 'Talking to yourself again, Henry?'

Her loving, if slightly mocking, tone made Henry smile as he turned, and his heart warmed at the sight of his wife's kind face, her sensible chignon and no-nonsense way of crossing a room. 'Not at all, I was just chatting with my father.' He nodded at the portrait on the wall closest to him.

Stephanie followed her husband's gaze. 'A fine man, I'm sure. He certainly raised a good son.'

Henry chuckled. 'If Mother's to be believed, my rearing was entirely the responsibility of Nanny.'

Stephanie held out her hand, which her husband took in his. 'Oh, come on, Henry – you know very well she only ever throws out that Nanny comment when she wants you to understand she disagrees with something you've said or done.'

Henry sighed as he pulled his beloved wife close. 'An effective ploy.'

'Well, don't let it get you down. Now – what did you want to talk to me about? Mrs Davies-Cleaner tracked me down in one of the rooms on the fourth floor and told me you were looking for me. She's stayed there to inspect a rather lovely chest of drawers for woodworm; I do hope it's not been got at too badly. I left her to it…so I could come to find out what you wanted . So – what is it?'

Henry felt a rumble grow in his tummy. Was he suddenly hungry? Or was it terror? Of his *wife*? He took a deep breath – it had to be said. 'I'm just a little concerned that all this activity – all this climbing of stairs, hunting about in rooms that haven't been in use for decades, all this shifting about of furniture – might be a bit much for the baby.' Too late, he realized what he'd said. 'For *you*, I mean. *You*. *And* the baby. *Both* of you. *Equally*.' He swallowed hard, wondering exactly what Stephanie's widening eyes signified.

The duchess smiled. 'My dear Henry, I'm not ill, I'm pregnant. We've had this conversation umpteen times, and I shall repeat what I've said before: I am a healthy woman, my pregnancy is normal, our child will be healthy. What I'm doing is not dangerous for me, nor for our baby. I don't move furniture myself – heaven knows we have enough staff to do that. But I do want to be the one who ensures this child is able to begin his or her life in the best possible way. I don't want to buy expensive and faddish items from fancy shops in Cardiff or London…I want to find the most practical and beautiful furnishings for what will be our firstborn's nursery from what's already here. And that room will be beside our own – not two floors away where it would be necessary to have another person tend to this little one.'

Stephanie rubbed her baby bump as she spoke, and Henry was tempted to do the same, but always felt it better to be invited to do so. Which he was. So he did. He was constantly amazed by the knowledge that a new life was coming into being, and that he and Stephanie would be parents probably before Christmas. He realized with a jolt that only a couple of months remained before the responsibilities of fatherhood would be added to those he already bore as a duke, and he felt his shoulders hunch a little.

It was already almost the end of October; from October until whenever Easter fell, Chellingworth Hall was closed to the public, which meant it was also when most of the necessary maintenance was carried out around the estate, so he'd been focussed on the repairs to the ornate plaster ceiling in the small sitting room which had begun a few weeks earlier, rather than upon his wife's condition. He rolled his eyes as he thought of Stephanie's response to his potential use of such a term.

'Henry, what's the matter?'

Henry shrugged. 'Nothing.' He'd wanted to say '*Everything*', but didn't have the heart, or gall, to do so.

As though she were reading his mind, Stephanie said quietly, 'You'll be a wonderful father, Henry. One day our child…this child…will stand here and gaze lovingly at your portrait, as you do at your own father's. Which reminds me – did your sister's chum ever get in touch…the portraitist she mentioned when she joined us for the harvest supper a few weeks ago?'

Henry's heart plummeted. 'Clementine's ability to propose her friends and acquaintances as suitable suppliers of various services is rarely matched by said friends' and acquaintances' ability or desire to do any such thing. She probably forgot to tell whomever it was she was talking about that we'd agreed now was a good time to consider having myself immortalized for this place.' He waved limply toward the surrounding walls.

'I dare say,' was Stephanie's response. 'But where would your portrait be displayed, Henry? Beside your father?'

Henry smiled. 'That would be expected. All the Chellingworths have been hung in order.'

Stephanie smiled. 'I understand what you mean.'

Henry realized why his wife was smiling and joined in.

Stephanie pecked her husband on the cheek. 'Right, I have to be off. Val Jenkins and the TV people are due to arrive in a quarter of an hour, and I want to tidy myself up, even though I know they'll want to put a bit of make-up on me before my interview.'

She tucked a stray whisp of her dark brown hair into her chignon as she spoke. Henry hoped they wouldn't plaster her lovely face with too much gloopy stuff; his wife was the sort of woman whose classic features were best left alone, he felt.

'They're back again?' Henry felt as though the chaos that accompanied the TV circus – as he liked to call it – was yet another thorn in his side.

'It's been a fortnight since they were last here to film the ceiling in the small sitting room as it was investigated by the specialist plaster restorers, and they said they'd be back today to record how the work is progressing. Hopefully they'll only be here for half the day, as planned. They'll be back again in another couple of weeks to film how it all looks – up close – before the scaffolding is removed, then again when the room's been redecorated and refurnished. You agreed to it all, Henry. You know you did. And the money they're paying us to do this – when taken with the fees we're receiving for the architectural magazine article – will cover about half the cost of the project. I've done my best to minimize the disruption, and with Val having been my chum since before I was even a duchess, as well as a close friend of the producer, it's almost all in the family.'

Henry sighed. 'I suppose so. Though why they have to keep coming and going, I don't know. What with all of them in the sitting room – as well as those plasterers being in and out of the Hall every day – I hardly feel as though we're closed to the public. At least they'll all be gone by Christmas.' Henry felt a knot in his tummy. 'They will all be gone by Christmas, won't they?'

Stephanie headed for the stairs. 'That's the plan, Henry. And it's only October, so please don't start fretting about Christmas already – we've only just put the harvest festival behind us, and we've still got a great deal of work to do on the nursery before Christmas – and our new arrival.'

Henry stared up at the portrait of his father, noted the way his own ruddy complexion matched that which the portraitist had captured, and shook his head. 'How I wish you were still here, to be our rock, like you always were.'

CHAPTER TWO

Annie Parker swirled the suds in the sink, and pulled out the plug. The water gurgled away as she wiped her hands on a tea towel. 'I've washed up the mugs and plates, Chrissy. Put 'em away when they're dry, eh? Ta. I'm off now. Said I'd drop in to see Mave and Althea at the Dower House on my way back to the village.'

Annie waited, hoping for a reply, but there was none. Gertie, her black Labrador puppy, was lying on the floor a few feet away; the puppy raised her head from her paws and whined, but didn't give her mistress much more attention than that, preferring to concentrate on the stuffed toy shaped like a giant bone that was currently the center of her world.

Annie mounted the first few steps of the spiral staircase that led to the apartment in the loft of the converted barn, which, on the ground floor, housed the office used by the WISE Enquiries Agency. 'Did you hear me, Chrissy? What are you doing up there?'

The Honourable Christine Wilson-Smythe's head was wrapped in a towel when it poked over the balustrade. 'Sorry, Annie – I was in the shower. Did you want me?'

'I said I've washed up the mugs, and I'm off to see Mave and Althea on the way back to my cottage. I need to pack before I leave for Swansea, and Mave's got some final instructions for me, she says. Though I'm the one who's been doing most of the talking to the clients, so I've no idea what she really wants.'

'Maybe she'll just remind you – one more time – to be careful on this assignment.' Christine rolled her eyes dramatically. 'You know what's she's been like since I got shot.' Her hand moved, unbidden, toward her arm.

Annie smiled warmly. 'Yeah, she's even more overprotective of us all than usual. But there, it's not every day that one of us takes a bullet, thank goodness. Though you think she'd know by now that I can look after myself.'

'Come on, Annie, you know very well *you're* the one doing this job because you're just grand at the undercover stuff. We all know how good you are at gaining a target's confidence, winkling information out of them, and getting yourself out of a tight spot if needs be. But, in this case, your job is to work out how a woman is managing to control a man to the extent that she's able to sell off his valuables – apparently with his consent. When his two daughters initially visited the office, they seemed truly worried about his health and wellbeing, not just the fact that his new girlfriend seems to be auctioning off their inheritance from under their noses. She sounds as though she's a tough nut who's onto a good thing. Could be dangerous, if cornered.'

Annie nodded. 'I know, I know. And I agree that our clients really did come over as being much more worried about their father, rather than just the stuff. Who knows what I'll find out when I get there, but, whatever it is, I'll be on my guard, doll. Promise.'

The women shared a smile and a wave. 'Right-o then, off I go,' said Annie, picking up Gertie's lead from her desk.

Christine leaned over the balcony as Annie attended to Gertie and her precious toy. 'Will you be seeing Tudor tonight, before you head off?'

Annie looked up and beamed. 'Yep. Dinner in his flat, not in the pub, then he'll drive me to Swansea tomorrow morning. Aled's going to look after the Lamb and Flag while Tude's on the road; I know he'll do a good job of it, as does Tudor…Aled's got an old head on those young shoulders of his. And Gertie will enjoy staying at the pub while I'm gone – Tude having Gert's sister Rosie there means they play nicely,' added Annie, as Gertie threatened to drag her out of the door. 'Hang on Gert, it's slippery out there in the rain,' she called. The pair skidded outside.

'Take care,' called Christine at the door as it slammed – but they were gone.

Returning to the bathroom, Christine Wilson-Smythe removed her robe, and examined the scar at the top of her arm in the mirror. It could have been a great deal worse, of course, but the wound the bullet had made was not insignificant, and she hoped that the deep, oily massage she was giving the whole area on a daily basis would mitigate at least the discoloration, over time. Her shiny, puckered skin wasn't sore any longer, and she wondered if maybe the dimensions of the lumpen mass were decreasing, ever so slightly. All she could do was hope. Fortunately, she'd only suffered what she'd often heard referred to in films as a flesh wound; no real damage had been sustained by her musculature or bones, which had allowed for an excellent prognosis.

As she washed oil off her hands, then returned the bottle to the medicine cabinet, she reminded herself that Alexander Bright (she hated it that her pulse quickened whenever she thought of him) kept telling her it was an 'interesting' scar, and that she'd be able to tell her grandchildren all about it, one day. She'd never allowed the conversation to veer toward the subject of whether it might be Alexander himself who would be the grandfather of those children, and had no intention of entertaining the topic, let alone the reality, for some time. They'd only known each other for about a year; hardly long enough for her to decide if he were the right man for her; though, on occasion, she was utterly convinced he was anything but.

Her thick, long, brunette hair finally dry, and her choice of a form-fitting, periwinkle blue cashmere dress made, she bounced down the staircase to the office below in excellent spirits; she was meeting Val and Stephanie at Chellingworth Hall for tea, and Alexander was due to join them when he arrived from London for the weekend – which, apparently, began for him on a Thursday.

She debated answering the office phone when it rang, but knew that, as one of the four partners who ran the agency – even though she hadn't fully returned to her duties – it was her responsibility to do so. Besides, a few minutes wouldn't matter, she told herself; her lack of punctuality was something she invariably managed to explain away with a winning smile.

'The WISE Enquiries Agency, how may I help?' Christine perched on a chair, and her mouth slowly formed an 'O' as she listened.

'I've phoned the police, and they've said there's nothing they can do. Can you pop by the shop and help me out? See, there's no real proof I even had it, let alone that it's gone. And they said even if I did have it, and it was all taken, it was probably kids. But I don't think it was. Mam says it couldn't have been, and I believe her, 'cos you know what she's like – she's usually right. Besides, what would kids want with it? So could you pop over, Carol, cariad, before you go home?'

Christine recognized the voice. 'Is that you, Sharon? It's Christine Wilson-Smythe here, not Carol. What's the problem – has something been stolen? From you? What was it? Is this something only Carol can help with, or will I do?'

Silence.

'Sharon?'

The voice that replied was hesitant, the previously chatty flow now halting, and unsure. 'Oh, hello there. I thought you'd be Carol. Yes…yes, it's Sharon here. At the shop. In the village. Yes…yes, it's me. Is…um…is Carol there, by any chance?'

Christine smiled as she replied, knowing that she and Sharon hadn't ever really had time to bond, and that – being the daughter of a viscount – she could sometimes be viewed as being one of 'The Hall' crowd as opposed to one of 'The Village' crowd. 'Carol's working from home today, Sharon. You could phone her there, or on her mobile. But I'm happy to help…if you think I can.'

Silence. 'Thanks…yeah, thanks…I'll phone Carol. Thanks.' Sharon disconnected.

Christine addressed the handset, 'I don't bite, you know,' then she shrugged, grabbed her coat from the stand near the door, and scampered through the rain to her Range Rover, which threw up pea gravel from the drive as she stamped on the accelerator, not wanting to get to the Hall any later than was absolutely necessary.

CHAPTER THREE

Althea Twyst, Dowager Duchess of Chellingworth, was snuggled into a large, comfortable armchair in the sitting room of her Dower House. She was napping. And snoring. Mavis MacDonald had allowed her to remain undisturbed for as long as possible; she knew the octogenarian hadn't slept at all well the night before, and also knew she'd need her strength for what lay ahead of the pair. A glance at her watch told her that the time for resting was over, however, because Ian Cottesloe would arrive in a quarter of an hour to drive the women to Chellingworth Hall itself. There they were to take tea with a television producer who was making some sort of documentary about one of the ceilings in the place. Mavis had some idea of what was going on, but – given her background as an army nurse, and current occupation as an enquiries agent – architectural restoration wasn't really her thing. Thus, she found it difficult to imagine that such a programme would interest her – though she admitted she'd probably watch it just because of the close connection to her current home, which was how she most definitely thought of the Dower House, despite the fact she was really there as the full-time guest of Althea, to whom she'd become attached during the past year or so.

Althea came-to a little grumpily, then beetled off to use the facilities before Ian arrived, just as Annie Parker presented herself at the front door. The greetings that ensued between Annie's puppy Gertie and Althea's aged Jack Russell, McFli, were – as usual – noisy and friendly, and both were sharing the delight of pulling at a wet and already rather ragged looking stuffed toy when Althea joined them.

Althea's eyes glinted wickedly as she asked, 'All ready for your undercover undertaking in the murky underbelly of Swansea, Annie? Nudge, nudge, wink, wink, know what I mean?'

Impressed by the dowager's ability to shoehorn a Monty Python reference into almost any situation, Annie laughed. 'Nice one, Althea.'

'Ach, there's no' much murkiness in the part of Swansea where she'll be working,' replied Mavis tartly, her Scottish brogue rolling delightfully. 'Though I'm no' familiar with it myself, I understand that Langland has pleasant beaches, a well-reviewed golf course, and some exceptionally delightful homes – one of which is owned by the father of our clients.'

Annie replied, 'Unless that new girlfriend of his has managed to sell it out from under him already.' She winked at the dowager as she spoke, and Althea's dimples puckered. 'She sounds like quite a piece of work – but you know I've got a good nose for a wrong 'un.'

Mavis piped up, 'And that's what I wanted to impress upon you before you're away: you're right, you've an instinct for the work we do at the agency, and your skills are more than up to par, but we need proof. Evidence of what she's doing. That's what we need. At least, that's what our clients need.'

Annie rubbed Gertie's wet head as she replied, 'I know, Mave. I've talked it through – in great detail – with each sister separately, and with both of them together: the police have made it clear they can't do anything because – as far as they're concerned – Frank Turnbull is giving his live-in girlfriend his permission to offer certain of his possessions for sale via various online forums. The fact that his daughters believe he's suffering from some sort of dementia, and that he's so gaga that this "floosie" – as they refer to Jeanette Summers, said live-in girlfriend – is able to talk him into agreeing to anything she wants is not something the police are able to act upon. It doesn't matter that she's sold a load of their late-mother's jewellery, and all manner of other family heirlooms; Frank Turnbull's told the local bobbies it's all kosher. So, unless his daughters can prove that Jeanette Summers really is some sort of con artist, the cops are out of it. Which is why his daughters are now our clients. I absolutely understand the need for evidence, Mave – and I also understand the sort of evidence we need to give to our clients to pass to the local uniforms.'

Mavis nodded sagely, and McFli presented himself to Annie, clearly feeling he, too, needed to be petted.

'You've the experience required to handle this job successfully, I know,' said Mavis to her colleague, 'but I'll remind you, once again, about the need to keep good records. I admire your abilities, Annie, but I'm no' oblivious to your shortcomings. Paperwork, my dear. Paperwork. It'll all come in useful, and no' just for preparing the invoices for the clients.'

Annie sighed as she stood. 'Yeah, Mave, I know, doll. Tell her not to worry, eh, Althea? And you two enjoy all the folderol up at the Hall; I was talking to Tude about it earlier today – he said a few of the telly people had an early lunch at the Lamb and Flag, so at least there's one person who's pleased they keep coming back.'

'Ach, they'll only be here until the end of the afternoon, so they say,' remarked Mavis.

'And Ian will arrive presently to drive us over,' said Althea. She gazed vaguely around the sitting room. 'Indeed, he should have been here already. What's become of him? He's usually reliable.'

Mavis tutted. 'Given that the Gilbern Invader you force him to drive you about in was manufactured in 1970, and must, by now, be held together by wishes and willpower, maybe he's no' able to get the old thing going, my dear.' She disliked the car, and found it uncomfortable, but understood – grudgingly – that Althea wanted the rare vehicle her late-husband had once given her as a wedding anniversary gift to remain as a functioning means of transport.

'It, too, is most reliable. Usually,' observed Althea, sounding more than a bit miffed.

'Aye, well, it has its moments,' was Mavis's pithy response.

Althea sniffed. 'As do we all, Mavis. As do we all.'

Mavis arched an eyebrow, and Annie saw her chance to escape. 'Right-o, I'm off. Wish me luck, and cross your fingers this Jeanette Summers is as thick as two short planks, and gives herself away within five minutes of me meeting her.'

Mavis waggled a finger in Annie's direction as she admonished, 'Now don't you go thinking she's a stupid woman, Annie; we know she's cunning enough to be doing what she's doing and getting away with it. We've had conversations about how she might have been doing this for some time, moving from one elderly mark to another – so think on that; she's clearly charming, and believable enough that she's been able to win over at least one gentleman. Take care.'

'Byeee!' Annie dragged Gertie away from McFli and into the entry hall, where Ian Cottesloe was standing, dripping on the ancient, tiled floor. 'Gordon Bennett! Look what the cat dragged in. Is it raining that bad now?'

Ian shook his head. 'Not really – but I've been out in it for a while. Couldn't get the blessed car to start, could I? All alright now, it seems. Which is a relief. Her Grace might have to do without it for a while, soon, though; I think it's time for a significant bit of work to be done on the electrics. This weather plays havoc with them.'

Annie peered through the half-open front door; it wasn't bucketing down, but she was going to be wet through by the time she made it back to her cottage in the village. 'Ah well, no use putting it off. Here we go, Gert – and mind you don't trip me up in the lane.'

'Enjoy Swansea,' called Ian, as Annie hovered on the doorstep and considered braving the elements.

Annie waved her reply to Ian and said quietly, 'Sounds like everyone here knows I'm off to do some so-called secret, undercover work, Gert…which is funny when you think of it.'

Gertie barked her agreement, picked up her scruffy toy, and carried it proudly as the pair made their way along the winding lane that would deliver them to the center of the village of Anwen-by-Wye. There, Annie knew her little cottage would be warm and welcoming…and half her wardrobe's contents would be spread across her bed, because she'd been unable to decide upon exactly what should be worn by a woman seeking employment as a live-in carer in one of the posher stretches of the Welsh coast.

CHAPTER FOUR

'Hiya, Sharon, what's up?' Carol Hill answered her mobile phone as she sat at her kitchen table, surrounded by laundry, and paperwork. Albert, her infant son, was gurgling happily as she bounced him on her knee.

'Oh *Duw*, Carol, I just spoke to that Christine at your office and she must think I'm *twp*. I thought I was talking to you, see, but it was her. What'll she make of it all?'

Carol paused her bouncing, but continued to snuggle Albert as she replied, 'Well, that depends on what you said to her, I suppose. But she doesn't bite, you know. She's quite normal – just like you and me.'

'But she's posh, Carol – not like you and me at all. Besides, she doesn't know me like you do; we see each other almost every day, what with you coming over to the shop so often or taking Albert for a walk past here, and what-not. Besides, you're Welsh, like me…well, like almost everyone around here, this being Wales, you know. And she's…well, I know she's Irish really, but she's such posh Irish she sounds English, if you know what I mean. Not that she's said much to me, really. Hasn't needed to.'

Carol sighed – if only people in Anwen-by-Wye knew Christine like she did, they'd think of her differently; Carol had met Christine years earlier at a networking event for female executives in the City of London, and they'd clicked – despite Carol having been brought up on a sheep farm in Carmarthenshire, and Christine being the daughter of an Irish viscount. She wondered what Sharon would have made of her and Christine, and Annie, when they'd all been commuting to their jobs in the City, rather than knocking about in a picturesque village in the Wye Valley.

Carol dragged her thoughts away from memories of long evenings spent in noisy wine bars that sold horrifically overpriced Chardonnay, to her present life. 'So…what did you say to her, then, Sharon? Why the call?'

'Oh, yes…right. Well, that's the thing, see, it's all gone, from the shed. Not one jar left. And the police said they couldn't help right away – because there's something happening in Brecon tonight that means they're having to close a load of roads, and that's not really fair, is it? Besides, they think it'll have been kids, which Mam thinks is *twp*, because what would kids want with it?'

'What would kids want with what, Sharon? What's missing?'

'All the preserves. In the shed. From the harvest supper. Gone. Not a jar left. See? What would kids want with pickles and jams and marmalades? Mam's got a point, hasn't she?'

Sharon's tone suggested that Carol should have known what she was talking about.

'Hang on a second, Sharon,' said Carol, squeezing the phone between her cheek and her shoulder. She plonked Albert into what her husband insisted upon calling 'his padded cell' – though Carol herself preferred to think of it as his safe-zone – then dropped a collection of brightly-colored cloth rings in with her son, so he could entertain himself. 'So you're talking about all those pickles and what-not that were entered into the preserving competition at the harvest supper?'

Sharon sighed dramatically. 'Yes. It's what happens every year; competitors submit ten jars of whatever it is they're entering, one of the jars is picked at random and gets judged, then the other nine all come to the shop where they're sold to raise money for local causes. This year the money was going to pay for a coach to take the village kids to Tenby for a day trip, after Easter. There were a lot of entries this year, so I had a couple of hundred jars in there.'

'A couple of hundred?' Carol sounded as amazed as she was.

'Yeah, I know, it's great, isn't it? Except that they've all gone.' Sharon sounded deflated. 'Can you help? I mean…you know…sort of as a friend. I…I mean we, you know, the organizing committee, we don't really have any money, you see. I know you and your lot are professional investigators – but, well, I suppose I'd be asking for a bit of a favor. As a friend.'

Carol was touched by how hesitant Sharon was being – not wanting to take advantage of a friendship, but really needing to, by the sounds of it. She decided on her best course of action. 'You say you've phoned the police about it? I mean, it's theft, they can act on that.' Carol was always mindful of the absolute rule they had at the agency: any police matters were to be handed to the police.

'The woman I spoke to said they're all in Brecon, like I said. They can't do anything.'

Carol weighed her reply. 'Well, how about you phone them again tomorrow, Sharon? I'm sure they'd all be back from their traffic duties by then. Maybe they'd send someone to take a look. You'd at least be able to file a proper report that way. I'm not sure that – until you've done at least that much – the agency could get involved, even as a favor.'

What Carol was really thinking was she knew very well that Mavis would have her guts for garters if she said anything else, and that she herself was already feeling a bit overwhelmed by a fast-turnaround case she was working on, that called for a deep dive into the background of a man who'd said he had the money to buy up a chain of hairdressing salons that extended across the whole of mid and south Wales. His aggressive, and apparently patronizing, attitude had annoyed the woman looking to sell her business so much she'd been prepared to pay the agency to check his credentials and creditworthiness with rather more depth and deliberation than would usually be the case. Annie – who was the one who always came up with the best names for all the agency's cases – had dubbed this one The Case of the Aggressive Acquisition.

Sharon sounded disappointed when she replied, 'But it's for the kids, Carol. And that's why I know it's not village kids who've taken it all – it was announced at the harvest supper that everything we raised was to go towards the day trip.'

Carol looked down lovingly at her son, then cast her eyes across her kitchen table, *aka* her desk. Her husband David was away at a conference in Brighton for computer systems managers, and she was feeling the pinch. 'I tell you what, I'll run it past Mavis, and see if she can drop by to take a look. Or maybe Christine could do it…though she isn't supposed to be working full time at the moment; she's still not a hundred percent, really. With David away, and me already on a deadline for a client in Aberystwyth, I think that's the best I can offer at the moment. How about that?'

'Oh, you're a star, you are,' gushed Sharon. 'I haven't touched anything, and I won't – I watch enough of those forensics things on the telly to know that. When will Mavis come, do you think?'

Carol panicked. 'To be honest, I don't know if she'll come at all, let alone when. I can't promise anything, see? I know she's up at the Hall this afternoon…'

'Of course! The telly people are there today, aren't they? I'd forgotten that. See? That's how much this has upset me.'

'I tell you what, let's assume she can't come today – so you try to get the police to show an interest by phoning them again in the morning, and I'll fill Mavis in, and we'll take it from there. Alright?'

'Fantastic! I'll see you and Mavis in the morning then. Got to go, got a customer.' Sharon shouted a greeting that got cut off, so Carol had no chance to put her right.

'Oh no, what's your Mam gone and got herself into now?' Bending to pick up her son, Carol couldn't help herself – she laughed aloud. 'That's it…that's right…your Mam's got herself in a bit of pickle! Oh – I bet that's what Annie would call this…The Case of the Purloined Pickles. Loves a bit of alliteration, does Annie.' Albert gurgled appreciatively at his mother's observations, and Carol kissed him for it.

CHAPTER FIVE

'But of course he must join us for tea,' said Stephanie to her friend Val Jackson, referring to the documentary producer. Turning her attention to the man in question, she added, 'Wouldn't you enjoy the chance to have a poke around the famous Chellingworth Library, Barry? It's never open to the public – too many opportunities for the books to sustain some dreadful damage, you see. A significant restoration project was completed earlier in the year; maybe His Grace could talk you through the finer points of the work that was undertaken.'

Henry didn't dare glare at his wife, though she suspected he'd have liked to, if his heightened color was anything to go by. Instead, he blustered, 'Not really my area of expertise, the architectural stuff, but I do know a great deal about the books. So many of them are works of art in their own right.' He smiled, and rolled on the balls of his feet.

Barry Walton was a small, bespectacled man, dressed in jade green jeans and an over-large Aran sweater; he looked uncertain, glanced at the phone in his hand, then looked alarmed. 'Time's pressing on, and I'd like to get back to London at a reasonable hour...' He licked his lips, thoughtfully, several times, then added, 'However, if there were a chance to have a look at the Chellingworth Bible, I'd be most interested. I've heard of it, of course, but to see it would be a treat.'

Henry brightened. 'Then see it you shall. I'll get Edward, our butler, to fetch some gloves for us after he's served tea, and we can browse at our leisure. It's a most fascinating tome...both rare, and exquisite. Shall we?'

Stephanie was relieved that her husband's mood had lightened; he'd scowled the entire time he'd been hovering at the door to the small sitting room where she'd been interviewed on camera, and he'd been hard-pressed to display any signs of true welcome toward the television crew.

As Henry and the producer made their way toward the library, Stephanie pulled at her friend Val's arm to signify she should hold back.

'Everything alright, Steph?' Val's expression was one of concern. 'All going well with the baby?'

Stephanie sighed. 'I'm fine. The baby's fine. I wish everyone would stop treating me as though I'm made of glass.'

Val smiled. 'Sorry – though it would be lead crystal now, in your case, wouldn't it, Your Grace?' She pulled at one of her rather wild, short, dark curls as though it were a forelock, and winked. 'Henry? First-time father problems? Not that I've any personal experience of such things, of course, but friends of mine who already have kids tell me that expectant dads can be quite tiring.'

Stephanie nodded. 'He means well, but you know Henry – he's never happier than when he's worried about something, and I'm an easy target for his concerns at the moment. But that's not what I wanted to talk to you about. It's this: how would you feel about becoming our child's godmother? I know you've got a bit of a jaundiced view of the church, because of your father's fondness for his, but I'd really like our child to have someone in their life who's accepted by all as having a formal role, but who's not...um...'

'Titled? Posh? Head so far up their own backside they wouldn't know whether the sun's shining or not?'

Stephanie laughed. 'Well, let's not forget I've got my parents to help with that too, but, yes, in a nutshell, you're right. I want someone who's Welsh, not English, and local, not living miles away like Mum and Dad are, in Spain. Someone who's normal, but also maybe just a little more worldly wise than a lot of the folk around here. You've done so well for yourself, Val, with your *Curious Cook* TV series, the books you've written, and how you made the Cooks and Crooks bookshop in Hay-on-Wye a real draw for people. You know what's what. That would be good for a child.'

Val Jenkins nibbled her lip. 'I'm flattered to be asked, of course, especially considering that laundry list of requirements you just rattled off' – she grinned at her old chum – 'but honestly, I'm not sure I'm well suited to be anyone's godmother. It's not just that I've been adversely affected by Dad's passion for his church, but I'm not the most religious of people in any case. Though I hope I respect dedicated Christians sufficiently well to know there's a specific role for a godparent in any child's life…which I don't think I'm up to.'

Stephanie rubbed her chum's arm as she said, 'Thanks for being honest, Val. But please think about it for a bit? I'm not under any pressure to offer up a shortlist yet, but that day can't be long in coming. Even if Henry doesn't see the necessity, I know Althea will be all over it – and possibly sooner rather than later.'

Val looked alarmed. 'A shortlist? Good grief, will I have to audition?'

Stephanie laughed airily and replied, 'Of course not – now come on, I could kill for a cuppa.'

As the women headed to join the rest of the group in the library, the Duchess of Chellingworth was thinking to herself, *This tea with Althea means you're already auditioning, Val, but maybe it's best you don't know that.*

'There you are – we wondered what had become of you both,' exclaimed the dowager when Stephanie and Val arrived at their destination. 'You'd better tuck in, or there might not be any cake left,' she added, eyeing up the remains of a large Victoria sponge on the sideboard.

Stephanie grinned; her mother-in-law's sweet tooth was a constant source of amazement to not just herself, but the entire staff at the Hall. She also knew her husband was concerned that diabetes might rear its head at any time, given Althea's constant nibbling of biscuits, indulgence in cakes, pastries, and desserts – as well as her habit of always having a few boiled sweets in the pockets of whatever she was wearing.

Stephanie replied, 'I'm not sure I could face a piece at the moment, but maybe a shortbread biscuit with a strong cup of tea will be just the ticket.'

Henry was immediately at her side. 'You're feeling quite well, are you, my dear?'

Stephanie sighed. 'Just tickety-boo, thanks, Henry. Both me, and the baby.' She managed to stop herself from rolling her eyes toward Val, who was settled on a leather armchair, blushingly allowing herself to be attended to by Edward.

The group was large enough that chatter among the entire gathering wasn't practical, especially given that the library had never been designed to host tea parties; the furnishings were dotted about the place. Althea and Mavis had been joined by Val – who lavished attention upon McFli – to take advantage of the warmth offered by the fire; Stephanie had been joined by Christine – who'd arrived just in time to stake her claim to the penultimate slice of sponge – and they were seated beneath one of the tall, shaded windows; Barry Walton and Henry were huddled over the Chellingworth Bible, both wearing white cotton gloves, with Henry turning the ancient pages slowly, and taking great pride in explaining the history of the book, which was over five-hundred-and-fifty years old, having been created by Dominican monks in the mid-fifteenth century, one of only two volumes of its type in the world.

A natural lull in the various conversations allowed the television producer's voice to ring out clearly when he commented to his host, 'I'm surprised the thirteenth duke didn't sell it, to support his addictions and predilections. I know he ran through a great deal of the family's wealth before he killed himself. Probably couldn't cope with the guilt, eh?'

Althea Twyst paused, her bone china cup hovering in mid air; Henry's back became rigid. He closed the Bible with great care, peeled off his gloves, and stuffed them into his pockets. His guests, and his wife, exchanged puzzled glances.

Eventually Val said, 'What do you mean, Barry? Are you talking about the thirteenth duke of *Chellingworth*?'

The producer's expression when he turned to face the room revealed he had absolutely no idea of the reaction his original comments had caused. 'Yes. The thirteenth. The Disgraced Duke – that's what he's known as, right? Or sometimes he's called The Batchelor Duke…which was probably more of a rarity than a disgraced one in those days.' He chuckled jovially, only then appearing to realize that both his host, and his host's mother, were absolutely not amused.

Henry said firmly, 'The family never speaks of the thirteenth. Correct, Mother?'

Althea sat very upright. 'Indeed, Henry, we do not. A blight on the family, and a dreadful man, by all accounts. Enough said.'

Stephanie stared at her husband, then at his mother, then at the television producer. 'Barry, tell me more about this man, my unborn child's ancestor.' She spoke as firmly as her husband had done.

It appeared as though Barry wished his sweater was even larger than it was, so that he could disappear into it. 'Oh, far be it from me to…elaborate…not really my place…but it's a fascinating story – I've been giving some serious thought to it…it might well prove of interest to viewers, you see. But if the duke and dowager don't wish…'

Stephanie put down her cup and saucer, and stood. 'Very well, then, Henry – tell me, now. I know of no scandals attached to any of your forebears, not beyond those which inevitably exist for every family of this type due to the fact it's had land, money, and a title for hundreds of years. What makes the thirteenth duke stand out from the crowd? Just spit it out, Henry.'

Henry addressed the carpet. 'He *was* known as The Batchelor Duke, even during his day. Not a lot of dukes remain without a wife and heir for very long, as you observed, Barry. Had a bit of a wild reputation. Potty about plants. Built the gardens as we see them now – the parts with beds and walls, in any case – not the general layout, because, as we all know that was done earlier, by Capability Brown.'

'When was he duke?' Stephanie retook her seat, Althea wriggled forward in hers.

'1835 to 1856,' replied the television producer with a half-smile that suggested he was trying to be helpful, though it made Stephanie realize the man had done more than a little research into her husband's ancestor.

'Indeed? Interesting times,' replied Stephanie. 'And? Simply not getting married, and planting a garden, don't sound like actions that would lead to a duke's "disgrace". So, what else did he do?'

Henry swallowed, took a deep breath and gabbled, 'It was a scandal. Terrible. Ostracized by his peers, and it's been said that the locals actually took up arms against him. The thirteenth duke hid here, at Chellingworth Hall, for several years after it all happened – never leaving the place. It was even rumored that he had to employ English servants and so forth, because none of the locals would set foot upon the entire Chellingworth Estate.'

Stephanie stared at her husband. 'And what, exactly, was so scandalous that it led to the thirteenth duke being ostracized and attacked?'

Henry's neck flushed red, then his words tumbled out. 'Rumor has it he killed two men, buried them somewhere on the estate, then, after years of hiding away, he finally killed himself.'

Stephanie's eyebrows shot up. 'He *really* killed two men and buried them here…or was it all just gossip, with no truth in it?'

Henry studied the fireplace, not meeting his wife's gaze. 'Possibly, yes. Or maybe not. There was a cartoon in *Punch* magazine about it at the time – quite a notorious cartoon, apparently. It showed him digging two graves, covered in the blood of his victims, and screaming that he'd bury the evidence where it would never be found. To be honest, I'm not terribly clear about it all beyond that – given that he's never been spoken of, openly, within the family. I'm so sorry I didn't tell you when I proposed, my dear…or even before. It's not something our family is proud of, indeed it's a stain upon our line. But there you have it – a killer's blood runs through my veins.'

He glared at the television producer who was sidling toward the door.

Stephanie sighed and crossed the room to hug her husband. 'Dear Henry, I can see this bothers you a great deal. Does the secret of this disgraced duke weigh heavily upon you?'

Henry nodded. 'It does. Always has. Did upon my father, too.'

Stephanie sounded amazed as she replied, 'But you don't know the full story? You don't know if he actually killed two people – or, if he did, why he might have done so? Nor if their remains are *really* buried somewhere on the estate?'

Henry shook his head. 'Frederick, the thirteenth, had no heir, so it was his cousin, Harold, who assumed the title. *He* knew what had happened; carried out an investigation at the time, they say. It was he who passed the facts to his son, and the story has come down from there, orally, but that's all I know…all my father would tell me, at least. Maybe he told Deveraux more, my big brother being the one who should have inherited the title, if only he hadn't died because of stupid measles. But even then, Father had a couple of years when he could have filled me in, had he wanted to, or had he known more himself. But he didn't, so that's all I know. And it's a dreadful knowledge to carry with one, secretly, not being able to discuss it. And Mother knows no more than I, isn't that right?' Henry looked at his mother whose expression was pinched.

Rather than reply to her son, Althea said, 'I can see that Mr Walton is anxious to begin his journey back to London, so let's all wish him a safe trip. I'm sure he'll understand that private family matters such as this should remain so.'

The producer had his hand on the door. His expression conveyed a mixture of nervousness and gratitude as he replied, 'But of course, Your Grace. Your Graces. I didn't mean to cause concern. I honestly only mentioned the matter because I came across some stories about him when I was doing my research into the history of this house…this seat. I truly thought that the information being readily available within the public domain meant it was something the family would have come to terms with a long time ago, which was why I felt able to mention it. So sorry…yes, I'll get going. See you in couple of weeks for the next…um…yes…maybe we could talk more about the thirteenth duke then…' He slipped through the door and pulled it shut behind him.

Val stood. 'Would you like me to leave? Time for family only?'

Christine also rose. 'But of course,' she added.

Mavis didn't budge.

Stephanie waved at Val. 'Stay, Val, and you too, Christine…we're all as good as family here. Besides, it seems "the public" knows more about my child's ancestors than I do, so I can't see how having a conversation about a man who died the better part of two hundred years ago can hurt anyone. Correct, Henry?'

Henry stared at his mother, who glared back at him. 'I don't really know anything else,' he all but whimpered. 'I don't know what Barry meant by there being public information available about the thirteenth duke. As I said, Father told me almost nothing. I recall the day the topic arose in most detail: we were in the Long Gallery at the time, and we were talking about each of the dukes, in turn, as we examined their portraits. Father had to explain why the title had passed through a cousin, of course, largely because it was the fourteenth duke who gifted his significant chin to the family, which – as we all know – has made its presence known even to my own generation. He was the one who stepped into the breach, and investigated the truth of it all. Unfortunately, he only lasted a few years, and was himself said to be somewhat bitter about having to give up his own rather comfortable existence to take on the responsibilities of a publicly besmirched title. His son was called back from his life as a mariner to become the fifteenth duke, it seems, and felt a similar antipathy toward the thirteenth.'

Stephanie sounded annoyed when she said, 'Right then, so the people who investigated the thirteenth duke bore a grudge against him? In that case there's nothing for it, but we'll have to carry out our own enquiries. Not knowing what really happened is not an acceptable state of affairs: I want to know the full story – inside and out – so we can tell our child why his or her ancestor is known beyond this family as "The Disgraced Duke". Or else we are able to restore the thirteenth duke's reputation and lay the rumors to rest, once and for all.'

Henry bleated, 'But what if it's true? What if we discover he *was* a murderer, who was found out by the locals, and took his own life, wracked with guilt? What then? If we discover that's the truth of it, that's a good deal worse than merely suspecting it to be the case.'

Stephanie's eyes shone in the firelight, her head was held high. 'The truth needs to be unearthed, Henry. We owe it to our child. And look, Mavis and Christine are right here, on the spot – two professional investigators…sorry, I know you prefer the term "enquiry agents", Mavis. So let's all put our heads together and come up with a plan. When Barry Walton returns, I want to be able to present him with *all* the facts, whatever they might be…because you can put money on our conversations here this afternoon being replayed in any number of pubs around London for the next couple of weeks – and that's not at all a good thing. Nor is the fact that Barry's interest has probably been piqued by our reactions here today.'

Henry sagged as he took a seat in a corner. His wife was right, of course.

CHAPTER SIX

'Really, Tude, I've got to get going. My suitcase in't going to pack itself, and I want an earlyish night to be fresh when you pick me up in the morning. You're the one who wants to get going by nine, so you've got to let me have me beauty sleep.'

Tudor Evans reached across to touch Annie Parker's hand; beneath the table Gertie and Rosie seemed to sense a change in the mood, and two heads popped out – one black, one yellow – sniffing for scraps.

'First of all, you don't need any beauty sleep, Annie, and secondly, I only suggested we head off early so we've got a chance to have a spot of lunch beside the sea before your assignment begins. I've read about a new little place overlooking Swansea Bay – almost literally on the sand; their menu's been getting a lot of praise in the local press, so I thought I'd like to take a look for myself at how they do things. You know, presentation, that sort of stuff; I'm not afraid to admit there's a new trick or two out there I could learn.'

Annie smiled as her heart warmed. 'That's the sort of comment that might make me refer to "old dogs", Tude, but I know what you mean. And good for you; your pub's got a good reputation locally, but all of this "destination dining" thing might not hurt, neither. It's a lovely run out this way; folks might come for the drive if they knew there was a great place to have a bite before they head off again…either home, of maybe to the Hall, when it's open. Lunch here, tea there, that sort of thing.'

Tudor nodded. 'Exactly. So – fancy a nightcap before I walk you home? I know we agreed we're both too full for afters, but what about a nice Irish coffee? Sweet, and it'll help you sleep; decaf coffee, of course.'

Annie gave the idea some thought. 'Nah, Tude, I'm chock-o-block. Your shepherd's pie in't just the stuff of legends, it's also the most filling thing I can imagine. And you don't need to walk me home, doll, I can mange to cross the village green on me own, ta…though it's so wet tonight I think me and Gert will be walking around the green, not across it, 'cos it's going to be no more than a muddy mess.'

Tudor settled back into his seat. 'Not only do I enjoy accompanying you home, but it'll give me a chance to give Rosie her walk, too. Two birds, one stone, that sort of thing.' He grinned and winked, leading Annie to tut loudly.

'Know how to make a girl feel special, don't you? And yes, I'm well aware I'm stretching the "girl" thing beyond its breaking point. But there – with both of us in our fifties, we're far enough over the hill to agree we're going to do all we can to enjoy the trip down the other side, right? At least, I know I am.'

'And I couldn't hope for anyone better to share the ride with – even if it's a bit of a bumpy one.'

Annie mugged a frown. 'Oi, what do you mean a bumpy ride? I'm the easiest-going person I know – not a bump in me.'

Tudor laughed heartily. 'Says the woman who's just about to lie her face off to all and sundry so she can find out if some poor old bloke is being ripped off by a glamorous, young gold digger. No bumps? You? Sometimes you're nothing but bumps, Annie Parker.'

'Got any more compliments tucked up that sleeve of yours, have you? Look, I know that being brought up in the East End of London means I might be a bit more ready than the born-and-bred locals to speak my mind, and you know how hard it is for a Townie to fit in out here in the wilds because you're one yourself. But, bumpy? Me? Come on, Tude, you know I've got to tell the odd porky or two when I'm undercover, and this job's an important one. The Case of the Suspicious Sisters – which is what I've chosen to name it, by the way – will be a challenge, I know, but this is the part of the job I love best. If this woman's doing to our clients' father what they think she is, then she deserves to be stopped, *and* she should have to pay for what she's done. It's not nice, taking advantage of older folk. It won't be too long before we're both in our dotage, and how would you feel if some young woman came along and charmed you out of everything you own?'

Tudor chuckled. 'Tough question, that...I might be happy to be charmed by some bright young thing when I'm feeble and all alone. But there wouldn't be much for her to get out of me, and I don't think now that I'll be alone in my "dotage", after all. But that's one of the things that makes me love you, Annie – that you feel so passionately about your work.'

Annie froze. The silence that enveloped the pair was intense. Tudor had never before said that he loved her. Did he mean he *loved* loved her, or that he loved her like a friend?

Annie panicked, and all her defence mechanisms kicked in at once; she pushed back her chair, scraping it across the ancient wooden floorboards, and stood to her full five-eleven. 'Come on, Gert, let's get you home. This one wants to get me drunk on Irish coffee and take advantage of me afterwards, no doubt, when he hardly knows me. Can't have that, can we, my girl? You stay and clear up, Tude. I'll see you in the morning. Thanks for dinner, it was lovely. Come on, Gert.'

Annie had made it across the small room in two long strides, was already pulling on her coat and waggling Gertie's lead as she finished speaking, and was down the stairs before Tudor had a chance to say goodnight. She stopped to attach Gertie's lead to her collar just before stepping out into the horizontal rain, which at least cooled her face, though it didn't help with the hot flash running down her back and making her feel both helpless, and annoyed.

As she quick-marched her surprised puppy along the road she shouted above the wind, 'What do you think he meant, Gert? Love...or *love?*' Gertie chose to keep her opinion to herself.

FRIDAY 21ST OCTOBER

CHAPTER SEVEN

Albert Hill had bawled through the night, and it seemed he was intent upon bawling through the morning, too. Unable to pacify him any other way, Carol had finally resorted to strapping him into his seat in the car and had spent the last couple of hours driving him along country lanes with Tom Jones's Greatest Hits on the CD player, because that was all that seemed to quieten her son. She'd realized, about a quarter of an hour earlier, that she'd reached the point when even one of her favorite songs grated on her nerves, but reducing the volume of the CD player led to an increase in volume from her son, so she kept it turned up, and did her best to tune it out.

Just as the now overly-familiar opening bars of 'Delilah' began again, Carol noticed she'd need to fill up with petrol before too long, so she took the next turning, and headed for the nearest pumps she knew of, wondering how Albert would react when she switched off the engine, thereby robbing him of his entertainment. But she decided she'd cross that bridge when she got to it. And getting to it was going to be no easy task; the narrow road ahead appeared to be blocked – a snaking queue of cars stretched around the next bend, their brake lights gleaming red through the heavy rain.

'Oh no, Albert – a traffic jam? We don't need that, do we? No, we do not.' Carol spoke softly as she peered at her son's finally peaceful face. She felt the love swell inside her – those cheeks, those fingers, he was absolutely adorable – when he was asleep.

The next twenty minutes were spent nudging along, with Carol's anxiety increasing exponentially when the warning light told her she was truly short of petrol. She tried to calm herself by imagining her husband telling her he'd happily drive all the way to Brecon with that much in the tank, but she felt an enormous relief when she eventually pulled up beside a pump.

She didn't take her eyes off Albert as she turned off the ignition; he didn't stir. As she unfolded herself beside the car she was startled to be tapped on the shoulder.

'I thought it was you.' Marjorie Pritchard was dripping wet, and beaming madly. Carol's heart sank as she shut her door as quietly as possible; Marjorie's reputation as the ultimate village sergeant major was well-deserved, and Carol wondered what instructions were about to be barked in her face. Indeed, she wondered why on earth Marjorie was at the petrol station at all – she didn't even own a car.

'What a surprise to see you here,' was the least offensive greeting Carol could muster.

'I know – I don't usually come out this way, but I've been to Builth Wells with an old chum from school to visit another girl from our crowd back then who's going through a bad time. Breast cancer. Dreadful. But she's strong, and she's fighting it, and she's only got two more treatments to go until they check to see if it's working. But we're all banding together to visit and cheer her up.'

Carol wondered how she'd feel if Marjorie Pritchard came to visit if she was poorly, but shuddered at the thought – then grappled with the idea that the woman actually had any friends at all.

As if she'd read Carol's mind, Marjorie added, 'I haven't been the best at keeping in touch with the people I was in school with, but that business a couple of months ago made me think about them, and I've been renewing old friendships ever since. It's an ill wind, and all that. We stayed over last night – terrible weather, and you know what these lanes are like at the best of times after dark, so we're just going back to Anwen-by-Wye now. Diane had to fill up, and I thought I'd stretch my legs; now I'm hoping I don't drown. Hard to imagine where all the rain comes from, isn't it?'

Carol nodded politely, and pulled up the collar on her raincoat, hoping to stop more rivulets sneaking down her neck. 'It's certainly wet enough,' she replied, then she and Marjorie did a few balletic moves to allow her to stick the hose into her car.

'I can watch him while you go inside to pay,' offered Marjorie when Carol had finished. 'Diane mentioned something about needing the loo, but she won't mind waiting if she's back before you are. Go on, you leave him sleeping where he is…I'm wet through already, and my skin doesn't leak.'

Carol thanked Marjorie, and rushed to the little cabin that housed a shop selling a bizarrely wide range of items, at laughably high prices, as well as a sullen young man who operated the till, and a so-called 'coffee bar' where desperate motorists were able to help themselves to either a small bucket of brown liquid, or an absolutely massive one. As she paid her bill, Carol couldn't help but wonder why on earth Marjorie had seemed so normal. Not at all like her. Had the events that had transpired through August made the woman – so entrenched in her own perceived position at the top of the pecking order in the village – really reconsider the way she interacted with others? Or had Carol just caught her in an uncharacteristically charitable mood? It was hard to tell, but she noted the change nonetheless; her colleagues would be interested to hear about it.

Upon returning to her car, she was delighted to see that Albert was still sleeping soundly, Marjorie was on duty beside the driver's door, and all was right with the world.

'That's Diane, over there,' said Marjorie waving cheerily toward a cherry-red roller-skate of a car, where a large woman with a shock of lime green hair was jammed in behind the steering wheel. 'Lovely woman. Got seven children. Seven! Can you imagine?'

Glancing at her firstborn, Carol knew she couldn't begin to imagine what that would be like, and prepared her 'I have to get going now, Marjorie' speech in her head, but her companion beat her to it.

'Mustn't hang about – Diane needs to drop me off, then she's going to pop to Sharon's shop to pick up a whole box of the preserves we're selling there to raise money for the young 'uns to enjoy a day in Tenby next spring. She's a good sort, is Diane; said she'd take them to her village to try to get us some income from people who aren't…well, you know what it's like when we're fundraising around our village – it's always the same people putting their hands into their pockets, isn't it? A bit of outside money would be nice. Anyway – see you around, no doubt. Bye now.'

Carol was relieved that Marjorie had dashed away before she had a chance to tell her about the missing marmalades, jams and pickles; she was pretty certain that Marjorie Pritchard's affable mood wouldn't survive the news of the loss of the entire fundraising stock.

CHAPTER EIGHT

Christine was worried about Alexander; he'd texted her the evening before to say he'd been delayed in London on an urgent matter so wouldn't arrive at her place until around ten in the morning. She knew that meant he'd have set out from his flat on the south bank of the Thames pretty early, so she'd made sure she was ready for the day by half nine, and that there was a pot of coffee awaiting him when he arrived. But he hadn't arrived. Nor had he texted. And he wasn't answering his mobile.

She paced the office, poking at papers on desks, and sighing. She was as annoyed with herself as with him, because she knew, absolutely, that she should not have to worry about a man who had his own life to live, and his own businesses to run. Yes, by anyone's standards they were, indeed, a 'couple'. However, Christine had enough experience in life, she felt, to not believe her happiness depended upon a man – even though she was what Mavis always irritatingly referred to as being 'only in her late twenties'…as though that were the same thing as being a teenager. She tried his number again. Nothing. Sighing away her exasperation, Christine decided against a third mug of coffee, and was starting to regret having drunk a second, when she saw Alexander's car pulling up outside the converted barn. She smoothed down her skirt and plopped herself onto the sofa, hastily picking up a magazine.

When Alexander Bright burst into the building, she was able to glance toward her watch nonchalantly and say, 'Oh, is it that time already? How was the drive?'

Alexander shook his umbrella and stuffed it into the stand. 'Almost fatal, thanks…but, as you can see, I made it in one piece.'

Christine couldn't help herself, she leaped to her feet and felt her entire body vibrate with horror as she exclaimed, 'What do you mean, "almost fatal"? What happened? Are you alright? The car's okay it seems – are you?'

Alexander grabbed a mug and the coffee pot. 'It is, and I am, thanks. But it was a close thing. Terrible pile-up on the M4 behind me…by about two cars. I saw it all in my rear-view mirror, just about – the rain was coming down sideways at the time, and I reckon a bit of aquaplaning might have been involved. I couldn't help – in fact, I'd have probably caused another accident if I'd done anything but keep going. So I did. But I took my time after that. Best to reach your destination alive, even if a bit late, eh?'

Christine allowed him to place his steaming mug on the table before she flung her arms around him. 'I've been worried to death about you,' she admitted after they'd kissed. 'I hope everyone involved in the accident was alright, but I have to say I'm glad you were ahead of it, not in it, or behind it. Come on, have a sit down and catch me up with what's been going on. Why couldn't you make it last night? Your text was cryptic, to say the least.'

Alexander excused himself before he settled, but Christine noticed that – when he finally rejoined her – he wasn't his usual self. He sat back on the sofa as he sipped his coffee, but was clearly distracted. Christine wondered if the close call had shaken him more than he'd admitted. 'Penny for them,' she prompted.

The man Christine Wilson-Smythe loved a great deal more than she'd admit to herself, let alone anyone else, rubbed his face with both hands, and shook his head. 'Nothing I can't cope with – just a bit of a thing going on at the antiques place. You know the reason I bought it was because the current Coggins – Bill – was the last in his family, and he didn't want the business to disappear? Well, in a bit of a turn-up for the books, Bill's gone and found himself a lady friend, and it seems she's…well, it appears that both he and she are rather surprised to discover that, at the age of forty, she's pregnant. There will, indeed, be another generation of Cogginses to take on the business, after all, it seems. So he's asked me if he can buy me out.'

Christine was surprised. 'But I thought it wasn't just that he didn't have any heirs to inherit – I thought he'd needed the money. Wasn't the business teetering on the brink of collapse when you bought it? You've put so much work into it – I thought things were going rather well nowadays. Do you think it's the right time to sell? Isn't it a good little earner now?'

Alexander chuckled. 'Just listen to the Right Honorable Miss Christine Wilson-Smythe talking as though she was dragged up in the bowels of Brixton, like I was. Is it a good little earner, you ask? Indeed it is. Now. Though, as you say, it wasn't when I took it on. But, to be fair, while I do believe the business problems were largely down to the fact Bill hadn't been as enthusiastic about putting in the hours as he might have been, I reckon that was because he realized he was the last of the line that had run the place since the 1700s, and he felt like a bit of a failure because he hadn't managed to produce anyone to train up to take it forward.'

'From what you told me that wasn't for lack of his trying, though,' remarked Christine with a wink. 'I'm pretty sure you sanitized the stories you used to tell me about his escapades and entanglements, but it sounds as though he's finally found Ms Right. When's the baby due?'

Alexander waved an arm. 'No idea…no, hang about, he mentioned May.' He paused, and counted his fingers. 'Oh, that must mean she, and he, have only just found out about it. Early days yet – though, of course, he's eager to make plans.'

Christine was doing a bit of mental arithmetic of her own. 'I see what you mean about him making plans, but – and don't take this the wrong way – isn't Bill a bit old for all this? I don't know his exact age, but he's got to be around sixty…ish. Isn't he going to be a bit past it when his child is of an age to be able to learn the trade?'

'He's sixty-three, and yes, I agree with you – which was something we went around and around about last night. My initial point was that his child might not be interested in the business anyway – which Bill poo-pooed as being genetically impossible. He reckons it's in the blood; the generations of both male and female Cogginses who've inhaled the dust from all those antiques have magically downloaded it into the family's DNA, he says, and there it shall reside for ever more. So I wasn't going to win on that point. But eventually I persuaded him to talk through another aspect with his "girlfriend"…though one hesitates to use the term in these circumstances.'

Christine giggled, and said playfully, 'Should I not refer to you as my boyfriend then?'

Alexander smiled broadly. 'With me in my forties and you not yet thirty, I think we can get away with it for a few years yet…if that's still what you want to call me in a few years' time.'

Christine chose to not pursue that line, but countered with: 'What's the aspect you persuaded him to consider? That without you at the helm, being the driving force behind the business and able to use your contacts the way you have, going forward, that there might not be a business for his child to inherit in any case, especially given his advancing years?'

Alexander snorted coffee. 'I don't think Bill would take kindly to your characterization of his age, but – essentially – yes, that's what I made him consider. Because I think it's the truth: a child for a couple at their stage of life – though they aren't yet ancient – is bound to require a good deal of time and energy…which means he'll be either distracted from the business, or from his family – and neither would be good for a family business. I think he and Nat will see sense.'

'Nat?'

'Natalie. Nat.'

'Have you met her?'

Alexander shook his head. 'Not yet. They've only been seeing each other for a few months he says. Met at the V & A, of all places. He was there day after day, getting up close and personal with a twentieth-century pottery exhibit they were displaying on rotation, learning all he could about a specific method of making pottery…because the number of fakes is increasing in that area like you wouldn't believe, and we certainly don't want to get stuck with anything we can't be certain is real. Anyway, Nat bumped into him – quite literally – and almost sent him hurtling into a display case. They bonded over some sort of quinoa salad in the café, and have been – it appears – inseparable ever since.' Alexander sighed. 'He rather overused the term "soul mate" during our talk last night.'

'I like eating at the V & A, though all those majolica tiles in the Gamble Room make it too echoey for a really intimate atmosphere.'

Alexander chuckled. 'Damning the world's first ever museum restaurant with such faint praise, Miss Wilson-Smythe? They'll drum you out of the posh totty club before you know it if you carry on like that.'

Christine gave him a playful thump. 'So what was the upshot of this chat…was it worth having to stay in London, then brave the M4 this morning?'

'The way the weather was last night, at least I faced it in daylight today – if you can call it that – but there wasn't a resolution to our conversation. Bill will think about what I said, and he'll talk it through with Nat. Then we'll talk again.'

'So why do you keep looking at your phone all the time?' ventured Christine. 'If you're not expecting to hear from Bill Coggins imminently, why do you keep staring at it on the table over there?'

'Can't get anything past you, can I? I dare say that's the price I have to pay for allowing a professional enquiry agent to become my very significant other. Okay, I confess, I'm expecting some information…maybe by text, or maybe an email, can't be sure. But the person who promised to get it to me is late…and he's never late. It's surprising, and disappointing.'

Christine didn't miss the change in Alexander's tone, and it worried her. 'This is nothing to do with Coggins, is it? Is it connected to your other businesses…the property development and rentals side of things?'

Christine knew that was the gray area of Alexander's life – not that she hadn't been incredibly grateful, on several occasions in the past, that he had any number of slightly shady connections. However, it unsettled her to have to face the fact that – in some of his dealings – he sailed a bit too close to the wind for her liking.

Alexander nodded. 'Don't worry, it's nothing bad…just a bit of an issue I'm having with a roofing company we've been using; haven't shown up at a few jobs they're supposed to be doing. I know the weather's not ideal for roofers, but they're not on site, and no one's answering the phone or responding to emails either. They're usually reliable – which is why I use them. Anyway, I've got someone looking into it, now, and it's not the sort of enquiring you and your colleagues do, so no need for you to have to become involved. At all. But, speaking of enquiring – what's on the books for you at the moment? I know you're still building up to going back to work full time, so is there anything for you to do right now – or is Mavis chaining you to the laptop to type up reports or some such useful, though safe, endeavor? You know it's alright for you to take a bit of a back seat for a while, don't you? You don't have to be front and center, on every case, all the time. You understand that, right? You can still be a valuable team player even if you're not the star today…benched, but waiting, coiled and ready to perform.'

Christine brightened – not too much, she hoped – and replied, 'I absolutely understand that I am not always going to be the star of the show. But it's interesting you should mention being coiled and ready to act, because something's just come up at the Hall that needs all hands on deck for a bit of a burst of activity – and I was wondering if you'd mind helping a bit.'

'Always pleased to help, if I can. You know that. What's required?'

Christine began to explain.

CHAPTER NINE

Henry Twyst cleared his throat several times, rather loudly, in a polite attempt to get everyone's attention. It didn't work. He scanned the library for something akin to a glass and a spoon – but nothing was available. Eventually he resorted to: 'I say, everyone…' which seemed to do the trick.

Althea peered across the library at her son. 'Spit it out, Henry – what's the plan? We're all present and correct – as requested.' She acknowledged her son and daughter-in-law, Val Jenkins, and Mavis, with individual nods of her head, then continued, 'Except for Christine, who's been delayed, and Carol who's working on something terribly important and time-sensitive for the agency, and Annie, of course, who's off to work on some skulduggery in Swansea. Otherwise, we're all here.' She mugged a salute in her son's direction, eliciting an uncomfortable chuckle from him as he rolled on his toes.

Clearing his throat once again, Henry announced, 'I've asked Edward here to join us so we can agree on how we'll set things up, then he can make the necessary arrangements for our needs to be met. I know our initial conversations determined that the library makes greatest sense in terms of a location for our campaign HQ, so to speak, because there's a general belief that most of the information we're seeking is to be found in this very room. Isn't that right, Stephanie?' Henry hoped his wife would speak up; he lacked her natural talent as an organizer and leader.

Fortunately for Henry, Stephanie did step into the breach, and within half an hour Edward had been dispatched with full instructions about what furnishings would be needed for the library, to supplement those already present.

Althea suggested the group might take elevenses in the yellow sitting room while the installation of said furnishings was undertaken. Everyone agreed, though Stephanie made sure that writing materials were to also be sent to the yellow sitting room, so everyone would be able to make notes as they discussed their plan of attack.

When they arrived at their destination, Althea grinned when she saw that seed cake was being served. 'Just a small slice, or two, for me,' she said coyly, as Edward passed her a plate that already had two slices set upon it.

'Just tea for me. I'll pour,' said Stephanie.

Mavis said, 'No cake for me, thanks, Edward; I don't care for the flavor of caraway seeds. Never have, never will. Thank you. And I'll see to my own coffee, thanks.'

'In that case, would you care for some of the shortbread biscuits?' Edward spoke softly, as he always did.

Mavis nodded. 'Aye, go on then, but just two. They're rich enough.'

'And for madam?' Edward turned to Val, who blushed.

'Some cake would be lovely, thanks. I've heard the seed cake here at Chellingworth Hall uses a recipe that predates even Mrs Beeton's famous one.'

'Cook favors a recipe that's been used here since the early 1700s, pre-dating Mrs Beeton's by a good fifty years, I believe,' replied Edward as he served.

'Thank you, Edward,' replied Val. Henry wasn't sure why the woman seemed so excited at the prospect of eating a piece of cake, until she added, 'Imagine being able to consume cake that's been made using the same recipe for over three hundred years, in a place where it's been eaten for all that time, and even created in the same kitchen. It's like…it's like eating history. Wonderful.'

'I'll take what Mother had,' said Henry, sounding distracted, as he contemplated what Val had just said, never having thought of seed cake quite that way before, 'and, as my wife said, she'll look after the tea. Thank you, Edward.'

A few moments after he had left the group, Edward returned to announce, 'Miss Wilson-Smythe, and Mr Bright, Your Graces.'

Christine and Alexander wafted into the sitting room smiling.

'Thanks, Edward, we'll sort things out for ourselves,' said Christine cheerily as she kissed Stephanie on the cheek, then blew kisses to everyone else. 'Sorry we're later than we thought we'd be – Alexander almost had an accident on his way from London this morning, because of this dreadful weather. But, as you can see, he made it in one piece, and we're finally here. So – what's the cake today? I'm ravenous.'

After the kerfuffle that, necessarily, followed Christine's announcement about Alexander's unpleasant experience, and with everyone enjoying their refreshments in a sitting room where the yellow walls glowed and created something close to a sunny atmosphere, Henry was relieved when Stephanie finally called the group to order.

'There are some things we know, and some things we suspect,' she began. 'First and foremost: I want to invite Val to share her knowledge about the television producer Barry Walton. I think she can give us some idea of what we're up against. Over to you, Val.'

Val Jenkins looked a little uncomfortable to find herself put on the spot, but rallied. 'I've known Barry since he was the original producer of the television series for which I was the presenter, *The Curious Cook*. Of course, that hasn't been on the air for some years, but we've kept in touch, and I know Barry's been working on various factual programming series since then. Just in case you're not clear why he was here in the first place, when Stephanie told me about the plans to repair the plaster ceiling in the small sitting room during the months when the Hall is closed to the public, I mentioned it to Barry during one of our texting conversations – that's how he seems to habitually communicate – and he showed an interest in filming the restoration process as part of a short series he's producing. He was particularly pleased to be able to include a project being undertaken in Wales, there now being more interest in what they call "regional" content. And, yes, I know – it's not a flattering way to refer to our country, which has its own distinct and unique history, and future…but that's the term they use. Though I suppose it's a step forward that they're even recognizing Wales exists at all.'

After a general nodding of heads, Henry eventually spoke up. 'Has he talked to you again about why he's so interested in the thirteenth duke?'

Val shook her head. 'I haven't heard from him since he left here yesterday afternoon, and I've no idea why he's interested. I know that this series he's currently working on was always planned to be a one-off...though I also know that producers always hope the format they've created will be so popular that further series will be made. That being said, I suspect the research he said he'd done into the Chellingworth seat's history prior to coming here was pretty thorough; I know from experience that he enjoys the research aspects of his work. Clearly – from his comments – he's come across the information he mentioned about the thirteenth duke. It's the sort of scandalous story that would catch his eye; not because he's an unpleasant person, but because he's a good producer...he knows what sells, and knows how to put together a proposal that will get the backing it needs. And a scandal always draws good audiences, I'm afraid. That's all I *know*...but I'll add my opinion, if I may: Barry Walton is persistent and determined; if he thinks he's found a saleable idea, he'll pursue it and follow through. He's not the sort of man to let an opportunity pass him by.'

The occupants of the room sat in silence for a moment as everyone digested what Val had said.

Henry was the first to speak. 'You're saying you think he's going to give the idea some serious thought? Do a bit more ferreting about into our family's secrets?'

Val nodded.

'Like McFli, when he knows there's a rat in a hole,' said Althea quietly. She looked up from her cake and added, 'Not that I wish to imply that the thirteenth duke was a rat, of course...though, if what my dear, departed Chelly said to me was true, then the thirteenth carried the stain of two murders on his soul to his final resting place which – in case anyone is interested – is, in fact, in the family vault beneath St David's Church, in the village. That would not be the case if it was known at the time of his death that he'd committed suicide.'

'I thought it was just the Roman Catholics who didn't allow suicides to be buried on consecrated ground,' said Henry.

He noted that his mother looked shocked. 'For heaven's sake, Henry, do you know nothing? The rules for *our* churches changed more than a decade ago, but in the time of the thirteenth duke there'd have been no question about a suicide's remains being accepted – not even if the corpse in question was that of a duke. And that's why I think the rumors are wrong; the thirteenth duke is with the rest of the family, though he only has a small, engraved stone on the church wall close to the side chapel, and there's no commemorative monument, either. However, I have made my point, I believe.'

'And that's exactly the sort of information we need,' said Mavis emphatically. 'You see? We've begun. So – someone needs to talk to Reverend Ebenezer Roberts and check the records at the church; there might be some proof there that the thirteenth duke didnae kill himself.'

Stephanie said, 'I wonder if we might consider referring to the man some other way, please? He was a person, after all, not just an anonymous number. I dislike it intensely when someone assumes that my husband is not worthy of recognition as an individual besides his ability to be the eighteenth person to bear a title.'

Henry glowed, and beamed at his wife. 'He was named Frederick, though that's not an uncommon name in our family,' he offered.

'Frederick Algernon Devereaux Henry Charles,' said Althea. 'There have been several dukes using each of those names and, with the fourteenth duke having brought the name Harold into the line as well, that's the pool of male names we've traditionally used.' The look she bestowed upon both Henry and his wife told him his mother was Making a Point. 'I suggest we use Frederick – though maybe we could take a leaf out of Annie's book and just call him Fred. Awful Fred? No…Frightful Fred.' Althea sat up and her dimples puckered. 'I'll give that some thought…but let's use Fred. It would be like a sort of code name, just within this group. If anyone were to hear any of us chattering about "Fred" they'd be unlikely to guess we meant the thirteenth duke. That would be good, don't you think?'

Henry suspected his mother would have her way – she usually did – and his supposition was proved correct. With a general nodding of heads it appeared that his ancestor was to be referred to as 'Fred' for the foreseeable future, which made him feel inexplicably uncomfortable.

'We still need someone to volunteer to talk to Reverend Roberts about...Fred,' added Stephanie.

Althea's hand shot up. 'I need to speak to him about the arrangements for All Hallows' Eve, and *Nos Galan Gaeaf*,' she said, 'so I'll tack on the Fred thing to that conversation.'

Henry panicked. '*Nos Galan Gaeaf*, Mother?' Henry felt his body sag a little. 'I thought you and the reverend had reached an agreement about all that a couple of years back. You know he sees your proposals as...well, I heard him whisper the word "heathen" to the church warden when they were discussing it last time, and I can't imagine his views have changed, since then.'

Althea looked smug. 'They might not have done, but there's been a few changes on the parochial church council, and there's a new church warden now, too. I believe my suggestions might carry the day this time. Besides, if we don't make sure our cherished Welsh traditions are observed, they'll die out completely. And I use the word "our" having lived here in Wales for over fifty years, though I acknowledge I was unfortunate that only one of my grandparents was Welsh. Despite that oversight on my part,' she said with a smile, 'I'm aware there are generations who know nothing of the ancient Celtic rituals, and if we allow them to be observed, they are more likely to be continued.'

Henry did his best to sound calm as he replied, 'You see, Mother, it's your use of words like "rituals" that gives the reverend pause. "Celebrations"? Or possibly "enactments" might be better – those words smack less of religious overtones. You must see that, Mother. I'm all for traditions being maintained,' he lied – he wasn't even aware of most of them, until his mother brought them to his attention, 'but they need to be framed as ancient and harmless, not as a set of entrenched beliefs that are ready to go toe to toe with Christianity.'

Stephanie cleared her throat. 'I fear we might be going off at a bit of a tangent here,' she said, smiling, 'so let's agree that Althea will speak to the Reverend Roberts about any church records that might throw light on the facts of the…Fred's…death, and move on.'

'I'll go to see the vicar with Althea,' said Mavis. Henry felt relief wash over him, and he beamed at Mavis, trying to thank her with his eyes. She'd keep his mother on the straight and narrow – he hoped.

'Anyone else want to offer anything more?' Stephanie's expression suggested to Henry that his wife felt a little exasperated.

Christine waved her hand in the air.

'No need to do that,' said Stephanie, 'but what did you want to say?'

Christine turned to Alexander as she began. 'Edward told us when we arrived that he's getting things set up in the library for the team to work there. I'm guessing that means you think it's a good place to root out a lot of family information – but I know how many volumes that vast room houses, so who's the person who'll be in charge of telling us all where to look? I mean, who's our "librarian" in all of this? I wouldn't have a clue where to start.'

Val waggled her hand. 'I think I can help there. When my father did the restoration work on those books in the library, I visited him several times while he was beavering away. Both of us being bibliophiles, and bookshop owners, I couldn't help but trawl through the index card system, and poke about on the shelves, so I've a decent working knowledge of how the books in the library are sorted, and I can certainly search out what might be useful. Whomever it was who set up the system did an excellent job.'

Althea said, 'That was undertaken during Chelly's time – the entire library was in the most dreadful state; books had been organized by size rather than any more useful designation. He used a chap from Aberystwyth University, I recall, though he'd be long gone by now – he looked as though he were a hundred years old back then, and that was…oh my…almost half a century ago.' She sighed and seemed to shrink into her seat. 'How time flies…all this…this life…was so new to me then. I still had one foot in my life in London…my old friends from my days as a professional dancer would come for the weekend. What sparkling times those were.' She sighed, and Mavis patted her hand.

Henry felt his brow furrow as he stared at his mother; he'd never really come to terms with the fact that she was a person, with her own history. She was Mother, and that was that. He'd never been able to imagine her as a young dancer, living a dancer's life, in London. For no particular reason he wondered why she'd never shown him any photographs of herself back then, nor shared any of her memories.

Stephanie's comments drew him from his reverie. 'Thanks, Val – you're hired,' she quipped. 'So how about we all go back to the library now? Edward's just given me the nod at the door that the room's ready for us. Val, you could begin by searching through the indices to find anything that's related to family history; maybe Christine and Alexander could volunteer to run up and down the ladders to gather together the relevant volumes; you and Mavis can get in touch with the reverend, Althea, and make an appointment to see him. Oh, and Henry, could you please go to see Bob Fernley? As estate manager he might have access to estate records from the time. Bring anything useful he's got to the library, please.'

Henry muttered, 'Sounds like a military operation,' to himself as he nodded and sauntered toward the estate office, where he hoped he'd discover Bob Fernley.

CHAPTER TEN

Slipping away from the group making its way to the library, Althea whispered to Mavis, 'Why don't *you* make the appointment with the reverend? He's likely to agree to see you more quickly than he would me.'

Mavis was surprised. 'And why would that be? You're the dowager; I'm just a retried army matron who happens to share your home.'

Althea hesitated, and pulled Mavis aside, so she could sit on one of the Jacobean needlepoint chairs that lined an alcove in the Great Hall. 'He doesn't like me, Mavis. Never has. Not since we had that run in over him insisting upon calling the service "Midnight Mass" the first Christmas he was here.'

'Hasn't he been here for…well, decades, at least?' Althea nodded. Mavis squared her shoulders and added, 'Well, in that case, you'd think he'd have got over it by now. It was called "Midnight Eucharist" this past Christmas, wasn't it?' Althea beamed. 'Ah, so you got your way then, in the end.'

Althea stood. 'It's been called "Midnight Eucharist" since his second Christmas here: I wrote to the then bishop, and he sorted it out.'

Mavis sighed, and followed Althea patiently, as she took things slowly, heading for the library. 'Ach, well now, maybe what you said about him is a little more understandable then, but I'll no' lie to him; he's a man of God, whatever you might think of him…or him of you.'

'You won't have to lie to him at all; just tell him we want to visit the church to look something up in the church records, that's all. I'll broach the topic of *Nos Galan Gaeaf* while we're there, when he can't escape.' Althea's eyes twinkled.

'Sounds like you're wanting me to set a trap for the poor, wee man. I'll phone him, and make an appointment, but be it on your own head, Althea.'

Mavis noticed that Althea was fizzing with glee as she spoke. 'Excellent. And do it now, will you? There won't be any dusty old books for us to trawl through for a little while – Val's got to locate them, then Alexander has to climb up to get them all…though I wouldn't mind watching him do that.'

Mavis was shocked. 'Althea Twyst, what's got into you? I've never heard you speak of Alexander that way before. It's unbecoming.'

Althea paused, resting on her cane. 'Oh for goodness' sake, Mavis, I'm old, not dead. Alexander Bright is a desperately good looking man – it's no wonder Christine is so drawn to him. Dangerous too, which is part of the attraction, I suppose. As I was sitting there with my seed cake, and my title, and my son…and the prospect of my first grandchild ahead of me…I realized I have almost forgotten the woman I once was. The woman who was lithe, fearless, and sometimes even a little reckless. I wonder if you'd have liked her as much as you seem to like me, Mavis; I'm not sure the young Althea and the young Mavis would have become such firm friends as we have done in later life.'

Mavis could see the wistfulness in her friend's eyes. 'Ach, away with you. You cannae have changed that much; people don't, not in the important ways, at least. Besides, you can cause worries enough these days, so don't go thinking you've become a goody-goody' just because you're a dowager; I can spot a troublemaker when I see one, and my money's on that never having been any different – at any age – in your case.'

Althea's cheeks dimpled. 'You'll be pleased to know your money's safe with a bet like that.' She leaned toward her friend and added in a whisper, 'But maybe what you don't know is that I'd have had a chap like Alexander eating out of my hand in a fortnight, back when I was in my twenties. That Christine had better make up her mind about him soon, or he might reckon he'd be better off moving to pastures new.'

Mavis nodded her agreement. 'Now that's where I'm with you. She appears to lead him a bit more of a dance than I think he's prepared to take – for much longer. Though, to be fair to the girl, I don't think she's doing it on purpose. No, I think Christine is wondering if she could stick it with him for the long haul, because the fact that he's got that edge to him, and that he's mixed up in so many enterprises that might operate in the gray areas of the business world, mean he's not just dangerously good looking – which I'll grant you – but that being partnered with him for the long term might become uncomfortable.'

'But life without risk, without taking chances, can become so boring, Mavis,' chided Althea.

A penny dropped for Mavis. 'Is that what all this nonsense about *Nos Galan Gaeaf* and the vicar is about? Are you really intent upon saving Welsh traditions that have slipped into obscurity, or do you just want to bait Ebenezer Roberts? Come on now, be honest with me. I'll no' take any nonsense, as well you know, nor shall I play a part in you causing mayhem, just for sport.'

Althea suddenly sagged, to the extent that Mavis steered her toward a seat set against the wall. Once she was down, Althea looked up at her friend and said, 'My dear, I am biologically old enough to be your mother, so listen to what I'm telling you. One day, you'll realize you've become a shadow of the person you once were. Your body won't do what you will it to do, your memory will let you down when you least need it to, and your future will seem…well, let's just say not as extensive as it once was, nor as full of possibilities. The horizon one sees as far off in one's youth is suddenly close, and the sun is setting into it – and that's when you have to fight, or die. I shall always do my level best to make life exciting, and as full of new things as possible. Sometimes new things can be old things – and, as I grapple with what I hope will one day be my legacy, I can see more clearly now that one of the things I *can* do is to use my not inconsiderable local influence to refocus the attention of at least our small community on something that isn't anodyne, diluted by the influence of the global societal lens the young have today, nor messed about with by those who say they are bringing the past to life, when all they're doing is presenting the world with a fantastical reimagining of something that would work well as a graphic novel.

And, yes, I do know what I'm talking about, because I surf the internet as well as anyone. So, while I don't deny there are aspects of this potential battle of wills with the Reverend Roberts that appeal to me on a purely personal level, I must impress upon you my heartfelt desire to bring Welsh traditions back to life, to the extent I am able.'

Mavis reckoned Althea was being honest with her, so nodded and replied, 'Aye, well, I'll phone him then, and back you up, if needs be. But I'll take the chance to check in with Carol, too – she's earning the WISE Enquiries Agency a crust, while I'm getting involved with all this, so there's that to consider.'

'Of course, Mavis, pragmatism has its place.'

'It does that.'

CHAPTER ELEVEN

Annie found it difficult to be her normal self with Tudor following his possible declaration of love the previous evening – if that was what it had been, because she kept reminding herself she still couldn't be sure. Thus, the drive to Swansea had been tense, to say the least; she'd made a few attempts to engage him in conversation, but he hadn't bitten. By the time they reached the part of the M4 that swept down toward the sea, the atmosphere in the car was so thick Annie suspected she'd have needed a chainsaw to get through it – and then it would have taken a while.

'Here we are, then.' Annie thought Tudor sounded tired when he announced their arrival and finally turned off the ignition, having snagged the last parking space in the small car park behind the restaurant that was their lunch destination.

'It looks...um...nice,' observed Annie. She was lying; the place looked small and almost shed-like, and they'd parked beside an industrial-looking attachment to the building that housed...well, she hoped it wasn't the kitchen, anyway.

Tudor replied, 'Hmm, not quite what I'd been expecting, I have to admit. Anyway, we're here now, so let's go in. To be honest, I'll be happy to inspect their facilities, if nothing else – so, if we don't like the look of it, how about we just have a coffee then find somewhere else?'

Annie agreed it was a good plan because she, too, needed the loo.

Rounding the building it was clear that its main feature was its location – on the paved promenade that ran between the miles of sandy beach and the grassy banks which led down to the main road. The heavy rain had stopped, but there was still drizzle in the air. Tudor gleefully informed Annie that such weather was locally referred to as 'Swansea Mist'; what it meant was that all the tables outside were unoccupied, and the place looked quite full inside. They were greeted at the front door by a young woman with two-thirds of a head of long magenta hair, the other third being almost clean-shaven.

'Two for brunch – or will it be lunch?' she asked as she led Annie and Tudor to a table beside the floor-to-ceiling windows.

Annie shrugged. 'Not sure yet, it depends what's on offer for which.'

The woman smiled. 'Okay – I'll leave you both menus in that case, but I'll warn you that we stop serving from the brunch menu in a quarter of an hour. After that it's just the lunch one. Alright? Your server will be along in a few minutes.'

The couple nodded their understanding. 'Ta,' replied Annie, 'but, before I pick anything, can you point me toward the loos, please?'

'Down there, on the right.' The hostess looked Tudor up and down and added, 'Unisex.'

'After you,' said Tudor, gallantly.

Annie tossed her scarf onto her chair and said, 'Just leave that there, it'll be alright. You don't have to wait – come on…'

Refreshed, and reseated, Annie and Tudor turned their attention to the menus, both deciding they fancied the brunch menu more than the lunch one. Tudor managed to get the attention of their server, then ordered the Welsh Eggs Benedict. The description told Annie that Tudor's choice somehow involved the use of laverbread and bacon; she preferred to avoid the local delicacies, so plumped for scrambled eggs on sourdough toast, with field mushrooms and sausages. Two mugs of coffee arrived with a small jug of milk as the pair settled into their modern, yet comfortable chairs, and took in the sea view – through the shifting lens of the Swansea Mist.

'That tide's a long way out,' observed Annie.

Tudor smiled. 'Second biggest tidal range in the world we have here…eight-and-a-half metres, which is almost twenty-eight feet. I'd say there are parts of the bay where it goes out about a half a mile or so. I used to love low tide when I was a kid growing up here – loads of open space to play rugby or cricket.'

'Did you live far from the beach…the bay…what do you call it, exactly?'

Annie noticed a wistful gleam in Tudor's eyes as he replied, 'The entire expanse is Swansea Bay, but each of the areas has its own name – this part being Swansea Beach. There's Aberavon Beach right over at that end, beyond Port Talbot – the big steelworks we passed on the way in – then Baglan Bay and Jersey Marine Beach, and over there' – he pointed in the other direction – 'is Mumbles Beach. You're going to be staying around the corner from there…in Langland Bay, which is properly part of the Gower Peninsula. I suppose Swansea Bay itself is about twenty-five miles all the way around. I was a lucky kid; we didn't have much, but bus fares were cheap back then, and my mam let me go with my friends to whatever beach we liked through the summer holidays.'

Annie tried to visualize Tudor as a small boy, but it seemed impossible – his features were so individual. 'Must have been nice. The East End of London was a bit different to this place, though we did get away to the seaside sometimes. Eustelle and Rodney – bless them, they were picky parents – preferred Brighton over Southend, but it was easier to get to Southend from our part of London, so we went there more often. Never went in the sea itself, though, of course.'

Tudor set aside his steaming coffee. 'What do you mean "of course"? Sea too cold for swimming there?'

Annie almost snorted coffee. 'Swimming? Me? In the sea? You must be joking. Eustelle and Rodney hate the sea. They let me go for swimming lessons at the local public baths with the school, but they'd never let me anywhere near the sea itself.'

Tudor looked puzzled. 'But your parents are from St Lucia; loads of lovely beaches there, I'd have thought. Didn't they swim there, when they were young, before they migrated to England?'

Annie weighed her response, and decided to be honest. 'Look, I've told you before that I don't like having to speak up on anything on behalf of all Black people, just because I'm Black myself. I'm just me – with my own experiences of what it's like to grow up as a Black woman in the East End. So all I can tell you is what I know. Personally. And the way my family sees it is like this…you might not understand it though; when they were dumped on the islands in the Caribbean, the slaves were taught – over generations – to be terrified of the sea. The slave owners didn't want them thinking they could escape by sea, and I don't think that the poor people who'd been chained in the bowels of some rickety old ships transporting them from Africa needed much convincing. So Eustelle and Rodney – like all their friends – grew up with hundreds of years of terrible tales about the dangers of the oceans being passed down to them. The way they tell it, most people of their age on the islands don't swim, because they just won't go into the sea.'

Tudor's expression told Annie he was working out how to react. Eventually he said, 'Sorry.'

Annie reached for his hand. 'Aww, it's alright, doll, no need for you to think it was your fault that my ancestors were seen as a less valuable commodity than a dog that was really good at killing vermin…it weren't you who did it to me, it was them, back then. But ta, anyway.'

She was relieved when the food arrived, because it allowed there to be a natural break in what could have become a difficult conversation.

'Fancy a bite?' Tudor offered his plate.

'With that slimy green laverbread slathered all over that bacon, no thank you very much. You caught me out with that stuff once before; I get it that it's a cultural thing, but – Gordon Bennett! – it looks and tastes as disgusting as you'd think boiled seaweed would. And it sticks to your teeth something rotten. Never again, Tude. I'm quite happy with what I chose.'

She nonchalantly reached into her handbag for the bottle of hot sauce she carried everywhere with her, and drowned her eggs and sausages with it, leading Tudor to wrinkle his nose and shake his head.

'Talk about a cultural thing…I'm surprised you've got any tastebuds left,' he said, then popped the bacon covered with laverbread into his mouth, grinned, and 'Mmmm'd' his way through his brunch.

As they ate they chatted more naturally than they had done on their drive, and Annie felt the weight of her confusion about Tudor's use of the word 'love' the evening before lift a little.

Tudor wiped his mouth and pushed away his completely spotless plate; he'd mopped up every bit of slime, Annie noted.

He said, 'Any chance you've rethought the idea of you having to get a taxi to arrive at your digs? I'd love a look inside the place.'

'I don't know about that…my cover story is that I've come on the train, then by taxi. Why?'

Tudor sat back in his seat. 'The building you're staying in used to be a convalescent home for coal miners before they changed it into luxury flats. I'd love to see what it looks like on the inside – and what the view is like. I used to look up at it when I was little and be amazed – I thought it was magical. A fantasy building.'

'The photos make it look dead posh,' replied Annie. 'Apparently it's built in the Scottish Baronial style – which is a bit odd, considering it's in Wales.'

Tudor chuckled, 'You can trust an Englishman, put in charge of a Welsh ironworks in the late 1700s, to build a Scottish-looking summer home overlooking a Welsh beach, I dare say. I could drop you off…you could say I was a friend of a friend, if anyone challenged you.'

Annie could see how eager Tudor was. 'Sorry, doll, I can't risk it. The house our client's father owns is on the hillside above the place I'm staying, so my target could be looking out of the window and see us. It's too much of a chance to take. I've been working on my background story, and it doesn't allow for friends of friends in the area; I'm supposed to be visiting to explore the place, and hunt down the most profitable position as a carer that I can. Luckily, my research shows there are several expensive care homes in the area, and I'm going to make a show of visiting them…if I have to. Jeanette Summers has to think I'm on the make when I bump into her and attempt to befriend her – that's the plan, and I've got to stick to it.'

Tudor's brow furrowed. 'But if you're supposed to be a care worker, how come you're also supposed to be able to afford to stay where you're staying? I can't imagine those flats are cheap to rent.'

Annie smiled. 'Good point, and I've taken care of that...in fact, I've even woven that thread into my cover story as a way to strengthen it. I've come into a bit of money, see, left to me by the last old lady I worked for. Nice touch, eh? I want my target to think I'm happy to more than profit from my charges...so maybe she'll see me as being more like her – on the make, and on the take.'

Tudor shook his head. 'I'm still not happy about this,' he muttered. 'It could all be...well, it sounds unsavory, and it could be dangerous.'

Annie felt her back stiffen. 'I'm quite capable of taking care of meself, Tude. I'm no damsel in distress, and don't go forgetting that. I've managed perfectly well to make my own way in the world for the past half a century. It took some doing to work my way up from the mail room in one of the biggest Lloyds' insurers in the City to be their senior receptionist...before the old so-and-sos unceremoniously made me redundant – so don't think I suddenly need taking care of.'

Tudor's face fell. 'I didn't mean...it's just that...you're quite right, of course. I know you're competent, and professional, and you'll do an excellent job. Now – dare we go and face those menacing monkeys again?'

Annie was completely baffled. 'You what?'

'The monkeys on the wallpaper in the loo.'

'I didn't have no monkeys in the loo I used...gold wallpaper with peacock feathers in mine. Very nice, actually.'

Tudor smiled. 'Ah, well maybe I'll try that one this time – because mine had purple monkeys climbing scarlet trees, and the expression on some of their faces was quite alarming.'

Annie chuckled. 'Yeah, hard to tell if they're smiling or planning how to chew your face off with monkeys, innit? But you're right – best to go before we go...then I'll phone for a taxi and you can leave me here with my bag. I'll take it from here, Tude, you head off home.'

As they went about their business Annie suddenly realized she'd referred to Anwen-by-Wye as 'home', and had meant it. She'd surprised herself, because she hadn't even been away from her beloved London for a year, yet it almost seemed as though the life she'd lived there had happened to a different person.

CHAPTER TWELVE

Carol stared out at the rain lashing sideways across the village green, worrying that it might disturb Albert as it beat against the windows, then reasoned it was just as likely to be soothing him, because at least he was napping. She was grateful for the break, and took her chance to settle back in the nursing chair in his room, stroking Bunty, her beloved calico cat, who'd decided that Carol's lap was by far the best place for her to be. As she enjoyed the feeling of Bunty's silken fur, Carol admitted to herself that she felt ragged around the edges, and knew she looked it, too. Her usually-casual blonde curls looked as unkempt as she felt, she had stains on the front of her burgundy sweater, and her leggings were definitely being discarded this time; all the give in them had gone. She calmed herself with the knowledge that there was no one to see her, except Albert – and he certainly didn't care what she looked like, which helped her to discount her appearance as utterly immaterial.

Her watch told her it was coming up to lunchtime, and she knew she had to eat something, though she wasn't sure what. As she considered what might be in the fridge – knowing she was too tired to get up and look – her phone vibrated on the changing table. Her annoyance levels immediately hit the roof, because it meant she had to leap up – terrifying poor Bunty – muffling the sound of the vibration as she moved as fast and as quietly as possible across the creaking floorboards, pulling Albert's door closed behind her.

She hissed, 'Mavis…just a second,' into the phone as she tiptoed down the stairs, trying to avoid the really noisy ones. 'You know what, Mavis – David and I thought the way this old house creaked and squeaked was charming, until we had Albert to consider. I've never known a place to be able to make so much noise when you're just doing the bare minimum in terms of living. It's incredible.' She paused, plopped onto a kitchen chair, and added, 'Sorry about that. What can I do for you?'

Mavis replied tartly, 'Aye, well, as I always say, bairns'll sleep when they need to, and their parents have to sleep when they can.'

Carol sighed, silently. 'Yes, that's exactly what you always say, Mavis, I know. So, what did you want? And why are you puffing and panting? Are you alright?'

Mavis said, 'I am, thank you. I'm up at the Hall starting to look into something that's…well, it's interesting enough, but nothing for you to worry about at the moment. We have a paying client, and I thought I'd best check to see how you're coming along with the work for her – the deep dive into the prospective buyer of her hairdressing empire she doesnae like the smell of.'

Carol rolled her eyes, hoping Mavis couldn't hear her doing it – though she feared she might. 'I've started, but there's a long way to go yet. I know she needs my report – *our* report – tomorrow, and I'll hit my deadline. A fast turnaround, with a full briefing on a Saturday, means we're getting well paid, I know, but some processes take the time they take – and I need to get the information that's only available on weekdays while I can, then I can focus on the analysis. I've already requested all the data I need…now I have to wait for it all to come in, and start chasing toward the end of the day if it hasn't arrived. Until then – well, I can carry on sifting through information that's publicly available online, but I'll be at it right up until the last minute, I should think.'

Mavis sighed. 'You're a talented woman, Carol. Thanks. And you're right, this job's a good earner for the agency. Your efforts are appreciated. I'll no' interrupt you any longer.'

'Hang on a sec, Mavis – there is something else.' Carol explained the situation regarding the stolen preserves.

Mavis didn't respond immediately, then said, 'It's a police matter until they say it isn't. We cannae make a decision until after they make theirs. Let me know what they say. And impress upon Sharon that this position will not change; she has to get the police to either step up, or step away. It's our policy, as you know, even if the job's something you're suggesting we do as a favor. Which, in itself, is something you know I'm wary of; once we're seen to be doing something for free for one lot, there'll be more wanting us to do it for them too. It's a slippery slope, Carol.'

Carol's voice conveyed her resignation and relief. 'Yes, I know Mavis. I'm sure Sharon will be nagging the police to do something – even if it's to confirm they can't help, so I'll wait to see what happens with them, then let you know. Right then, I'd better get back to my research, if you don't mind, Mavis. Was that all?'

'Aye, and I'll be getting back to mine too, after a spot of lunch. Give that bairn of yours a hug from me – but only if he's already awake. Bye.'

'Bye.' Carol disconnected, then woke up her laptop and checked her inbox. Yes, it was filling up nicely. Not too many more jigsaw pieces to come in – but some of the more critical items of financial background data still hadn't arrived.

She looked at her watch; Albert had been asleep for a whole hour, and she hoped he'd stay that way for a couple of hours more, so she decided to make the most of her opportunity to get something done.

Carol hardly noticed the time passing, she was so utterly focused on her tasks. Although she had wanted nothing more than to become a mother, Carol Hill – even before she'd married and become Carol Hill – had loved data. She'd thrived on it from an early age, and had found its trawling, manipulation, and interpretation to be the most fulfilling activity possible. That love of data had led her to programming, and that had led her to systems management, and – when that had proved too highly pressurized to allow her body to do what she wanted it to do, and conceive – she had happily replaced managing systems with managing different types of data…the information required for their cases by a team of enquiry agents. Now Carol wondered how she'd ever found systems and programming to be at all interesting, when facts about people, places, and happenings were so riveting.

And this case – The Case of the Aggressive Acquisition – was giving her the best possible opportunity to burrow into the all-encompassing background of a person, and a group of companies, to work out what the truth was. She was pleased that her colleagues recognized that her type of enquiring – while not something any of them had a great deal of interest in or aptitude for – was as relevant to their agency's portfolio of offerings as any of their skill sets, as well as being a much relied upon service she provided to the whole team. Sadly, they usually all wanted her to do something urgent, just for them, at exactly the same time but – with a client needing her full attention and being prepared to pay through the nose for it – she was relishing the opportunity to focus on one project from start to finish without any distraction, except, maybe, for the puzzling theft of a shed full of preserves...and Albert.

Carol's fingers stopped flying across the keys as she listened to the baby monitor; would Albert settle again, or were his grizzles going to become a full-blown meltdown? She hardly dared move as she waited, and hoped Bunty would stay where she was, too, not wanting the errant creak of a floorboard to stop him from settling – though she knew it wouldn't be long before he'd need feeding, so it was unlikely she'd have much more time to herself until he, maybe, napped that evening. She sat there, her hands hovering above her keyboard, her screen displaying a dizzying array of figures, listening to her son in the room above her, and feeling the connection between her professional and home life in every cell of her body.

CHAPTER THIRTEEN

Mavis thought Edward looked a little shocked – for Edward – when he opened the library doors to announce that luncheon would be served in the dining room in fifteen minutes. As she looked at the chaos surrounding her she wasn't surprised that even the usually stoic butler had been unable to completely disguise his alarm.

Val, Christine, and Alexander had worked as a team to locate, then retrieve the volumes in the library that the group hoped would shed light on the pertinent period of the Twyst family's history. While Alexander had done the lion's share of scaling the ladders which rolled along each wall, Christine had done all the steadying at the foot of the ladder, as Val had called out reference numbers to identify the appropriate volumes. Some had been difficult to bring down, being heavy, and – in some cases – more frail than they appeared when they were simply sitting on a shelf, where they had been largely undisturbed for half a century. The wearing of white cotton gloves during the entire operation didn't therefore just protect the books, it also protected the hands of the threesome, as well as those of Stephanie, who'd been 'allowed' to move books around into a manageable order, once they'd been placed upon cloth-covered tabletops. The dust being produced by the undertaking hung in the air and besmirched faces.

Mavis and Althea had watched the proceedings from the fireplace end of the library; Mavis had begun by ferrying books to tables, but she'd found herself inexplicably puffed, so Christine had taken those duties upon herself, and Mavis and Althea had retired, until the responsibilities for actually reading the books were allocated.

Mavis had successfully made an appointment with the vicar for eleven the next morning, when he had said he'd be honoured to meet with herself and the dowager for tea, and she'd also spoken to Carol, who seemed to be well-focused on the work she was undertaking for the agency.

As Mavis accompanied Althea to use appropriate facilities before lunch, she commented upon the progress. 'Ach, it's no wonder yon Edward was almost goggle-eyed when he saw what's happened in the library. Who knew such a change could come over a room so quickly.'

Althea shrugged. 'Books are merely decorative when all one can see is their spine on a shelf. It's not until they're opened and read that they become what they truly are, dear – which is *magical*. The library, as it was before we started pulling down books, was just a room lined with leather and a bit of gold lettering – now it's starting to come alive, with insights, information, and family history. It can all be put back as it was just as quickly, and can return to being a slumbering creature, guarding its hoard of treasure, soon enough.'

Mavis smiled. 'You're having an especially poetic day today, Althea. What have you been reading?'

Althea twinkled. 'Oh, this and that, dear. Don't worry, I don't have William Wordsworth under the stairs, ready to recite his poem about daffodils when the poet inspector calls. Nor is Thomas Hardy camped out in my bedroom.'

Mavis paused. 'Well, I dare say I'm pleased about that – because if you claimed they were I'd be more worried about you than I am at this moment, but what is it you're on about, dear?'

Althea sighed as she disappeared into the WC. 'You really do need to watch more Monty Python, dear. The Poet Inspector sketch? That lovely Welshman Terry Jones dressed up as a woman always makes me laugh.'

Mavis availed herself of the use of the facilities, too, and the women joined the rest of the group at the dining table, where Edward immediately began to serve a light beetroot and goat cheese salad, which Mavis enjoyed very much.

'Excellent choice for lunch,' she said to Stephanie.

'Thanks,' replied the duchess, 'the cheese is from our own goats and the beetroots are from the vegetable garden, of course, and the lemons are from our orangery...though I expect Cook used oil from Italy for the dressing. A few too many food miles on the plate for my liking. I wonder where the nearest place is where they're able to grow good olives, to make oil,' she mused aloud.

Mavis noticed that Henry sounded quite disinterested when he muttered, 'You should look into that,' in reply to his wife's comments.

'What fish will it be, Stephanie, dear?' Althea had already cleared her small salad; Mavis could never get over how quickly the dowager managed to vacuum up her food, while still observing all the niceties of table etiquette.

'Hake; Cook says it's a delight to work with, and I understand she's used mushrooms, rosemary, and lemon today – all our own, of course, and the vegetables are ours too. So just the miles for the fish to consider, but I do feel that's offset against the fact that hake is a wonderfully sustainable fish, so please don't feel too badly about it.'

Mavis was pretty sure she heard Althea mutter, 'Wasn't going to,' under her breath, but she chose to ignore it.

Instead she looked toward Henry and asked, 'Any joy in the estate office? Was Bob Fernley able to help?' Everyone had noticed that Henry hadn't returned to the library before lunch, and Mavis found it hard to believe she was the only one who wondered why that had been the case.

Henry looked down at his hake with approbation as he replied, 'He was out and about. Had to wait for him to come back. Didn't want to miss him. Busy man. He's going to have a hunt about for us – bring anything he can find to the library after lunch. Said he'd work through to accommodate us.'

Mavis edited several responses she felt inappropriate, and made do with: 'Aye, well, if we're back in there as soon as possible, I dare say we'll all be happy to crack on, to get this done.'

'There's such a lot to get through,' observed Christine. 'There must be about fifty volumes we've found so far…do you think we're going to have to read them all, Val?'

Mavis noticed that Val was relishing every mouthful of her meal, which she supposed was to be expected of a woman who was known as a specialist in regional Welsh recipes and therefore the person at the table most likely to be both sensorily, and academically, interested in the food with which they had been served.

Val opened her eyes, which had been closed in concentration, and replied, 'The records I've been accessing only mention titles and topics in the broad sense, though I know we all believe the half-dozen volumes of the family history could be our best bet. I suggest our first task should be to check each of the other volumes to assess their pertinence, then we can focus on those we don't discard – though maybe we shouldn't return them to the shelves until we're certain we don't need them, since Alexander's gone to so much trouble to bring them down for us.'

'My absolute pleasure,' replied Alexander, beaming. 'I miss the gym I have at home when I'm away – but I don't feel as though I've missed my workout today after all.'

Mavis couldn't help but overhear Christine whispering, 'You said you set out from home this morning; didn't you exercise before you left?'

Having accidentally heard Christine's comment, Mavis's ears went out on stalks to catch Alexander's reply which was a terse: 'Didn't have the chance. Early start.'

Mavis wasn't convinced he was telling the truth, and her reading of Christine's attack on the poor, defenceless fillet of hake on her plate told her she wasn't alone in her assessment.

'I think Val's given us a good plan for this afternoon's endeavors,' commented Stephanie airily. 'I planned a light lunch to get us through to tea – for which everyone will stay, I hope, before we call it a day. Edward, the lemon mousse now, please – I believe we've all finished. Thank you.'

Mavis wondered if Althea would make it to tea time without a nap; she usually grabbed forty winks in the afternoon, though she looked perky enough at that moment.

Althea threw one of her most winningly dimpled smiles toward her daughter-in-law. 'Oh good, I very much enjoy Cook Davies's lemon mousse; how she manages to make it so light I'll never know. I wish she could teach my cook how to do it, because hers could do with some help. By the way – do you think there's a chance we might have a Victoria sponge for tea, Stephanie?'

Stephanie chuckled as she replied, 'Cook Davies knows you'll be here, so I have no doubt she'll make one for you – and we'll all do our best to force down a crumb or two to help you out. But, before that – once we've finished here – let's do our best in the library.'

Althea whispered to Mavis, 'If only we could have a gorilla as a librarian, and not just a human dressed up as one.'

Mavis tutted. 'That Monty Python lot again?'

Althea winked. 'Clever girl.'

CHAPTER FOURTEEN

Annie entered the bar of the Seaview Hotel with a bit more of a clatter than she'd intended; it had been her plan to skid through the doors so everyone would look at her, thereby allowing her to not only catch the eye of her target, but also to be able to naturally gravitate toward her when she settled herself. As it was, a slight puddle inside the door meant Annie ended up on her backside looking up at a smiling woman who was doing her best to not laugh.

'Come on, I'll give you a hand up.' She giggled, then added, 'You alright?'

Annie was thrilled that Jeanette Summers had apparently been sitting just inside the doorway, and was therefore the closest person to be able to offer to help her up from the floor. It was also quite natural for Annie to flop onto a chair at her target's table.

'Ta for that – what a twit I am,' said Annie, beaming. 'Let me buy you a drink, to say thanks.' She didn't want to miss the gold-plated opportunity, and suspected Jeanette was the sort of woman who wouldn't turn down a free drink.

Jeanette smiled. 'Alright, thanks. But I'll go to the bar, you stay there. What do you want?'

'G & T,' replied Annie. She reckoned that was what was in the half-empty glass on the table.

'Me too. Doubles for both of us? We're worth it, aren't we?' Jeanette stuck out her hand, into which Annie deposited a twenty-pound note.

As Jeanette waited at the bar, Annie made a show of fussing to get herself comfy while she studied her target. The Turnbull sisters had shown Annie a strip of photo-booth pictures of Jeanette with their father. She'd been wearing a KISS-ME-QUICK hat and holding a stick of candy floss. He'd looked...happy, had been Annie's impression; an elderly man with a horseshoe of white hair, kind eyes, and an impish grin. Having only seen Jeanette's head, Annie's imagination had added the standard 'floozie' body...curvaceous, clothed in bingo-chic, with a bit too much bling. But that wasn't at all how Jeanette Summers presented herself to the world: she sported a sensible navy jumper, serviceable gray slacks, and flat, comfy shoes. Her hair wasn't as blonde as it had been in the photos Annie had seen – it looked darker in real life – and she wore almost no make-up.

As Annie fussed, she heard Jeanette say to the barman, '…least I could do, poor thing. Yes, just time for one more…' then she brought the drinks across to the table, nodding to the handful of other patrons who were dotted around what Annie thought was a cozy, nautically-themed bar. Annie made sure to look perky at the sight of the drinks.

'Can't beat a G & T,' she said as she picked up her glass. 'Cheers. Thanks for the help. I'm Annie. Annie Porter. New around these parts. Nice to meet you.'

'Cheers yourself. I'm Jeanette Summers.' She didn't hand Annie any change from the drinks.

Annie noted that the first thing Jeanette did was finish the drink she'd already had on the table, then she glugged down about half the fresh one. Annie was taken aback; she enjoyed the odd gin now and again, but this woman knew how to knock it back. It was almost as though she were afraid someone might take her glass from her, so firmly did she grasp it on the table. Annie made a mental note: Jeanette Summers was a drinker, no question about it.

Annie made a snap decision, and polished off her drink in record time. 'I needed that. Been gasping for it all day. Fancy another?' Before Jeanette could reply Annie was on her feet saying, 'My turn to go to the bar – you stay there. It's the least I can do. Same again?'

Her target's expression told Annie there was no way she was going to look a gift horse in the mouth, and she nodded her agreement. Annie stood at the bar, smiling and nodding at everyone who made eye contact, rolling her eyes and shrugging, recognizing they'd all seen her eventful arrival.

Leaning toward the young barman she said, 'Same again, please. Doubles.' As he prepared the drinks Annie dared, 'She seems really nice – kind of her to help me up.'

The barman opened bottles of tonic as he replied, 'Jeanette? Yeah, she's one in a million. Heart of gold.' He leaned in. 'Drops in every night, just for an hour or so. Needs a break from her partner.' He leaned even closer. 'Poor thing's got dementia, you know? Leads her a right old dance he does, sometimes. This is the only break she gets, when she's put him to bed for the night. Best to do it early, she reckons, then he can get the rest he needs.'

Annie forced a smile. Her clients had told her about Jeanette's evening ritual, which was why Annie had known that the Seaview Hotel was the place to 'bump into her', but their take on it was that Jeanette was drugging their father with sleeping pills so she could have at least twelve hours a day when she didn't have to interact with him at all.

'Oh, the poor woman,' was Annie's comment, 'the things people do for the ones they love, eh? Terrible thing dementia. So hard on the whole family. Isn't there anyone who can give her a hand?'

The barman rolled his eyes and chuckled wryly. 'I've only been working here for a month or so, so I don't know the bloke myself – lives up on the cliffs, in one of those big houses. She says he's got a couple of kids who don't care about him at all; never phone or visit. Not even a birthday card. Terrible that, isn't it? I know I'd do better if it was my dad. How can kids abandon their father like that? Jeanette's an angel. Never complains. Deserves her little break.'

Annie paid for the drinks, knew immediately that Jeanette had hung onto almost four quid she should have given back to Annie, and returned to the table. Jeanette drained the glass she already had, and took her fresh drink, once again immediately gulping down half of it. Annie realized she'd have to gird her loins – and start using her credit card – if they were going to keep up the drinking for much longer.

Noticing that Jeanette was looking at her watch, Annie asked, 'You got to be going? Surely you can stay a bit, it's early yet. And I don't know anyone around here.'

The woman looked distracted. 'I suppose one more after this wouldn't hurt, but I've got to get back before nine, at the very latest.'

Annie braved, 'The barman mentioned you're a carer – pop in here for a little break. That must be difficult.'

Jeanette looked at Annie, looked at her drink, and sighed. 'Hmm, maybe he shouldn't be so mouthy about other people's business, but, yeah, I thought I was going to have a fantastic life here with my new partner. But he's developed dementia, and I look after him now, so I make sure he's comfy in bed every night, then pop down here for a little bit of me time. But I don't like to leave him too long – he wanders.' She hesitated for a moment, and Annie thought the woman was making some sort of decision. Eventually she added, 'There's a lot of stairs in the house, and it's dangerous for him.'

Annie adopted the sincerest expression of sympathy she could muster. 'Oh, you poor thing. It's a terrible disease, isn't it? So hard on the family. I recently had a lady with it myself. But I'm paid for my duties – that's what I do…professional carer. Live in, usually. I don't suppose you're looking for someone, are you? That's why I'm here, see – on the lookout for a new position. I heard through the grapevine there's a lot of folks in these parts who aren't short of a bob or two that they might be happy to spend on someone who's qualified to give them the attention they need. Thought I'd spend the weekend here first, have a bit of a look-see, then start a proper bit of research on Monday.' Annie hoped she hadn't pushed too far. How would Jeanette react?

Her target picked up her glass and took a couple of swigs. 'A paid carer, eh? How much do you charge?' Her eyes glinted as she quickly added, 'Just out of interest – not that I'm looking.'

Annie shrugged. 'Shame. How much? Well, it depends on the arrangements – you know, living in, costs covered, all that sort of thing. The specifics of what's needed matter too…how much lifting, washing, that sort of thing. Some folks don't need as much help as others, see, so it's hard to charge them as much. But my last post was a good example – she was the lady I mentioned, needed a lot done for her, so that was twelve hundred a week, but I can go as low as eight hundred, if all they need is someone on the premises, so to speak, who can make a cuppa, have a chat now and again, keep them company, and know what to do in an emergency. It varies.'

Jeanette nodded at her almost empty glass. 'Twelve hundred a week? So that's what I'm worth on the open market, eh? Some people should realize that.'

'How long have you been looking after him for free then?' Annie felt herself settling into her fake persona.

'Almost three months.'

Annie saw an opportunity to gather some insight. 'That sounds like a quick decline. Were there no signs before then? Did he just get bad, fast?'

Jeanette's eyes narrowed. 'I didn't see any signs, but maybe I wasn't looking, I'm not a professional, like you. But now he can't walk without falling, needs bathing, and wears adult nappies that I have to change. Lost control of it all, he has. Horrible.' She sighed. 'But I love him, so I do it.'

'His family can't help at all?'

Jeanette snapped, 'How do you know he's even got family?'

Annie tried to take Jeanette's suspicious glance in her stride. 'The barman again – mentioned some kids. Though, in my experience, the kids don't want anything to do with it all. They're usually the ones who find me, then get the ones I care for to pay my wages. Sometimes the kids do it, yeah, but not if the parents can afford it.'

Jeanette drained her glass, and rolled it in her hands. 'Yeah, he's got two kids. Never hear from them. Glad to be shot of him. No idea I'm saving him, and them, a fortune…going by what you charge, anyway.' She chuckled to herself. 'Maybe I should give you one of their phone numbers so you can offer your services, and tell them what you cost. That would show them.'

Annie pretended to bite. 'If you think they'd be interested…'

'Just joking.'

'Another?' Annie sighed internally at the thought of having to knock back another large gin, wishing she'd eaten more than the two sausage rolls that had been her evening meal.

'Go on then, why not? I like you, Annie Porter…but when you get back from the bar this time, let's talk about something more uplifting than washing old people and making sure they've taken their tablets, alright? That's a London accent, proper Cockney, if I'm not mistaken. I've got a few friends in London and I spent a lot of time there before…this. So let's chat about that instead, right?'

'Absolutely, doll,' said Annie grabbing her handbag. 'Oh there's some stories I could tell you.'

'And me you,' replied Jeanette.

Good, thought Annie as she waggled her card at the barman and signalled she wanted the same again, *because I want to find out as much as I can about you before I stagger back to my fancy rented flat for the night.*

CHAPTER FIFTEEN

Christine never liked to challenge Alexander outright. No head-on attacks for her; she'd learned, when negotiating as a broker at Lloyds in the City of London, that men would defend themselves once they knew they were under fire – it was much better to lull them into a false sense of security first. Thus, she preferred a course of action that allowed her to whittle away at Alexander's position until he was left with almost no possible defence – then go in for the kill.

It was late, and both she and her quarry were relaxing after a delicious dinner she'd prepared in the surprisingly useful kitchenette in her loft apartment. Christine was well aware that food didn't have to be exotic to be tasty and enjoyable, so her simple, homemade pasta dish, using aged parmesan, just a small amount of truffle, and good prosciutto, had done the trick. She'd chosen the best Amarone wine she had to hand because Alexander liked its intense flavor, and she knew it tended to put him in a good mood.

They'd chatted about the problems posed for the Twyst family by having a potential murderer as an ancestor, which had inevitably led to conversations about Alexander's lack of knowledge about his own father – and thence the equally inevitable suppositions about who he might have been.

'If my mother hadn't been so full of wildly entertaining stories, and booze, I'd have a better idea of what to believe. Maybe he was a Jamaican *gangsta*, or even a Nigerian prince…I have no idea, because she told me quite earnestly, on different occasions, that he was both. Or neither. It's just as likely he was one of the stall holders at Brixton Market. I'll never be sure. But I can't help wondering how my life might have turned out if he'd stuck around.'

Knowing from experience that this was a conversation that threatened to take them down some very bleak paths, Christine raised the topic of Bill Coggins and his unexpectedly bright future.

'Do you think you'll get to meet the mother of Bill's future child?' she asked, languidly pulling a blanket over her feet on the sofa.

'I'm sure I shall. Though I'm not sure when.'

'Is she from London, too? I know you said they met at the V & A, but that doesn't mean she's an actual Londoner.'

Alexander lifted his glass, examining the candlelight through the ruby wine. 'It didn't come up. He didn't say where she was from. Though, since they've been seeing so much of each other since they met, I suppose she must live in London now, even if she's not from there originally. Why do you ask?'

Christine shrugged, and picked up her own glass, aiming to appear as nonchalant as possible. 'Just curious. You don't think it's a bit…well, a bit convenient that this woman bumped into him, and now she's pregnant. It all seems a bit…quick. After all, anyone meeting Bill, and knowing about the Coggins antiques business, might think he's loaded; your involvement as the company's real owner isn't widely known about, is it?'

Alexander put down his glass, empty, then swivelled to face Christine. 'I know that Annie's off in Swansea looking into a situation that involves some sort of gold digger – as Althea put it, anyway – but do you think that's what's happening with Bill too? You don't think there's such a thing as love at first sight, between soulmates, who were destined to meet – even if they've left it a bit late in life to do so?'

Christine sat up. 'Love at first sight? No, I don't think it exists. If there's a connection from the off it has to be chemical, not emotional. You can't love someone, not in the real sense, until you know them. Before that point it's all pheromones, and lust.'

Christine didn't like the way Alexander chuckled. 'For a young, intelligent, beautiful woman, you're horribly cynical, you know. I never thought of myself as a romantic until I met you…you're the anti-romantic, aren't you? And it turns out that I'm the one who leads with his heart, when he should let his head play a bigger role.'

Christine didn't want to lose the ground she felt she'd gained by serving such a good dinner, so countered with: 'I am a romantic. Look at us – good food, excellent wine, candlelight, blankets on the sofa…what more can a girl do to create the perfect atmosphere?'

Alexander rose, his tone suddenly sharp. 'Okay then, yes, you're right, this has been a wonderful evening, and, if you want to, why don't you dig into Bill's girlfriend a bit? You're good at that, aren't you? All of you are. I know that her name is Natalie Smith, and that's all I know. Good luck with that. Let me know how you get on.'

Christine also stood, knowing she had to recapture the mood somehow. She stroked Alexander's arm as she purred, 'I'm sorry, I didn't mean to annoy you. I clearly have though – so why is that? Am I a horrible, hard-hearted woman?'

Alexander sighed and smiled. 'Not hard-hearted, but sometimes it's so clear that we differ in fundamental ways. You see, I truly think it's better to expect the best of people, knowing that sometimes – and only sometimes – you'll be disappointed. You seem to believe that everyone's going to let you down, and that you have to pitch in as though whatever it is you want, you're going to have to fight for it from the off. Not everything's a battle, Christine. Sometimes life is more about give and take than you seem to believe. I really hope that Bill and Nat have a healthy baby, and a wonderful future together. But, if something happens that means that's not the case, then it'll be no worse, or easier, to cope with if they've been dreading it happening.'

Christine could tell that the couple had somehow ended up having an important conversation – when all she'd wanted was to create a route to the place where she could confront Alexander about her suspicion that he hadn't spent the previous night at his flat in London, as he'd said he had. She had to decide how to proceed, and decided to follow his lead.

'Maybe I'm the way I am because I've been disappointed so many times, in so many ways, in the past,' she replied seriously. 'And I'm not bleating, just saying.'

Alexander's smile appeared cold to Christine as he replied, 'Oh my dear, you've been disappointed? Do you mean by men who haven't been as interested in your Mensa membership as much as your long legs? By men who've turned out to be just the same as all the other City and titled types you grew up mixing with? Because I don't know of any other ways you've been let down. Your parents are incredible people: your father's built a business by leveraging his contacts, yes, but he's built it from nothing, nonetheless; and your mother's done some amazing things for all sorts of charities, again, using your father's title, because being a viscountess means she can move in circles not available to everyone – and those circles contain quite a number of people with deep pockets, and an ability to make things happen because of what's in those pockets. You were well educated, blessed with a good brain, beauty too, and let's not forget an upbringing that was gilded, in every sense of the word. So how have you been disappointed? In what ways? By whom?'

Christine was taken aback. Alexander had never spoken to her in such a confrontational manner before. She'd always managed to sway him; bend him to her will. She was concerned about what it meant.

Deciding that it was best to be as open and honest as possible, she replied, 'For example, then…why did you lie about where you were last night? You told me you were at home, that you left to drive here this morning. But there's no way you'd have left your flat without having your daily workout, and you let it slip at the Hall today that you hadn't done that this morning – so where were you?'

Alexander chucked wryly, and plopped down onto the sofa. 'I get it now, that's what this evening's been about. Buttering me up to get me where you want me. Got it. Well, if you must know, I *was* at home last night, but I left earlier than I implied. Too early for even me to exercise. And, yes, you've got me…because I went down to Chelsea Harbour, to the office at the antiques warehouse, to see if I could find out a bit more about Bill's new consort. In fact, that's the only reason I even know she's named Natalie Smith, because Bill had been doodling it on some bits of paper when he'd been on the phone there. And…and I suppose the reason I've been pushing the "love at first sight" thing is because I want to believe it's true…maybe I even need to believe that it's true, that it's possible. But I fear it might not be. So, yes, you've got me. Right where you want me, as always.'

Christine felt bad. Alexander had been a complete rock since she'd been shot; he'd supported her emotionally, as well as being solicitous in the extreme when it came to her physical and mental well-being. And now here she was trying to game him – because that's what she'd been doing, no question about it. She sighed and joined him, pulling the blanket around her knees.

'Sorry,' she said, simply. 'And, yes, I could try to find out something about Natalie Smith, aged around forty, from somewhere, who now probably lives in London – but I might not get very far. Carol's our whizz at that sort of stuff, and Mavis has her chained to her laptop at home doing something for a client in Aberystwyth. But I could try. I have my moments.'

Alexander kissed her hair. 'You certainly do.'

'So who's let you down then?' Christine wanted Alexander to know she cared. 'That roofer you mentioned?'

'Him? Yeah – well, I'm not so bothered about him letting *me* down, that's just business…there are, literally, dozens of other roofing contractors I could have on those sites tomorrow morning…and I've sorted that part of it, because I can't have my tenants let down that way. It's not that. My problem with him is that he's disappeared completely, and I've found out that his wife and children are sitting in their home in Clapham without a clue where he's gone, and with a bank account that's got only half the amount of money in it that should be there. And that's not on, Christine. He's walked away from his business obligations which is bad, but that's nowhere near as dreadful as abandoning his family. I've met her quite a few times over the years – his wife – nice woman. Solid. Dependable. Now he's done a runner, and left her and the kids high and dry…not short of a bob or two, but utterly devastated.'

Christine was puzzled. 'Sorry to hear that. But, surely, that's not your problem, is it? I understand that you need to replace him in the business sense, but…well, I know it's very sad, but if a man choses to walk away from his family, how's that your problem?'

Alexander sighed heavily. 'Oh, come on, Christine – I thought you understood me well enough by now to not need to ask that. The people who know I'm in property development and rentals imagine I'm involved in the world of high finance and building glittering office blocks. But you know my life's really all about building and renovating houses and flats for people who need a hand up; safe, sound homes for folks who can't afford astronomical rents, and who'll take a pride in the place where they live. I also hire subcontractors who share those principles…or so I thought. You see, when someone you think is on the same wavelength as you, goes and does something that illustrates they just don't get it that we are, in fact, all living in the same world, all connected, and all responsible for each other in at least some ways, then it's not a stab in the back, it's a wound to the heart.'

Christine hoped he wasn't thinking of her as he spoke. 'So, who's the roofer?' She wasn't sure what else to say.

Alexander shook his head, smiling sadly. 'Ronnie. Ronnie Right, the roofer. And, yes, it's his real name. Everyone jokes about it, but at least it's memorable, and he's played on it for years. Dierdre, his wife, always used to quip about how she'd found her Mr Right. And meant it. Five kids they've got. Five.'

'Where's she from?'

Alexander smiled. 'Back in your "Old Country" originally, I believe. And yes, I'm aware she has the same name as your mother – has a different strength than your mum, though; not an outgoing woman, only attended social functions when it was absolutely necessary. Hated being away from home and the family for a minute.'

'Oh dear…'

'I know. It's terrible – and that's the thing, you see; I know what it's like to grow up believing my father left us because I wasn't worth sticking around for. Now Ronnie's kids will feel the same way about him, and that's not good. I know a couple of them are in their teens already, so maybe they'll get it that they weren't to blame, but the others? I worry about them. What paths they might choose to follow if they grow up thinking their own father thought they weren't worth his time…his effort.'

Christine felt the weight of Alexander's emotions. 'How can I help? Whatever it is, I'm in.'

Alexander kissed her tenderly. 'I'd hoped you'd say that.'

SATURDAY 22ND OCTOBER

CHAPTER SIXTEEN

Carol Hill looked down at her son with a smile as she rocked him in his swinging cradle with her foot. She sang softly – a lullaby-like version of 'The Green, Green Grass of Home' – hoping he'd drop off, but his smiling face and busy hands and feet told her that might take some time, though Bunty was already curled in a ball beneath his swing, fast asleep.

Outside her cozy kitchen the weather was just about as dreadful as it could be; the dimness enveloping the village was the best that could be expected, given how heavy the rain was, and she'd had all the lights on in the house since first thing, trying to make her home feel as jolly as possible. Taking a break from her rocking duties, she turned off the overhead light in the kitchen, hoping that would soothe Albert, but he was quiet, and happy, and she reckoned that was maybe the best she could hope for.

She'd been up with him several times during the night, but that hadn't been a bad thing, because she'd been working until gone two in the morning anyway, and was happy to be back at her laptop by six. All of which meant she'd already been able to contact the agency's client in Aberystwyth to explain the key points of her findings on the phone, as well as emailing off her full report, ahead of schedule. The client had been suitably impressed not only with the speed and depth of Carol's work, but also with what she'd discovered, which had put Carol in a good mood before she enjoyed a few fig rolls and a cup of tea around ten.

David had texted to say that his presentation of a paper at his conference had gone 'as well as could be expected'; they'd spent half an hour on a video call around eleven the previous night, when Carol hadn't been able to quieten Albert at all, and his father had offered to sing him lullabies so she could have a bit of a break. She'd been concerned that David's late night might have meant he was less than fresh for his presentation, so she'd been glad to hear that it had gone well.

With Albert dozing, Carol stepped into the sitting room to take a call from Sharon.

'I can't get hold of anyone who'll take any notice of me.' Sharon was cross, no doubt about it. 'I know it doesn't seem like much to them, but why can't the police see that theft is theft? Said someone might come around next week. I mean, what's the point of that, Carol?'

Carol gave the matter some thought. 'I tell you what, I know one of the local constables, personally; how about I try to get hold of her, and ask her to help?'

'Oh, you're magic, you are – though I'm very sorry Mavis says you can't help me yourself until the police have had a look.'

Carol sighed inwardly. 'Let me try to contact her, and I'll phone you back, alright?'

'Ta. Got to go. Customer.'

Carol peered out of her front window across the green; Marjorie Pritchard was shaking her umbrella – to death, by the looks of it – in the doorway of the shop, so she could imagine the mutual moaning that was about to begin between the two women, possibly under cover of Marjorie choosing a packet of biscuits, or a tin of something.

She punched Constable Llinos Trevelyan's number into her phone; they'd exchanged personal numbers having discovered a mutual interest in quilting when they'd been working on a case together months earlier, and – since then – had enjoyed chatting with each other, and many fellow quilters, in online forums connected to their hobby. It meant there was an international dimension to their friendship, though not a local one, which was both bizarre and yet strangely comforting; neither expected any great in-person interaction in Anwen-by-Wye, yet both felt the bond their online conversations had built.

'Carol?' Llinos sounded surprised. 'Is everything alright?'

'Don't panic, no problems,' said Carol hurriedly. She hoped she wasn't going to step over some invisible boundary in their friendship, but felt she had to do what she could to help Sharon. 'Just phoning for a chat. How's the "purple power" quilt coming along? It's your sister's birthday soon, isn't it? Will it be finished in time?'

Llinos laughed. 'If they stop sending me off to do overtime directing idiots who can't work out that a "ROAD CLOSED" sign means that a road is actually not open, no I won't…but I'm off today so, yes, I'm getting a good bit done right now, as it happens. Back on tomorrow though, so I'll just do the best I can. My sister won't mind if I take a photo of it, unfinished, and give her an IOU on the day. It won't be the first time my job's interfered with a family occasion.'

'I've just sent a report to a satisfied client, but I think the rest of the day will be mine. Until I start on a bit of a local thing…you know, a bit of a problem in the village. If Mavis allows me to work on it, that is – because she won't let me do anything until you lot have said you can't touch it.'

Llinos chuckled. 'Go on…what is it? We both know I owe you a favor – is this you asking for it back?'

Carol smiled, and hoped her friend could hear it in her voice. 'Yeah, I am, actually. It's a bit weird – a load of jars of preserves have been taken from the shed behind the post office and general shop, you know, Sharon's shop, in the village. The preserves were going to be sold to raise funds for a community project, see, so she's really hoping she can get them back – but…well…I suppose it's not a high priority for your superiors…' She didn't finish her sentence, hoping Llinos would jump in.

'My shift starts at one tomorrow. How about I pop into the shop to pick up something for my lunch around ten thirty? I dare say Sharon would take the chance to mention it to me when I'm on the spot, wouldn't she? How would that work for you?'

Carol beamed. 'Thanks, Llinos – it would mean the world to her…and, by extension, to me too. I'll see you then. I'll have Albert with me, 'cos his dad's away at the moment. You won't mind too much, will you? I know you're not big on kids.' Carol's laugh sounded forced even to her own ears.

'Hey, I said that in general terms; just because I don't want any kids myself doesn't mean I can't appreciate other people's. I can smile at them, and make them smile back, but I don't have to do anything else. So, yes, it'll be lovely to see you and Albert…and Sharon…tomorrow morning. Let's make sure our plan doesn't reach "official" police ears though, eh?'

'Mum's the word,' said Carol, then she giggled at her quip. 'See you tomorrow – I'll have to tell Sharon about our plan so she stops bothering your lot at the station, but I'll make sure she doesn't share it. See you then – and thanks…oh – before you go, I'll bring what I've got left over of that lavender mini-print for you, alright? Bye.'

'Thanks, great, bye.'

Carol glowed at her son and said, 'Mam's done two good things today, Albert, and look, it's only lunchtime. Speaking of which…' Carol busied herself around the kitchen – quietly, and in the half-light – before sitting to check her emails.

She munched on a ham sandwich as she read a promising report from Annie, who seemed to be making good progress with her case in Swansea, as well as one from Mavis – who was asking Carol to phone her later in the day to discuss how she might be able to help with the matter they were looking into at Chellingworth Hall – though she didn't say what that was. There was another email from Christine, who was asking if Carol might have any 'free time' to be able to help with some background research for her and Alexander. The thought of 'free time' almost made Carol choke on her lunch, but she'd recovered by the time her phone rang. It was Annie.

Having had a nice chat with her chum and colleague – who she missed a great deal – and with a full tummy, Carol sat staring at her son, and didn't feel herself dropping off to sleep in the chair until she slipped, knocked her plate onto the floor with a crash – which sent Bunty screeching away in a panic, which woke Albert, who also started to scream. Carol suspected she'd end up driving around in the rain listening to Tom Jones before too long.

CHAPTER SEVENTEEN

Annie Parker was already pooped, and her day still had a long way to go. She'd spent the morning in the swish flat that belonged to a friend of her clients; the bloke in question worked for an oil company, and was away every other month – which meant his place was available at a 'friends' rate' to Tina and Tanya Turnbull, Frank's daughters, so they were paying for it, and Annie was reaping the benefits.

The bay windows surrounding the small dining table Annie had covered with her laptop, paperwork, and various electronic devices, overlooked Langland Bay itself, which was bounded by green space at one end and a more rugged cliff face at the other. Beneath her she could see the waves crashing onto the rocks, as well as rushing across the sand, all beyond a serried row of roofs, which sat atop delightful green-and-white wooden cabins used as day huts during the summer months. Exotic-looking palms waved in the blustery wind, and the rain had finally stopped. There were clouds massed on the horizon; Annie reckoned she'd be going out in her waterproofs again that evening, when she was to meet Jeanette Summers, as arranged, at seven, in the bar of the Seaview Hotel.

She settled to speak to Carol, the WISE women's designated collector and collator of all daily reports. She'd already sent an email, but fancied hearing Carol's voice. They'd chatted the previous day, but Annie missed her chum more than usual, though she wasn't sure why. Maybe she just needed to hear the voice of someone who would speak to Annie Parker, real person – not Annie Porter, fictional unemployed carer.

'Hello Car, doll, how you doin'?'

'Annie, lovely to hear from you. I got your email, thanks. How's it going – ready to sally forth and capitalize upon the great start?'

Carol's tone was warm, but smacked of the conversation being all business, so Annie steered it as best she could. 'All in hand, Car. How's Bertie? You two managing alright with Dave away?'

'*Albert* is just fine, thanks. As am I. A bit busy though, truth be told.'

Annie sensed that something wasn't quite right. 'What's up? Summat is – so spill the beans.'

She heard Carol sigh. 'Can't get anything past you, can I? Don't know why I try. You knew I had that thing to do for the worried client in Aberystwyth, didn't you?'

'Hairdressing woman…wants financial background and business credentials check for a bloke who wants to buy her out and is a bit too pushy about it. The Case of the Aggressive Acquisition. Yeah, I know about it. Hasn't he got the money after all? All hat and no cattle, as I believe they say in the good old US of A.'

'More likely to say all sheepdogs and no sheep around here – but, yes, he's got the money. Pots of it – which he seems to have made by buying up chains of service companies then getting rid of half the staff, and working the ones he hasn't fired so hard that they all leave of their own accord, saving him money in the process.'

'Ah – so the client's not pleased, then?'

'Deliriously happy: she's got a good enough reason to turn him down now, which I think was what she wanted all along.'

Annie was puzzled. 'Sounds like you did a great job, Car, and we've got another satisfied client then. So that's not what's got you sounding a bit off – so what has?'

When Carol sighed again, Annie added, 'You sound like a balloon with a leak. Come on – out with it.'

Carol explained about the theft from the shed behind Sharon's shop, and how anxious she'd become that she'd had to get on with the paying client's work before being able to give her attention to the missing preserves.

'Well, if Constable Llinos Trevelyan is doing you a favor by agreeing to examine Sharon's shed in the morning, it seems you've done all you can to get the ball rolling,' said Annie, when Carol stopped to draw breath. 'You know we can't touch that sort of case with a ten-foot bargepole as far as Mave's concerned. It's theft, and it should be the police who get called in first.'

'I don't think Llinos will be able to do much, but I'll be there when she arrives, so we can see what's what together, and at the same time. If she can't help, then maybe Mavis will okay me putting a few hours into it – as a sort of community service effort. You know Althea's big on that sort of thing, so I might be able to get her on my side...though they're both a bit more difficult to get hold of than usual at the moment – seem to be spending all their time up at the Hall. Not sure what they're up to, but when I spoke to Mavis yesterday she sounded quite out of breath.'

Annie chuckled. 'Probably chasing McFli around the place.' At the thought of Althea's dog, Annie's thoughts turned to Gertie; she'd had no idea she could miss a gangly ball of fur so much. 'You haven't happened to see Tude out walking Rosie and Gertie, by any chance, have you?'

'I've been glued to my laptop and phone all day and more or less all night; it seems Albert's only happy to sleep when his father's actually in the house. David sang him lullabies on his mobile from Brighton last night just so I could get a bit of a rest, but even that didn't really do the trick for long.'

Although she really wanted to, Annie hesitated to tell her friend about what Tudor had said about 'love' when they'd been having their farewell dinner in his flat, because she reckoned Carol had a full enough plate. Instead, she soothed her friend with: 'Well, he's quiet now, so maybe just rest when he does, eh? I'd offer to sing to him for a bit myself, but that would just set him off bawling. If he's as much of a fan of Jones the Voice as you say he is – why not try playing those songs for him in the house, not just in the car?'

'Tried it, and it didn't work. Wish it did...though I'm not sure how many more times I can listen to "The Green, Green Grass of Home" without wanting to be under it myself.'

'You'll be alright, doll. Strong as one of those little Welsh pit ponies, you are...so I know you'll put your head down and get through this. When's Dave back?'

'Not until Monday night. And you're right – I'll be fine. Albert's got to sleep at some point...so I'll sleep then too. But listen. Before you go…good luck this evening. Just get into character, and use your intelligence to make sure you're safe, okay?'

'Got it. Will do. Be safe yourself. Talk soon. I'll email you; wouldn't want to disturb a sleeping baby by phoning his mum. Hug Bertie for me.'

Annie hung up before Carol could tell her off for not using her son's proper name, which Annie judged to be a mini triumph.

CHAPTER EIGHTEEN

'I'm glad we made an early start,' said Henry, 'and I do understand it's not even time for elevenses yet, but I'm beginning to wonder if we're ever going to find anything even remotely useful in this lot.' Henry was exasperated. Dusty *and* exasperated, which was even worse. He'd had to step away from the books spread across several tables on many occasions to tend to the explosive sneezing from which he was now – and possibly for life, he feared – suffering. And he wasn't the only one; even Stephanie had resorted to wiping one book at a time with a duster, then sitting with it splayed on her lap, turning the pages exceptionally slowly, to try to keep the dust where it lay.

Alexander seemed to be the only one among them not brought low by fits of sneezing. Indeed, it annoyed Henry more than a little that both Alexander and Christine seemed to be able to read so much, so quickly, and that Alexander was the one who'd found the parts of the family history pertaining to the fourteenth duke, and had also been the one to confirm that the entries about the thirteenth duke amounted to little more than a few lines about his having installed the gardens.

Not that Henry felt any real animosity toward Alexander; he'd been kind enough to sacrifice his plans for the weekend to help out, and Henry was grateful for that. No, what irked Henry about the chap, and – he admitted silently to himself – what had irked him since he'd first met him, was the ease with which he appeared to be able to do everything. Alexander Bright was sporty, well built, and quick-witted – all of which Henry knew he, personally, wasn't. The fact that he was also knowledgeable about antiques, books, literature, and even art was what really got Henry's goat, but he knew it shouldn't, which made the way he felt about Alexander even worse.

Henry knew an amount about the man's background, and didn't begrudge him the rewards of what must have been a supreme effort to lift himself up and out of the notorious council estates in Brixton, to reach the heights he had, not only in terms of his acquisition of knowledge, but his application of all his talents to the world of business, and property development in particular.

Now, as he sat watching Alexander read aloud from the family history – *his* family's history – he felt somewhat detached from his surroundings. As Alexander spoke of Harold, a man who'd had to turn his back on his career as a gifted musician, with connections across the whole of Europe, Henry couldn't help but think of the parallels with his own situation. Harold had taken the seat when his cousin had died; Henry had been summoned back to the seat when his older brother had died before even acceding. Harold had given up his music; Henry had given up his art. And both of them had had to face the uncomfortable specter of Frederick, their ancestor.

Henry sighed; the only passion he'd ever had in life was art, and his only real desire had always been to be a creator...to live the carefree, yet intense, life of an artist. But, no – here he was trawling through dusty books, desperate to save the family's reputation, all as part of his duty to the seat, the name, and his predecessors.

Looking across at his wife, Henry pulled back his shoulders, and sat up a little straighter; he reminded himself that he wasn't doing all this for the people who had gone before him, but for his child – and his dear Stephanie, of course. He wanted his firstborn to be able to start life with a clean slate, to not have to carry the burden of suspecting the thirteenth duke – 'Fred', for heaven's sake! – of being a cold-blooded killer, or to maybe understand the truth behind his crimes, had they been committed.

Henry had to admit he was clinging to the thinnest thread of hope – or was it merely a wish? – that they might manage to turn up some sort of evidence that Frederick hadn't killed anyone at all, that it had all been a dreadful misunderstanding – but he sagged again as he realized they were just as likely to discover that the man might have been a completely appalling person, with innocent blood on his hands.

'Are you feeling quite well, Henry, dear?' Henry's mother was peering at him across the library, poking Mavis's leg with her cane to try to get her friend's attention. 'Mavis, put those rather out-of-practice, but still no-doubt quite useful, nursing skills of yours to the test to see if Henry's alright, would you, please.'

Mavis turned to face Henry; Henry straightened his back and attempted to stare the woman down – but he felt the full force of her years as the matron overseeing the Battersea Barracks for retired service folk bearing down on him as she approached.

'Your eyes are bloodshot, and your nose is pink. You're no' liking the dust, are you?'

He noticed that Mavis never referred to him as Your Grace, but she never used his name, either. In fact, he struggled to recall her addressing him as anything; it was as though she felt she didn't need to use the former – due to the fact she'd now been his mother's live-in companion for almost a year – and felt uncomfortable using the latter.

As Mavis peered into Henry's face he spluttered, 'You're quite right, Mavis, and Stephanie's been sneezing terribly too.'

Before he could add more, his wife snapped, 'If you suggest that my sneezing isn't good for the baby, I might explode, Henry.' Stephanie tutted loudly, then added, 'And, yes, I realize that's a poor choice of words, but you know very well what I mean.'

'I wasn't considering saying anything of the sort, dear,' said Henry, glad that she'd cut him off just as he was about to say that exact thing.

Christine said, 'It is all a bit dusty, I'll grant you that, but we might be starting to see a little light. That passage Alexander read aloud tells us that Harold really did commission a report about Fred, right, Alexander?'

Alexander peered at the page in question. 'Yes, it's quite clear, but the family history also says: "While it was felt appropriate for the family to know the truth about Frederick, it was agreed that, thenceforth, no mention should be made of his tenure, neither within, nor beyond, the family circle. The report was commissioned, received, and its contents noted. It will not be referred to hereafter. To draw a line beneath Frederick's time, and make no further mention of him, is agreed as the best course of action". Now, to me, that suggests the report's been stored away somewhere it won't be easily found by someone casually looking around the library – so, maybe we need to search further afield for it.'

Henry said, 'This might be an opportune moment for you and me, Stephanie, to go up to the rooms used by Harold to see if there's anything there that might be of relevance. Alexander makes a good point: Harold might have kept those records somewhere private, rather than on display here, for all to see, so I would suggest his personal rooms would be a likely place to search.'

Henry was a bit miffed that Stephanie looked surprised when she replied, 'An excellent idea, Henry. It would be good for me to move about a bit. Do you know where his rooms were?'

'Indeed, my dear, I am familiar with their location. And, as I recall, there's a delightful blue wallpaper in his bedchamber that might be an inspiration for our own child's room, were you to produce a boy.'

Henry's confidence wavered as his wife's expression clouded. 'Whatever I "produce", Henry, our child will have a yellow-and-green room, that decision has already been made, if you recall.'

Henry nodded. 'Of course.'

'We'll manage alone,' said Stephanie, rising from her seat. 'Come along, Henry, lead the way.'

As her son and daughter-in-law left the library, Althea said, 'Mavis, Young Ian will be here to drive us to the rectory to take morning tea with the Reverend Roberts in a few minutes, why don't we prepare to leave now too?'

As Althea and Mavis were escorted down the front steps by Edward, Henry and Stephanie set off to the second floor.

Stephanie chided, 'Go on, Henry, get a move on. You're supposed to be leading, but I could jump over your head.' She overtook him on the first landing and marched off toward the stairs to the second floor. 'It's this wing, correct?'

'Yes, dear.'

Henry was dawdling on purpose, because he couldn't imagine they'd simply walk into Harold's rooms and light upon a secret report, about a secret investigation, to discover the truth about his family's enormous secret just…well, just handily lying about on a desk, or tucked into the unlocked drawer of a nightstand.

Stephanie screamed, 'Henry!'

'Yes dear. Coming.' He sighed, and plodded on.

When Henry eventually reached the top of the second staircase, feeling a bit puffed, he rounded the corner beyond which his beautifully pregnant wife had disappeared – and was horrified to see her curled on her side, on the floor, groaning.

'Stephanie! My darling!' He rushed to her side. 'Help!' he shouted with all his might. 'Somebody help!'

CHAPTER NINETEEN

The Reverend Ebenezer Roberts had been most accommodating. Not only had he served the dowager and Mavis with an excellent selection of biscuits, but he'd also committed himself to hunting out all the records kept at St David's Church concerning the thirteenth, fourteenth, and even the fifteenth, dukes.

As he went to the rectory's kitchen to make a second pot of tea, Althea whispered to Mavis, 'Don't you think it was a good idea of mine to make him think we're interested in all three of them? That'll throw him off the scent.'

Mavis reckoned Althea was being unnecessarily cautious. 'Ach, the wee man doesnae care, Althea, you can see that. He's no clue about the scandal surrounding Fred.'

At that moment, Mavis was glad that the somewhat childish code name had been agreed upon for the thirteenth duke, because it turned out that the reverend was surprisingly light on his feet, and had entered the sitting room just as she'd made her remark.

'I say, a scandal concerning a chap named Fred? I don't think we have anyone by that name in our congregation…might this pertain to one of your so-called "enquiries", Mrs MacDonald?'

Mavis had to be content with a polite: 'Indeed it does, Vicar, one of our many successful enquiries.' Knowing full well that the Reverend Ebenezer Roberts hated being called 'vicar', allowed her to feel she'd won a point to match his – possibly unintended – sneer.

'So, when do you think we might have a look at those records, Vicar?' she added, pushing home her advantage. 'We're happy to wait if you'd fetch them now.'

The Reverend Roberts was aged, and not known for his vim, or vigor. Thus, Mavis wasn't surprised that her call for action left him nonplussed, and wittering.

'Well, I dare say I could go across to the vestry now, if you'd like. Indeed – if you didn't mind waiting for a second pot of tea, Your Grace, we could all go together. That way Your Grace would be able to read the records on the spot. I couldn't possibly let them leave the premises, you see, not even with Your Grace.'

Mavis admitted he made a fair point, though his 'Your Grace-ing' was getting on her nerves. 'Aye, well, that's a good idea, isn't it…Your Grace?' She stared at Althea, hoping the dimpling in the dowager's cheeks didn't mean she was about to burst out laughing, or say something she shouldn't.

The robust 'Capital idea, Reverend' that Althea all but shouted as she pushed herself up out of her seat made the man blink with shock, and brought Mavis to the verge of the giggles herself.

Ach, that wee woman can be an imp when she wants, flitted through Mavis's mind. She hovered beside Althea as the threesome made their way cross the graveyard to the door to the vestry, at the side of the church.

The reverend produced a spectacularly large and ancient iron key with which he opened the spectacularly large and ancient iron lock. Once they were inside, Mavis got Althea settled on what appeared to be the least uncomfortable chair among a host of wooden seats that all seemed to have been chosen because they offered the sitter no ease whatsoever. She herself perched on what looked like a block of wood – nothing more, nothing less – as Ebenezer Roberts dragged an alarmingly rickety set of steps across the flagstone floor. These allowed him to reach a large cupboard – which had another massive iron lock, requiring another massive iron key.

Annoyed that she couldn't make out what he was doing, Mavis waited impatiently, and noticed that Althea's hands were trembling a little.

She leaned over and whispered, 'If you have gloves in that handbag of yours, I suggest you put them on. It's freezing in here, and we might be some time.'

Althea brightened. 'Of course, you're right. I do.' She pulled a pair of hand-knitted luminous green mittens out of her capacious tangerine leather handbag. Mavis thought they sat uncomfortably with Althea's bulky teal coat, and was quite taken aback when her friend pulled a fluorescent yellow, fake-fur hat, with ear flaps that reached below her chin, onto her head as well. 'There, much better,' said Althea, looking happy.

When Reverend Roberts had descended the steps – without incident, Mavis was relieved to see – he turned to place a large volume on the table beside which the two women were sitting, and gasped aloud at the sight of the dowager. Mavis noted that he blushed, but didn't comment on Althea's startling garb. She gave the man credit for that, at least.

'This would be the volume of records in question. It covers the whole of the nineteenth century, so would encompass the thirteenth to the fifteenth dukes, in toto. Would you like me to open it to …was it 1835, Your Grace?'

Althea replied, 'It was, and that would be most kind. Will you require us to wear gloves while we're perusing the pages, Reverend, or will my mittens suffice?' She smiled sweetly, waggling her hands at the cleric.

Mavis shot a particularly withering look at Althea, who ignored her.

The reverend spluttered, 'Whatever Your Grace chooses. I'm sure Your Grace's hands are quite clean enough to be used, should you wish to remove your…hand coverings.'

'You may leave us. We'll return to the rectory when we've finished here,' said Althea, in her most imperious tone.

Ebenezer Roberts nodded and said, 'But of course, Your Grace.' He left the two women alone.

'Ach, the poor man all but shuffled out of here backwards, you wee scamp,' said Mavis, free to speak her mind at last.

Althea smiled too sweetly. 'Come on, Mavis – let's not hang about, this place is freezing. Can your phone take photos that are good enough for us to be able to read all this tiny writing? Take a couple and check – then we can just snap away, and give it our attention later on, somewhere warm – maybe after lunch, up at the Hall. I know that being eighty doesn't mean I'm about to drop off my perch at a moment's notice, but I do find it terribly difficult to warm up once I've become chilled through these days…so, go on, get snapping – even if you have to do it several times per page. It'll mean we can get out of here in double-quick time.'

Mavis congratulated Althea on her excellent idea, discovered it was a system that would work well, and the women spent the next quarter of an hour photographing pages of painstakingly formed copperplate.

Finally back in the comparative warmth of the reverend's sitting room, and with a fresh pot of tea to help ward off the chills, Mavis felt the tension in the room increase exponentially as Althea began her explanation of what she'd like to see happen to celebrate *Nos Galan Gaeaf.*

During her decades of nursing, Mavis MacDonald had seen many things – some of them quite dreadful – but the sight of the Reverend Ebenezer Roberts gradually crumbling beneath the weight of the Dowager Chellingworth's continual, and incessant, onslaught was unique. Whatever the man said, Althea had her response ready: he said heathen, she emphasized tradition; he pleaded inappropriateness, she countered with birthright; he mentioned the bishop's likely displeasure, she mentioned the bishop's wife, her goddaughter; he insisted no church property could be used, she offered the Chellingworth Estate in place of the church hall.

Mavis watched in silence, never doubting the outcome.

'I'm glad it's all agreed then,' concluded Althea. 'I'll make it known that this year there'll be a host of traditional celebrations taking place at the Hall on the evening of October the thirty-first, to mark the beginning of the Celtic winter season the next day. You are welcome to join us, Reverend Roberts, or not – as you see fit. Now come along, Mavis, or we'll be late for lunch.'

Mavis wondered if Ebenezer Roberts would need a lie-down after the women left – she knew she would have done, had she been him.

CHAPTER TWENTY

It was dark by the time Annie set out from the flat, and the rain was just about starting, so she bundled up and headed to the bar at a swift pace. Even so, she got caught in a bit of a downpour, so ended up entering the doors through which she'd dramatically fallen the previous evening in a gingerly manner, making sure to wipe her feet well, and examining the tiled entryway for signs of sneaky puddles.

Jeanette was standing at the bar, where Annie joined her with a cheery, 'Not too late, am I? Have you started without me?'

Jeanette Summers looked her up and down. 'Look, everyone, it's Annie. She managed to walk in like a normal human being tonight.'

A few friendly smiles met Annie's semi-comedic shrugs.

'Glad you could make it, Annie. And no, you're not late – it's bang on seven. Just an hour here for me tonight though – Frank's been really unsteady today, and I don't want to leave him on his own for too long. I wouldn't have come at all if it hadn't been for me saying I'd meet you. But, I tell you what, you could come back to my place when we leave here. We've got some wine there – or you could keep going with the G & Ts if you prefer; we're never short of a drop or two of gin back at the house. If I'm there I can keep an ear open, in case he needs me. I don't want him wandering around like he was all last night. It's not too far, and it's an easy walk back down to the place you're staying, even in the dark.'

Annie was a bit taken aback by Jeanette's booming, and unexpected, bonhomie, but decided to react to the idea with enthusiasm, so they settled themselves at a quiet corner table where Annie managed to turn on the digital recording device in her pocket to capture every word as they chatted over their drinks. She was aware she'd never be able to play the recordings for her clients, but she found them valuable when she was making notes.

'How's your day been? Not too bad, I hope.' Annie thought it best to begin with an open-ended question.

Jeanette bit. 'It's been a difficult one, I have no idea why some days are better than others, but this was a bad one, which is why I don't want to be away from him for too long. But I'm glad we'd arranged to meet, because I might not have come otherwise, and I do feel better for a little bit of a break.'

'Do you have to lock him up when you're away from him?' Annie made sure she sounded as though this were the most natural of enquiries. 'I've known some of the carers I've met have said it's the only way to keep them safe – you know, when they don't really know what's good for them anymore.' Would Jeanette confess to treating Frank Turnbull in such a way?

'He's not my prisoner, Annie. And I don't think he's that bad, yet. Though maybe it'll come to that one day.'

Annie tried a different tack. 'I bet it's a lovely spot, up there on the cliffside. Nice view and all that. I've had some positions where all I had was four walls to look at – or a brick terrace across the road. Hopefully you've got the wherewithal there to make him, and you, comfortable; I know that makes a big difference.'

Jeanette leaned in. 'Yeah, it's a nice house. But you'll be there later so you can see for yourself. All a bit old fashioned, but that doesn't bother me. His late wife used to collect gaudy Welsh china; hideous stuff, but worth a bob or two.'

Annie saw a glimmer of hope. 'I never know why they all seem to hang onto so much tat. They never seem to see the sense of getting rid of all their old bits and pieces so they can enjoy the end of their life a bit better. Makes no sense to me – nor to others I've spoken to. But they all seem to do it.'

As she spoke, Annie could see in her mind's eye her own mother caressing an ugly, shell-covered jar that she kept in pride of place on a sideboard in the family's small sitting room; it had been decorated for Annie's mother by *her* mother, and Annie knew Eustelle would never, ever part with it – nor would Annie, when it eventually passed from Eustelle, to her. As the fleeting thought of her mother's advancing years crossed Annie's mind, she inexplicably felt her eyes welling up with tears, which appeared to confuse and concern Jeanette.

'Hey, no need for you to go getting yourself all upset about it, Annie – it's their stuff, they can do what they want with it, after all.' She threw Annie a sideways look of consternation.

Annie did her best to cover with: 'Yeah, well – I don't like seeing them suffer more than they need to, see, and if only they'd turn some of their bits and bobs into cash, they could have a better quality of life all round.' She hoped she'd got away with it.

'Some of them do, sometimes, Annie, especially with a bit of persuasion.' Jeanette leaned in close, her voice becoming a conspiratorial whisper. 'There's a friend of mine – an old school friend, in fact – who was living with a nice local chap, in Pontardawe.' Annie shrugged. 'Don't worry about where that is, it doesn't really matter, but it's not far from here, really. Anyway, she eventually managed to talk him into selling a vintage car that was just sitting in his garage, and he got a good price for it. They were able to go off on a nice cruise to the Canaries…which was funny, really, because his name was Finch. He admitted he'd enjoyed the cruise more than he'd ever enjoyed the car – which was good, because the poor bloke didn't last much longer, as it all turned out. Had a bit of an accident when he went out for a walk on his own at a local beauty spot, the Cwm Du gorge, poor dab.'

Annie did her best to look sage. 'Glad he enjoyed spending his money before he went,' she observed. Then – hoping she wasn't pushing too far, too fast – she added, 'My last lady agreed with me that liquidating a few assets was a good idea, but she…had an accident soon after, too, which was very sad. Didn't have a chance to spend any of it. But, there, I'm putting it to good use right now, aren't I? Fancy another – just a cheeky one before we go?'

Jeanette nodded, and Annie could tell the woman was thinking about what she'd just said. Had she done enough to at least set Jeanette on the road to believing that the two women might share similar views about liberating the value of the possessions of the elderly?

When Annie returned with the drinks, Jeanette said, 'Let's not hang about – I bet you can manage to neck this one down. I hadn't realized the time. We'll get back to the house then, alright? And when we get there, we'll have to have a bit more of a chat about this last woman you worked for…like how it was you managed to get her to "liquidate her assets" as you so carefully put it. But there, you strike me as quite a careful woman, Annie Porter.'

Annie preened. 'They do say you can't be too careful, and I wouldn't be feathering my nest for a relatively early and comfortable retirement if I weren't just about as careful as I can be.' She felt an amount of satisfaction when she recognized the glint of greed in Jeanette's eyes, as well as a hint of curiosity. She hoped she'd hooked her…though there wasn't really much on the recording she was making that would prove useful against the woman as far as the two Turnbull sisters were concerned; she'd have to try harder when they got back to the house.

Polishing off her drink in double-quick time, Annie popped to the loo ahead of their departure and tucked away all her electronics in a plastic container in her handbag. When she got back to the bar, Jeanette was giggling with the young barman, and Annie heard her say, 'I know, I know but look at the time…I want to be back with him by eight tonight. See you tomorrow…' Then they were waved at by the barman and a few others as they set off into the lashing rain.

With Frank Turnbull's house being above the beach by some way, the road they had to walk up twisted and turned, to prevent it from being almost vertical; the water gurgled down it in dozens of rivulets, and Annie was glad she'd worn her rainboots, even if they weren't the best for hillwalking.

'This must keep you fit,' puffed Annie as they reached a gate which Jeanette threw open before she made her way along a short path to a wide front door. The jolly yellow paint glowed in the light from a pair of carriage lamps that illuminated Jeanette's struggle to find her keys in her handbag.

Just as she raised them triumphantly, she dropped her bag in a puddle. 'Damn! Can you open up while I shake this off, please, Annie

– I don't want the leather to get soaked through. You'll want the brass Yale key, not the silver one.'

Annie took the bunch of keys. 'Yeah, course I can, doll.' She unlocked the door and pushed it open. In front of her was an outdated, though richly carpeted, hallway and a carpeted staircase with gleaming wooden bannisters. But what really caught her attention was the crumpled body at the foot of the stairs. Annie felt her knees weaken, which annoyed her, and she let out an honest-to-goodness gasp of horror.

Jeanette pushed her aside. 'Oh no…Frank! I knew it…I knew he'd fall one day. Oh Frank, what have you done?' She stamped around the entryway, flapping her wet coat, and wailing.

Annie stood inside the door, stock still, staring into the man's eyes. They stared back, unblinking. She couldn't look away from his eyes: the eyes she'd thought had looked kind when he'd smiled in a photo booth; the eyes that had looked happy as he'd lunged to take a bite of Jeanette's candy floss. She croaked, 'Is he dead?', knowing the answer.

Jeanette snorted. 'Of course he's dead…look at him! How could he be that shape and not be dead? But try for a pulse – go on…you do it…I can't bring myself to touch him.'

Jeanette retreated to the end of the hallway; she couldn't get far enough away from the corpse of her dead boyfriend, it seemed.

Annie eventually gathered enough courage to step forward. She touched Frank Turnbull's neck. Nothing. No pulse, though she was surprised that his skin didn't feel as cold as she'd expected it to. She managed to say, 'I'll phone 999.'

'Yes, you'd better. After all, you were the one who found him.'

Annie didn't care for Jeanette's accusing tone, and she felt her tummy tighten, though she didn't know why. Maybe it was because she was still reeling from the shock of their discovery – or the sudden fear she might be about to face the police while using an assumed name and personality.

CHAPTER TWENTY-ONE

Christine had to admit that – even for her – it had been a strange day; what had promised to be a productive search for the truth about an old secret at Chellingworth Hall, had morphed into chaos when Stephanie had taken an unexpected tumble before lunch. Of course, everyone had been relieved when the doctor had arrived, examined her, and pronounced Stephanie, and the baby, as having come to no real harm, but Christine had found it difficult to cope with Henry spiralling out of control, so she and Alexander had excused themselves once she was certain there was nothing they could do to help. Not even offering to continue reading through the dozens of books they'd hauled off shelves in the Chellingworth library was a starter; Henry had made it clear to everyone that he felt a Peaceful Hall would be a Happy Hall for his wife, so the entire 'team' had been stood down.

The ploughman's lunch she and Alexander had agreed would suffice at the Lamb and Flag hadn't turned out to be a roaring success, either; Tudor Evans had run out of pickled onions – a major catastrophe, it seemed – and it appeared there were none at all to be had in the village. He'd dispatched Aled to Builth Wells to buy some, and *he'd* disappeared for much longer than it took the couple to consume their meal without pickled onions – not that, in the scheme of things, that had been such a loss, because, as Christine knew only too well, they did tend to linger on the breath. But, once again, chaos had reigned during their time at the pub.

Without their entire day being spoken for at the Hall, as they'd expected, Christine spent the afternoon in the office trying to track down the incredibly elusive Natalie Smith, with absolutely no luck whatsoever, while Alexander had paced about making phone calls and typing emails and texts with angry thumbs.

Over tea she announced to Alexander, 'I've checked all the Natalie and Nat Smiths on all the major social networks, but – without a photo, or knowing what she looks like – I still have quite a few contenders. People use avatars so often, and of course they don't sometimes give their ages...so she might be on there, but I haven't found anyone who mentioned Bill Coggins, nor anyone who has him as a contact, where I was able to see contacts.'

Alexander sounded grumpy when he replied, 'Don't worry. I'll see if I can get him to show me a picture of her, how about that? That might help, right?'

'How about inviting them both for dinner, in London, soon – our treat. It would be natural enough, wouldn't it?' Christine thought it sounded like a good idea.

Alexander didn't seem convinced. 'With Bill and me having to discuss him buying the business back, and on what basis that would happen, well, maybe dinner might not be as jolly an affair as you might think. You see, to be honest, I can't work out where the money would come from.'

'What's happening on that front then? Is it him you've been messaging and on the phone with upstairs all afternoon?'

'A bit. And a few other things. At least I've managed to get some crews to turn up at a few of the roofing jobs – the most urgent ones. Of course, it's tough for roofers when the weather's like this because there are so many emergencies, yet it's so dangerous for them to be up there, doing their job. The weather hasn't been quite as bad back in London as it has been here, but it's still been a bit of a scramble to get people out to urgent jobs, and there's more to do by Monday in terms of picking up the regular maintenance contracts. I put a lot of work Ronnie Right's way.'

Christine could tell he was distracted, so decided to not dawdle. 'Okay – we need to make a decision about dinner; pasta, just the way I made it last night – because, of course, I rather overestimated the amount of ingredients I'd need – or do you want to go back to the Lamb and Flag, to make sure we're completely abreast of the situation concerning the great pickled onion shortage in Anwen-by-Wye?'

Alexander smouldered. 'You, me, pasta, Amarone, early night – take two, please. With the same for dessert as last night, thank you.'

Christine had already said, 'But we didn't have any dessert,' before she realized what he meant. She giggled. 'Excellent plan.'

It was around midnight when Christine woke to find herself alone in bed. The rain was beating against the window, the wind was making something clatter outside, and she was cold. She stayed where she was, letting her eyes adjust to the dark, then realized there was a light showing under the bedroom door.

She padded to the bathroom, which was empty, then peered over the balustrade down to the office. All the lights were on, but it was deserted. So where was Alexander? Unless he was in the office loo, downstairs, she couldn't imagine where he could be, especially given the weather.

Christine had a horrible thought: what if he'd left, in the middle of the night? She went back into the bedroom, turned on the light, and hunted for a note. She even checked her phone for a text, then told herself she was being stupid; if he'd had to leave in the dead of night, Alexander would have woken her to tell her so, and why.

Pulling on a pair of socks and a heavy robe, Christine carefully descended the spiral staircase. Outside, Alexander's car was parked where it had been, and he wasn't in it, so she crossed the barn to the washrooms.

She could hear him, speaking on his phone. Alexander wasn't exactly shouting, but he was speaking with great vehemence. She stood beside the closed door and listened.

'Send Jerry over there, he knows Ronnie, they go way back…No…No, I can't…Jerry's more than up to it…Well track him down then – tell Jerry to take a photo with him, show it around. God knows Ronnie's so flash people will know him if he's in the area…How would I know…Yes…No…Let him know what's what…Yes, if needs be…Yes, I will…You know exactly how far to go…Yes, just stop him walking at all, that should do it…He needs to understand who's in charge…Tomorrow, yes…Good.'

Christine could tell that Alexander had ended his call, so sped across the office, up the stairs, and leapt into bed. When Alexander joined her, he slipped between the sheets and fell asleep quickly.

Christine couldn't help but keep replaying what she'd heard: had Alexander Bright just given orders for someone named Jerry to be dispatched to somewhere or other to break Ronnie Right's legs, thereby leaving the roofer in no doubt about who was in charge? She clutched the duvet beneath her chin, and eventually fell into a fitful sleep.

CHAPTER TWENTY-TWO

Annie reckoned that if she drank any more tea she'd burst. It had taken until gone ten for the major kerfuffle to be over, and she'd spent most of the time since then making gallons of tea for innumerable people who'd traipsed into and out of the late Frank Turnbull's house. It was almost midnight, and she felt as though she'd been dragged through several hedges backwards, then sideways again, for good measure.

The body had been taken away, and Jeanette Summers was bundled up in a blanket, fast asleep – and snoring loudly – on the couch in the sitting room, having been given something to calm her by one of the two doctors who'd arrived at the house. Annie was keen to get back to her rented accommodation, just so she could send some emails in private. Every time someone had asked her about who she was, and what had happened, Jeanette had been right there beside her, so she'd felt it her duty to her clients to keep up the sham of being Annie Porter. Now she was wondering if she'd done the right thing; she wasn't up on what the legal consequences might be of having lied about her name and persona to the police, but she had the feeling her decision might come back to bite her in the rear end at some point.

She'd already decided to ask Mavis and Althea to intercede on her behalf with Chief Inspector Carwen James of the Dyfed-Powys police, hoping they'd be able to make him understand why she'd done what she had, and thereby get him to speak to someone at his own level in the Swansea police service. Despite the fact the senior officer had applauded her significant input in solving a tricky case in Anwen-by-Wye a couple of months earlier, she didn't have the confidence to try to get hold of him herself – but she knew he'd always accept a call from the dowager. However, Annie was also aware she couldn't even get the ball rolling on that front until the morning, so felt her best course of action was to get away from the Turnbull home, to avoid having to answer anyone else's questions about anything.

Two uniformed officers remained in the kitchen, and Annie said as casually as possible, 'I really need the loo again before I leave – is it okay if I go upstairs to use the one in the bathroom now? The one I've been using out in the back garden's a bit...well, dark and smelly is putting it nicely.'

They exchanged a glance and the older of the two nodded. 'Okay by us,' he said.

Annie didn't waste any time, she scooted up the stairs, and made herself ready for the walk down to her flat. Upon exiting the bathroom, she couldn't help but see into the bedroom across the landing; the door was wide open, and the bedclothes lay on the floor in a tangled mess. Jeanette had told the police she'd put Frank to bed around a quarter to seven, as usual, before popping to the Seaview Hotel. Annie wondered what had made him leave his room – because she understood there was an attached bathroom, so he wouldn't have needed to use the one she'd just been in. The house was quiet, and Annie's natural curiosity directed her feet across to the open door, and into the dead man's bedroom.

She took a moment to work out where she should walk; she didn't want to touch or disturb anything, so navigated the narrow space between the bedclothes that had tumbled onto the floor and the shabby, though once-grand, heavy oak furniture that sat against the walls. As she tiptoed across the room, she spotted what appeared to be a large wet patch on the carpet. She squatted. Was it blood? Surely not. Frank Turnbull hadn't been bleeding when she'd found him, so why would there be blood? No...the liquid was clear; other than an overall darkening, none of the colors of the carpet had been changed. She didn't hesitate – she bent closer and sniffed. Nothing. As she crouched down at floor level something glinted under the bed, catching her eye.

Annie stood and grappled with her conscience: the police hadn't been treating the bedroom like a crime scene or anything – Frank had fallen down the stairs, the bedroom was only of any significance because that was where his bed was, out of which he'd obviously clambered before taking a header down to the entryway. So why shouldn't she go to the other side of the bed to kneel down and take a better look at – and some photographs of – whatever was under there? She couldn't come up with a good reason, so that was exactly what she did, though she couldn't make out what she was seeing and photographing: several shreds of shiny metallic stuff and white plastic were scattered on the floor between the bed and the bedside table. Annie stood and straightened her back. Should she grab a sample of the detritus?

Hovering beside the bed, paralyzed by uncertainty, Annie heard the call from below. 'We're off now, you alright up there?' One of the police officers was calling to her, and she made her decision.

Annie bent, blindly grabbed a few bits of whatever it was on the floor, stuffed them into her pocket and called back, 'I'll leave with you if you don't mind – you go on out, I'll be down in a tic.'

She peeped out of Frank's bedroom, and saw both officers lurking on the doorstep, peering up at the night sky. She took her chance and dashed to the top of the stairs, just as one of them turned.

Did he see which door I came out of? Annie wondered as she trotted downstairs as nonchalantly as possible. The fact she was offered a lift to her flat in a friendly way suggested they didn't suspect she'd been nosing about where she felt she shouldn't have been. Annie declined the chance to be delivered to her flat in the back of a police car, not because she didn't want to alarm her neighbors, but because she wanted to be alone as soon as possible, and didn't mind the idea of a downhill walk along a deserted coastal road, with a bit of peace and quiet allowing her to think. And think she did...

I can't do much tonight – but I should try to get some sleep. I'll phone Mave and Althea first thing and try to get them to talk to Carwen James who might be able to help me out of the pickle I've got myself into. Then I must phone Tina and Tanya Turnbull to check how they're coping with the news of their father's death. Oh heck, how are they going to feel about me being the one who found him? I was supposed to be finding out all about Jeanette – now...well, they're going to be absolutely grief-stricken that he's dead of course...but what if...oh no...Mave will want us to be paid in any case, and what if...

Annie paused at a hairpin bend in the road and told herself to stop thinking – she was making things worse...her mind was whirring. She took a deep breath and looked at the view ahead of her: the moon was nosing out from behind some ragged clouds, magically illuminating their edges and highlighting the white foam of the surf. It was a still night, with no sound except the waves beating against the rocky shore below her vantage point. The road glistened in the pale moonlight and she avoided a deep puddle, which made her think of the wet patch on the dead man's bedroom carpet.

Sighing, she strode out; she'd never met Frank Turnbull, but his daughters had described a man who'd been generous, affable and sociable, which had made them even more concerned when he'd cut himself off from all his friends in the area, preferring, instead, to stay at home with Jeanette. Then they'd started to hear about his dementia from those ostracized friends, and had noticed it during their phone calls, and less frequent visits – he'd taken to speaking to them through Jeanette, saying he wasn't up to seeing them. Annie couldn't help but wonder if his death had been a blessing...that he'd been saved from many months, or even years, of increasing confusion, disorientation, and, possibly, pain.

Recalling Althea's frequent quotations of poems by Dylan Thomas – a Swansea boy himself – Annie couldn't help but wonder if Frank Turnbull had been singing in his chains like the sea when he'd walked from his bedroom to the top of the stairs. She suspected no one would ever know. She just hoped it had been quick, and painless for him.

SUNDAY 23RD OCTOBER

CHAPTER TWENTY-THREE

Annie's opening salvo in her conversation with Mavis could have been better crafted – she knew that – but she'd been building up to it for a while, and it had all come tumbling out.

'Mave, hello doll, it's me. Now listen, I've emailed you, but I needed to talk to you first thing too. I know it's early, so I don't expect you'll have read my report yet, so here goes.'

'Good morning, Annie. I'm just fine, thanks.' Mavis sounded immediately irritated.

'Yeah, me too – well, no not really. Look, after I found the body I didn't know what to do, but I couldn't tell the police who I was in front of the target, so I stuck to my fake name and background, and now I'm worried in case that means I'm in big trouble. Could you get Althea to talk to Carwen James for me? Ask him to get me off the hook? I didn't lie about anything else. I thought I was doing the right thing.'

Mavis sounded alarmingly calm when she replied, 'And exactly what body would that be, Annie?'

Annie could hear Althea in the background shouting, 'Put her on the speakerphone…there's a body? Where? Who? Is Annie alright?'

'All good questions, my dear, just a moment.' Mavis's voice was muffled, then it echoed as she added, 'You're on speakerphone, Annie. Only Althea and I are present here in the breakfast room, you may speak freely.'

Annie referred to her notes and gave what she felt to be a comprehensive and thoughtful account of the events of the previous evening and night. When she'd finished she waited for a response. There was none.

'Are you two still there? Mave? Althea?' She wondered if she'd lost her connection.

'I've opened your email, and have been following your report as you've been speaking. That's terrible news about Mr Turnbull. Tragic. So, am I to understand you want me to ask Chief Inspector Carwen James to do something that means you won't get into trouble for lying to the police in Swansea?'

Annie took a deep breath. 'Yes, please. I thought I made the right call, sticking to my cover identity and background details, but now…yeah, Mave, I'm worried.'

'I'm sure that, between us, Althea and I will be able to make him see the sense of supporting you in this matter; he was impressed with your work regarding the Priddle case. However, I cannae speak for how his intercession might be viewed by the folk in Swansea. Maybe nor could he. But we'll do our best for you.'

Annie had hoped she'd feel more buoyed by such a response, but she didn't. 'Thanks, Mave. Teamwork, right?'

'Indeed,' replied her colleague, then she added, 'And Annie – I think you made the right decision; our contract is with our clients, and they were specific about Jeanette Summers not being made aware of their investigation into her, through us. I hope this can all be sorted out satisfactorily. I shall communicate with you by text when I have more information. Have the police asked you to visit them today?'

'At one this afternoon, they said, which is good, because I think I've got to get two buses to get there from here, and they in't that frequent in this neck of the woods, but I'll sort it. And I'm going to phone our clients now, too, okay?'

'You've been the lead on this case since we were approached, because we knew early on that it would require your special skill set. I think it's quite correct that you speak to our clients. Please pass on the condolences of the entire team. It will be a difficult conversation, speaking to the bereaved; trust me, with my background it's something with which I became sadly familiar, the residents of the Battersea Barracks being service people in the latter stages of their lives. But I have every faith you're up to it, Annie.'

'I hope you and Althea, and Carwen James, can help,' said Annie, in a voice that she was annoyed sounded like her eight-year-old self, 'and I'll be gentle with the Turnbull sisters – it's got to be terrible for them. Hope to hear from you soon.'

'Byeee…we'll make sure that the James person goes to bat for you, Annie, never fear; I'll phone him before we go to church, and make sure he listens to us,' called Althea before the line went dead.

Annie drank another mug of coffee as she steeled herself to phone her clients. She decided to try to reach Tina first, because she was the elder of the two. It was still early – but she couldn't imagine either of the sisters would have got much sleep, under the circumstances.

Tina answered her mobile phone on the third ring. 'Hello? What time is it?'

Annie was a bit thrown by the sleep-addled voice. 'Well…it's just eight o'clock, and it's Annie Parker calling. I didn't think I'd be waking you. I'm so terribly, terribly sorry.' She didn't need to try to sound sympathetic, because she truly felt it.

'Annie? Oh thanks. It's alright. Just hang on a minute, let me sit myself up a bit…there you are, that's better. Hang on, let me open the curtains.' Annie could hear swooshing sounds. 'Oh, it's already brighter this morning than it got all day yesterday. That's nice for a change.'

Annie looked out of the bay window at the heavy clouds sitting threateningly on the horizon, but knew that Tina lived some way inland, so might have different weather there.

Tina still didn't seem ready to focus on their conversation. Annie could hear huffing and puffing; she could only imagine how scattered and upset her client must be, so waited patiently.

Finally, Tina said, 'Righty ho, there you are then. So, what did you want, Annie? But can we make this quick, I need to get going; my husband likes a cooked breakfast on a Sunday, and it takes ages to cook sausages properly.'

The conversation wasn't what Annie had expected, nor was Tina's general tone. She cleared her throat and asked, 'How are you feeling? Did you manage to get any sleep? I'm so terribly sorry. For you *and*

Tanya, of course. Well, for everyone who loved him.' It suddenly occurred to her that maybe Tina wasn't aware it was actually Annie who'd discovered her father's body. 'Did they tell you I was there?'

A moment of silence, then: 'Sorry, Annie, I'm not following you.'

Annie was deeply puzzled. 'Your father. Last night. I was the one who discovered him. Well, Jeanette was there, too, of course. I'd gone back to the house with her for a drink, you see. And then…well, I'm so sorry.'

A longer silence followed. 'Are you telling me something's happened to my father?'

Annie's stomach lurched. 'No one's been in touch with you?' She could feel her hand start to tremble as she clutched the phone.

'No. No one.'

Annie swore silently, and began with, 'Oh Tina…I had no idea…'

The next ten minutes of Annie Parker's life weren't as bad for her as they were for her client, but they were bad enough.

CHAPTER TWENTY-FOUR

It was a beautiful morning in Anwen-by-Wye, and Carol revelled in it to such an extent that it almost made up for the terrible night she'd had with Albert. The curtains were all open, and sunshine flooded the gracefully proportioned Georgian rooms of the Hills' spacious home. It was on days like this that Carol had to pinch herself; to have ended up living in such an idyllic village, in such a beautiful house – which cost almost nothing to rent – and with her sometimes-perfect son in her arms, it was almost unbelievable. Now all she needed was for her husband to get home from his blessed conference in Brighton, and all would be truly right with the world.

Albert – who seemed none the worse for having bawled through much of the night – enjoyed being fussed over by his sleep-deprived mother as she dressed him to go out; despite the glorious sunshine, Carol was aware there was a nasty nip in the air, so she bundled up both her son and herself before she popped him into the contraption she carried him in, clamped him to her bosom, and off they set. Thinking better of braving the saturated grass of the green itself, Carol walked along the road that surrounded it until she reached Sharon Jones's shop. The sign outside had been washed clean of every bit of summer dirt by the recent torrential rain, and swung in the gusty wind, announcing the presence of not only a post office, but also a shop that sold 'A bit of everything you need…or fancy'. Carol knew the promise to be truthful.

The bell above the door announced Carol's arrival, and she was greeted by not only Sharon, but also by Marjorie Pritchard. Her heart sank a little.

Oh, no, not Marjorie, she thought.

'Surprise!' Marjorie was in full jolly-mode, which Carol found most alarming.

Carol couldn't help but wonder what Marjorie was up to, but she smiled and greeted both the village bossyboots, and Sharon with equal warmth. The expected and inevitable cooing over Albert followed, and Carol was relieved that Llinos's arrival cut short any more comments about his amazing cheeks, perfect little hands, or the similarities he bore to Carol and David.

Not sure if Sharon had told Marjorie about the 'secret meeting', Carol played safe and said loudly, 'What a lovely surprise to see you Llinos. Off to work on a Sunday, then?'

Llinos's expression told Carol she understood the situation, and answered, 'Yeah – the uniform's a dead giveaway, isn't it?' She laughed. 'But, there, crime doesn't stop at the weekend, apparently, so some of us have to go in. I thought I'd treat myself to a ham bap for lunch and wondered if you'd have any on a Sunday, Sharon.'

Sharon looked nonplussed. 'Baps? At the weekend? Well, um…no. No baps. Fresh baps are Monday to Saturday only. And they go like…well, I could say "hot cakes", but they go like fresh baps, which is a bit quicker, to be truthful. I could make up a sandwich for you if you've got five minutes.'

Llinos waved away the offer. 'Oh, don't worry, it's alright. I'll just have one of these pasties. Good excuse, really. Love a corned beef pasty, I do, and you not having any baps means I was supposed to have one all along.'

Sharon pulled out a pair of tongs and approached the pasty cabinet asking, 'Do you want it warmed up?'

Again Llinos waved away Sharon's offer, focusing instead on her little finger that was being clutched by Albert, who was threatening to chew on it. 'No point, it'll be cold by the time I get to eat it. If you pop it in a bag, I'll take it as it is, ta.' She looked directly at Sharon and added, 'So, how are things around here then? Everything alright? Nothing to report?'

Sharon and Marjorie exchanged a significant glance, which told Carol that Sharon had most definitely shared the news about their so-called 'secret plan' ahead of time with the other woman, hence Marjorie being present. She decided to be helpful, so said, 'Sharon's had a bit of a problem with some preserves going missing, haven't you, Sharon?'

The shift in the atmosphere was palpable as all four women relaxed, and Sharon explained the situation to Llinos. A few minutes later, Carol reckoned she could almost literally see Marjorie Pritchard spitting nails as she grudgingly agreed to stay where she was, to keep an eye on things, while Sharon took Llinos, Carol – and Albert – through the kitchen-cum-storeroom behind the shop and out into the garden; Carol thought the patch of muddy grass with a large, rickety shed in the corner hardly deserved the use of the term, but that was how Sharon had described it.

'And all the jars were being stored in here, you say?' Llinos was trying to pick less squelchy spots to tread on as she crossed the mud. She turned and looked at Carol's feet. 'Wellies? Sensible choice. Mine are at the station, more's the pity. Anyway, if you're coming too, take care, it's like glass.'

Carol followed, one arm cradling Albert, the other extended, for better balance, or so she thought. She was within about two feet of the shed when she slipped, and her feet flew out from beneath her. Her first thought was for her son, and she wrapped him in both her arms, which meant she couldn't break her fall. As she landed, Carol told herself it was a good job that her backside was as well padded as it was.

Sharon and Llinos were at her side in seconds, both fussing over her, and Albert gurgled happily at his mother's plight. With a bit of help, Carol got to her feet, and everyone was pleased, and even chuckled, when she announced that nothing was hurt except her pride, and that she didn't have much of that left, having given birth recently.

She poo-pooed the idea that she needed a sit down, and was relieved that Albert truly didn't seem put out by her tumble. She pushed all the ideas about how much worse it could have been to the back of her mind, and urged Llinos to get on with her inspection of the shed.

'There's no lock on it,' said Llinos. 'Was there one, and it's gone...or did you never lock it anyway?'

Sharon blushed. 'Well, it never occurred to me there was anything in there anyone would steal, see…so there was a bit of a latch on it, just to stop it banging about in the wind, you know, but even that dropped off a few weeks ago. Rust. So, no. Just a bit of wire holding the door shut.' Carol reckoned that if Sharon had been standing on anything but a couple of inches of mud she'd have been shuffling her feet with discomfort.

'I see,' was all Llinos said, then she pulled open the door using a latex glove – which Carol thought was a sign of the constable really going the extra mile for Sharon.

'All these shelves were full of, what, glass jars?' Llinos stepped into the shed, and Carol was at her shoulder.

The two women scanned the space: a few rusted and broken tools of indeterminate original purpose were piled in one corner; light came through innumerable cracks between the planks of the walls, though the roof seemed to be intact; shelves made of rough-hewn wood were affixed from waist- to head-height along three walls, and all were empty.

'Yes, every bit of those shelves was full. There is one good thing, though. I told your lot on the phone that I didn't have any evidence the jars were ever in there, but I remembered just this morning that I took pictures, which I can show you, if you like. Me and Marjorie were so proud we fitted them all in…and it was to show people how much we had for sale, see? I wanted to get rid of it all before the cold weather comes – it would freeze out here, and you've seen how full my stock room is.'

'I understand,' replied Llinos, thoughtfully. 'And when exactly did you realize that the shed had been emptied?'

'I was out here getting a bit of a variety to restock the display in the shop after we closed on Wednesday. About nine? And then I realized I needed two more big jars of pickled onions for Tudor at the pub on Thursday morning about ten, and that's when I saw that everything had gone. So, between those times.' Sharon looked pleased with herself.

Llinos peered over Carol's shoulder toward the back of the shop. 'And you live upstairs?' Sharon nodded. 'Sleep at the back or the front?'

'Front.'

Llinos nodded. 'Good to know, except it means you're less likely to have heard anything going on back here in the dead of night.'

Sharon nodded. 'Yeah, I know.'

'You need to see any more here, Carol?' Llinos pulled off her single latex glove as she spoke.

Shaking her head, Carol stepped away, allowing the constable to leave the shed. 'Nope. I'm good, ta.' She turned her attention to Sharon and asked, 'There are no houses behind you. That's because you're backing onto the lane that comes down from Chellingworth Hall, isn't it? Is that what's beyond your hedge?' Sharon nodded. 'Shame.'

Sharon agreed. 'I did ask around, and no one heard or saw anything,' she said, bleakly. She finally made eye contact with Llinos. 'There's nothing you can do, is there? No footprints – given all the rain; no fingerprints neither, I shouldn't have thought – except for mine, and Marjorie's…and whoever else has been back and forth in there looking for who knows what, over the years. No clues at all.'

'Let's go back inside,' suggested Carol, concerned that it might start to rain again at any minute. The women returned to the shop, where Marjorie's reaction to Carol's mud-covered coat was one of horror.

'Oh, someone's taken a tumble. You and Albert alright?' Marjorie looked almost gleeful as she spoke.

Carol stepped back as the woman appeared to be about to set upon her. 'Both fine, ta,' she replied, hoping to be able to get home soon to change her clothes; landing on her bottom had been all well and good, but her coat had flipped up and she felt a bit damp in parts that don't appreciate being damp.

Apparently satisfied, Marjorie stayed put and stared hard at the constable. 'Anything useful?' It was a loaded question.

Llinos Trevelyan shook her head. 'Look, I understand how important the supplies were to the village – I mean, they could have raised a lot of money for the kids' trip to Tenby if they'd all been sold – but there's nothing to go on at all. To be honest, Sharon, you stand as much chance of finding out from the people who live around here if they saw or heard anything suspicious as I would by going door to door – everyone comes in here, don't they?'

Sharon nodded her head with resignation. 'They do, and I've asked already. And, no, no one saw anything.' She shrugged. 'Don't stand a chance of getting it all back, do we?'

Llinos smiled sympathetically. 'Unless somebody knows something, that they're keeping quiet about, and they choose to tell you…then, no, I don't think there's much the police could do. But that's not an official response – feel free to keep trying to get someone to have a look around if you want. But, in my experience, this is the sort of thing that would end up being an official report of a theft, but without any action being possible – other than all officers being told to be on the lookout for an unusual amount of preserved goods either being stored, or offered for sale. Would you like me to make this official? Do that much for you at least?'

Marjorie squared her shoulders as she replied on Sharon's behalf. 'Please do. One never knows…'

Sharon added, 'Yes, thanks Llinos.' Then she turned to Carol, who knew what was coming next. 'So, do you think Mavis would be supportive of your lot helping us, now that the police have said they can't do anything?'

Carol and Llinos exchanged a look. 'I'll talk to her about it,' said Carol, hoping Mavis would agree.

Sharon grabbed the paper bag containing Llinos's pasty. 'Go on…on the house,' she said, pushing the bag into the constable's hand.

The young officer chuckled. 'Very kind of you, ta, but I must insist that I pay. Here's my email address. Maybe you could send me those photos you took. I'll write up the report when I get into work, and I'll drop by with it tomorrow, so you can check it and sign it, alright?'

Carol returned home with Albert screaming his head off, and the rain making its presence known again. She managed to get her son settled in his swinging cradle before she began to extricate herself from her muddy coat, which ended up making a mess all over the kitchen floor. She hung it up in her own garden shed – which was in much better condition than Sharon's – hoping she'd be able to brush off most of the mud when it had dried. She'd decide if she'd be able to save the coat after that; she hoped she could, because her parents had given it to her for Christmas a few years back, and she liked it very much. As did David, who always commented on the plum color whenever she wore it.

She hurried back to the kitchen, where Albert was struggling to reach one of the brightly-colored stars on the mobile suspended above his swing, assured herself he was safe, then raced up the stairs to strip off the rest of her clothes, get dry, and pop on something comfy, and appropriate for a Sunday afternoon when all she had to do was about three loads of washing, clear away all her working papers from the table, wash the kitchen floor, and clean the bathroom. She wondered if she'd have enough time to whip up the batch of curry she'd been promising David for weeks as well, but somehow doubted it.

CHAPTER TWENTY-FIVE

Usually, Christine adored Sunday morning breakfast, because it meant a lazy start to a day when she wasn't working. Having been sidelined for some time, due to her injury, Christine had been desperate to get back to some sort of enquiring, and she'd hoped that the case up at the Hall – even though it wasn't a paying case – would be a useful diversion. She was the first to admit she'd not coped well with her period of recuperation; she became bored easily, and books and television only helped to a certain extent. Her father had gone over to the house in Ireland to see to everything that had needed to be sorted out there, and had expressly forbidden her from joining him; her parents had insisted she stayed with them at their London house, instead of at her own flat there.

Of course it had been wonderful to spend some time with her mother, but even that had palled after a few weeks, so she'd returned to the loft apartment in Wales under the cover of being needed at work; though Mavis had made it quite clear that she'd be on desk duty, as she called it, for some time.

But now, as she considered the prospect of toast and coffee with the man she loved – but who had a side to him that quite alarmed her – she wasn't feeling as keen about a lingering breakfast as usual.

Which was why she was relieved when Alexander surprised her by announcing he was going out for a run. 'It's not raining, in fact, it's not a bad morning,' he said while she was still snuggled in bed, 'and there are some great runs around here, so I'll take the chance to blow off the cobwebs, okay? Back in an hour, or less.'

Because she was unable to set aside her unease about what she'd overheard Alexander saying on the phone the night before, Christine used her time alone to do something she'd never thought she would: she took Alexander's bunch of keys and fobs and went through the whole of his car looking for...well, she didn't know what, but she was convinced she'd know it when she found it. But she found nothing out of the ordinary. Then she'd located his tablet, but it was password protected so she couldn't open it. His phone was also locked. So she just ended up feeling horribly guilty that she'd even done such things, and frustrated that she couldn't work out what was going on with him, which meant that her shower didn't invigorate her, and – for some reason – she couldn't make her hair do anything reasonable.

Alexander returned, showered, ate toast, and drank the better part of an entire pot of coffee as he read the newspapers – online – before they set out for the Hall where they'd been invited for lunch. His conversation was about the news of the day, not about the personal and professional worlds in which he existed, and Christine didn't have a plan for how to bring up the topic of the worrying conversation she'd overheard – in fact, she couldn't even decide if she should let him know she'd heard anything at all.

The short drive to Chellingworth Hall was a tense one for Christine; Alexander seemed ridiculously upbeat, which both worried and annoyed her.

Eventually, just as they pulled up in front of the stately pile, Christine knew she could bear it no more. 'I heard you on the phone last night. I didn't mean to listen at first – I just wondered where you'd gone, but when I heard your voice, well, I admit that then…well…then I did listen.'

Alexander turned off the ignition. 'Well, I suppose I should thank you for at least being honest about spying on me.'

Christine couldn't work out if he was being lighthearted or not, so asked directly, 'What were you talking about? Did you send someone off to break Ronnie Right's legs, to teach him a lesson? Be honest – a woman knows when a man is lying.'

Alexander's eyes narrowed. 'So that's what you heard me say?'

Christine nodded. 'I did. I heard every word. And I was…shocked. I can't believe it. That you would do that. I've always known about your background, where you came from, what you used to do – and heaven knows you mix with some exceptionally dodgy types. But to do that? I didn't want to believe you'd go that far.'

Alexander's knuckles were white as he gripped the steering wheel of the stationary vehicle. He said coldly, 'And yet you do.'

He turned toward Christine with a look in his eyes she'd never seen before; usually they were full of warmth, fun, and even passion. Now she saw...flint. Steel. It shook her.

'We'd better go in, or we'll be late,' he said, and what she'd seen in his eyes, she heard in his voice.

CHAPTER TWENTY-SIX

The atmosphere at Holy Eucharist had been tense: the Reverend Ebenezer Roberts had seen fit to deliver a sermon that focused on the dangers of worshipping false gods, and Althea had all but snubbed him as she'd left the church at the end of the service. She'd then instructed Ian Cottesloe to take a poster she'd had made up and pin it to the noticeboard at the church's lychgate, inviting the entire village to the Chellingworth estate at six o'clock on October the thirty-first.

'That's a bit rich,' observed Mavis as they took their seats in the Gilbern.

'If Roberts choses to tear it down, so be it,' replied Althea. 'Now, come along, Ian, let's get up to the Hall as quickly as possible; I want to find out how poor Stephanie is feeling before luncheon is served.'

'I've been told by Edward that Lady Clementine is expected later today,' said Ian as he tried to find a gear that worked.

'Clemmie's coming to visit?' Althea sounded mildly interested. 'I'm surprised she bothered telling anyone – though she's certainly been a little more settled since she's been knocking about with that professor of mathematics. Not my daughter's usual type, though he seems to be good for her. Sadly, I have to admit that on the rare occasions he speaks I can't understand what's he's saying – which is not to say I can't understand what he's saying, I just mean I can't understand what he says.'

Mavis turned to her friend. 'Could you no' be a little more clear, dear?'

Althea tutted. 'He's so terribly intense, and seems to possess the ability to bring any subject back to some sort of complicated mathematical theory or other. How does he strike you, Mavis?'

'If I say, "not at all", will you chuckle, and let the subject rest?'

Althea tittered. 'Very good, dear, though I still think your humorous quips need a little more polish; not going to make much of a living on the variety circuit with that level of one-liner, are you?'

Mavis endured, rather than enjoyed, the journey to Chellingworth Hall; she managed to not complain aloud even once about how her back felt every bump that transferred through the non-existent suspension of the aged vehicle, nor about how the screaming of the gearbox set her teeth on edge. The fact that the windshield wipers couldn't keep up with the rain also concerned her – though she had to admit Ian did an excellent job of nursing both the Gilbern and its passengers to their destination.

Edward met them at the steps with a large umbrella, and they were relieved of their damp outer garments with little ado. 'Did Ian inform Your Grace that Lady Clementine has suggested she'll be arriving later today?' Edward passed the damp coats to a helpful assistant.

Althea nodded. 'He did. Did my daughter think to tell anyone if she'd be alone, or if her…well, I hesitate to refer to him as her "young man" – with him being in his sixties – will accompany her?'

'The subject was not mentioned, Your Grace,' concluded Edward, as he followed the women into the yellow sitting room, where pre-lunch drinks were being served.

'What's Cook Davies offering for lunch today, Edward?' Althea's eyes gleamed as she asked.

'I believe smoked trout, goose, and a fruit crumble. With custard, of course, Your Grace.'

Althea's cheeks dimpled with delight. 'In that case, Edward, I shall take a sherry – not too small – and please ensure there's a good Gewürztraminer at the table, for the goose.'

'Already arranged, Your Grace. Her Grace had put plans in place with the household earlier in the week.'

As Edward withdrew, Althea turned to her son and asked, 'Is Stephanie sufficiently recovered to join us for lunch, Henry?'

Mavis noticed that Henry blushed a little when he replied, 'I thought it better she had something light taken to her in her room. We…discussed the matter…and she's agreed, though she might come down for dinner. But, of course, she didn't know about Clemmie when she said that, so maybe…'

The arrival of Christine and Alexander was a muted affair; Mavis wondered if the couple had been arguing, as neither seemed to be their usual sparkling selves.

'Trouble for our young lovers, I think,' whispered Althea as she sipped her sherry beside the hearth.

'Ach, they're no' young – at least, he's not,' said Mavis with a nod toward Alexander, 'and she's got an old head on young shoulders, when she wants. But, yes, I think you'll right; there's some sort of undercurrent between them. I hope…well, I hope it works itself out.'

'Luncheon is served,' announced Edward, and the group proceeded to the dining room, where they were only five, Val having declined an invitation to join the group citing a previous engagement.

As they ate, Mavis couldn't help but notice that Henry kept glancing at the empty seat that was usually filled by his wife. Not wanting to bring up Althea's feud about Welsh traditions with the Reverend Roberts, and feeling the group needed a topic other than Fred to discuss, she dared, 'So the doctor's happy with Stephanie, and she'll be dining with us this evening?'

Henry perked up. 'Indeed. She's in fine spirits. Raring to go. But, of course, she understands the need to be careful.'

'There is such a thing as being too careful, Henry,' observed Althea, wiping her lips with her napkin and sipping from the cut crystal that glowed in the firelight. 'So, please, allow her to listen to her body, and then you listen to her. A woman knows, Henry.'

'As I was saying to Alexander just a little earlier,' said Christine. She smiled so sweetly as she spoke that Mavis immediately knew Christine was taking the opportunity to score some sort of point against Alexander, who grinned coldly, and raised his glass a little too high toward Christine.

'Indeed you were,' he replied.

Althea poked Mavis with her cane, and rolled her eyes toward the couple, with a complete lack of subtlety, but no one seemed to notice.

'With Stephanie's tumble putting a stop to things yesterday afternoon,' said Mavis, 'is there anything we could push on with after lunch today, do you think?' She didn't want this non-paying case to become something that would bog her down for too long; she understood the importance of it, but – after all – she was the one who got the word out about the WISE Enquiries Agency, and the one who pursued potential business leads, and she was keen to resume her duties the next day, if possible.

'Maybe Christine and Alexander could do the rummaging that Henry and Stephanie planned to do in the fourteenth duke's quarters,' suggested Althea.

Both Christine and Alexander nodded their agreement, and shrugged, without making eye contact with each other.

'Good, that's a plan, then' said Althea, rubbing her hands with glee. 'Best to get done what we can before Clementine arrives, eh, Henry? Do you think your sister might have a useful contribution to make to our endeavors?'

Mavis noticed that the duke sagged in his seat. 'Probably not, Mother.' He spotted the dowager's disapproving expression and added, 'Though, of course, as a family member she might have some knowledge I don't. And she might even decide to pitch in – it's her name, too, that we're trying to salvage, after all.'

Althea shifted in her seat and replied, 'But of course, Henry, your sister's well known for "pitching in", whenever possible. Did you ever hear from that chap she mentioned, by the way? The one she said might paint your portrait?'

'Not a dickie bird,' replied Henry, 'though I shouldn't be surprised if she'd forgotten to mention it to whomever she was referring to. I forget the name she gave me at the time. Probably not a very accomplished artist, in any case.'

Mavis could see that Henry was sulking, as he always seemed to when his sibling was present, or was even being merely discussed.

Althea said, 'His name was…something-or-other Blanche. I know I remembered it when she first told me, because I looked him up. Online. He's very good. His portraits seem – well, almost photographic, one might say, though I believe his website used the term "hyper-realistic", which is much the same thing, I dare say.'

'There's no real hurry,' said Henry defensively.

Althea rearranged her shoulders. 'You don't want to have gone completely to seed before your image is captured for posterity, Henry. Your father had his done at about the same age you are now – best you don't leave it too much longer. I think it's important that a duke's portrait shows him at an age when he's already achieved something in life and for the seat, but one doesn't care to gaze at a dreadful old has-been, does one?'

Mavis forced herself to not smile as she watched the duke's expression grapple with his emotions as they swung between hubris, and defeat.

Christine had finished her dessert and was leaning back from the table when she said, 'Ducal portraits often show their subject within surroundings they have chosen to be significant, to frame their legacy, as they hope it will be seen. What setting would you choose for yours, Henry?'

Henry looked thoughtful. 'The roof? That took up a great deal of time and effort for the first five years that I was duke, and one hopes a good enough job has been made of it that it will last for many decades to come.'

Alexander joined in. 'The roof's important, certainly, but not terribly pleasing, aesthetically, as a backdrop. What about having yourself portrayed with some of those wonderful watercolors you used to paint? Or with a few of the delightful objects d'art from some of the collections here?'

'The tea shop – you should be painted in the tea shop; you were significantly involved with that coming into being, dear,' suggested Althea.

Henry looked dreadfully lost, thought Mavis, and she decided to come to his rescue. 'Well, there's a lot of thought can go into that one,' she opened, 'but, taking Christine's point about the settings and backgrounds chosen for ducal portraits, what's shown in the portrait of the fourteenth duke? Might that suggest somewhere he could have hidden away the secret report he commissioned about Fred? After all, the family history told us he had one written – so his portrait might give us a clue or two, right?'

Mavis beamed at each of her four tablemates in turn; only Althea responded with an encouraging expression as she replied, 'As I recall, the fourteenth is shown in an unspecified room within the Hall, standing beside a desk, upon which sits a clock, with only one hand. It's an odd detail that always fascinated me. Is that the sort of thing you mean? Should we be searching the Hall for a one-handed clock? Or might some helpful soul have had it repaired in the intervening years, do you think?'

Henry stood so abruptly that his guests were all surprised. 'Let's stop talking about it and do something,' he snapped. 'I'm off to the Long Gallery to take a look at the portraits of the thirteenth, fourteenth – and even the fifteenth – there, to see if any of them can suggest anything useful to us.'

With their host leaving the table, Christine and Alexander also stood, while Althea was helped to her feet by Edward, with Mavis in full hovering mode. 'We'll meet you there, presently,' called Althea as she and Mavis made their way upstairs more slowly than the rest of their party.

Mavis and Althea finally joined the three others standing between the portraits of Harold, fourteenth Duke of Chellingworth, and Frederick, his immediate predecessor, just as Christine was observing, 'Fred's in the garden – the hedged garden, not the walled garden. I have to say the poor chap looks dreadfully miserable, and he's holding a large bunch of…what are those flowers? They look a bit, well, weedy, I suppose one might say.'

'They're common cudweeds, I believe my dear, and thank you, Henry, yes a chair would be most helpful,' remarked Althea pointedly. Once seated, Mavis, Henry, Christine, and Alexander allowed the dowager a clear line of sight, while they stood aside, all five of them peering at the wall of portraits.

'The one hand on the clock in the fourteenth's portrait was well remembered, Althea,' said Christine. 'Does anyone recognize the clock? I don't think I've seen it anywhere.' All heads shook. 'And what do you think the one hand means? Is that a common allusion within portraiture?'

'It's not,' replied Alexander thoughtfully. Mavis noted that the duke glanced sideways at Alexander spoke, and could see that Alexander himself had also spotted Henry's expression. She was impressed when Alexander paused, and added, 'But I'm sure Henry's knowledge of art and artistic allusion is just as comprehensive as my own, if not more so. Do you know of any meaning traditionally ascribed to a clock that's missing – well, I'd say it's missing its minute hand, but I suppose that could be a shortish minute hand and it's meant to be missing an even shorter hour hand. Henry, what do you think?'

Henry puffed out his chest, then peered at the painting with his nose not an inch from it. 'I'd say that's the minute hand, so the hour hand is missing – but I'm baffled; other than the inclusion of a clock to signify the passing of time, it can be used to suggest that the sitter is aware of the finite nature of his or her life. Holbein was the master at this sort of thing, as I'm sure we all know. His works are absolutely fascinating, and set the tone for much portraiture that followed. Of course, if one examines this piece, one can see how the fashion of the day – not just in terms of the sitter's dress, but also in terms of a slight elongation of the face and body – has been employed. The fourteenth only took the seat in 1856 and died in 1860, so this must have been painted within that short window. At the time, if one didn't look like Albert, Queen Victoria's Prince Consort, one grew facial hair to resemble him, and he certainly set the tone for men's fashion, of course. It's no surprise, therefore, to see Harold looking rather like Albert in this portrait. We might also be safe in assuming that the staging of the portrait is significant – on many levels.'

'Impressive,' commented Althea, smiling at her son.

Mavis noted that Henry straightened his shoulders as he added, 'I cannot fathom the clock, but the swathes of velvet curtain are not of a color I have seen here at the Hall, and the desk upon which his fingertips are resting does not look familiar. It's not a piece that's contemporary to the portrait; the style clearly puts it as a Sheraton design, so something that was already here, I'd say.'

Mavis mused aloud, 'Do you think there might be some records back in the library that deal with furnishings purchased for the Hall?'

Althea was sucking the end of her thumb. 'I have a feeling I've seen that desk somewhere, Henry. But where, and when, I cannot say. I can tell you it's not at the Dower House, that's for sure. Those spindly little legs are not a bit of use when you have dogs in a place; the Queen Anne pieces are much more practical. I know I only have my trusty McFli these days, but time was when there'd have been half a dozen animals running about. They'd have had a Sheraton desk over in no time at all. But, you know – the other thing Sheraton designs were renowned for, other than ethereal legs, was secret drawers, and compartments. Might Harold be telling us he's hiding something?'

'I think Sheraton's designs were rather more sturdy than you seem to imagine, Mother,' replied Henry, then clearly thought better of saying more.

Mavis thought it worth asking the obvious question. 'So are we saying there's a chance that this desk might be where Harold hid the report he commissioned into Fred's misdoings? And what about the torn sheet music on the desk, and the trumpet nestling against, or almost hidden by, the draped velvet curtain? What of them? Are they clues? Might the desk be in the music room?'

Henry rolled on the balls of his feet when he responded, 'As Alexander read aloud to us, from Harold's own writings, we learned that he was both a musician and a composer,' replied Henry. 'He turned away from his passions to take up the seat. I would suggest that these items refer to that loss.' He glared at his mother, who ignored him. 'If this man' – he waved at the portrait – 'who dedicated his life to Chellingworth once called upon to do so, chose this desk to appear in his portrait, I would suggest that is significant. But I can't recollect seeing it in the music room. Why would there be a desk in there?'

Mavis couldn't see why there wouldn't be a desk in a music room. 'So, should we start to search the Hall for this desk, maybe beginning with the music room? If it's all we have to go on, I mean.' Mavis couldn't imagine how long that might take if it weren't in the music room, given that Chellingworth Hall had 267 other rooms.

'I say, have I arrived just in time for some sort of treasure hunt? How exciting…can I play, too?'

Everyone turned, except Henry.

Althea smiled. 'Ah, Clemmie, dear, I see you've changed your hair again. Do you think electric blue is really you? Especially with that straw-colored dress you're wearing. You remind me of something…what is it? Oh yes, a matchstick…you know, out of a box of matches. Ah well, come and give your mother a kiss in any case.' Althea didn't stand, but held out her arms toward her daughter – something Mavis thought extremely odd, for Althea.

'Hugs, Mother, but I'll stay where I am – I have a slight head cold. Greetings to you all,' said Clementine, waving to the group. 'So – anyone want to tell me what's up?'

As Henry and Althea brought Clementine up to speed, Mavis listened to their briefing with one ear, while her other strained to hear what was passing between Christine and Alexander. She could only catch words being hissed, but their facial expressions, and especially Christine's clenched fists, spoke volumes.

It didn't surprise her at all when Alexander stepped away from Christine and said, 'Henry, Althea, I'm afraid I've been called back to London. Urgent matter, demanding my personal attention. Nothing for anyone to worry themselves about, but I need to leave now. So sorry I shan't be able to help with the hunt for the desk after all, but I'm sure Christine will be up to the task. I'll keep in touch and shall return, if I'm needed, when I can. Cheerio.'

Mavis watched Alexander as he marched the considerable length of the gallery; the man looked as though he were striding into battle, she thought. Christine appeared to want to follow him but understood she wasn't wanted; at least, that was how Mavis interpreted her body language and expression.

Christine then said, abruptly, 'Right then, Clemmie, let's you and me start at the top of this stately pile and work our way down. I, for one, am taking a photograph of that portrait so that I don't go hunting for the wrong Sheraton desk in a place I suspect is crawling with them, and maybe you'd like to do the same, in case we decide to divide and conquer.'

Lady Clementine looked bemused. 'Very well. And I can tell you about my latest, Very Exciting News, as we hunt. I must say, I hadn't expected to be drawn into a search into my family's dirty secrets from the past, but I'm game.'

As the pair left, Althea observed, 'You'd think she was fifteen, not fifty, wouldn't you?'

'I dare say that's Nanny's fault,' replied Henry tartly, then added, 'I'm going to see how my dear wife is coming along.'

CHAPTER TWENTY-SEVEN

Annie told her knee to stop bouncing under the table, but it wouldn't listen. She'd been waiting in the small, plain, windowless room at Swansea Police headquarters for what felt like hours – even though her watch told her it had only been forty-five minutes since the smiling constable had left her there – to stew. And, boy, was she simmering away.

Mavis's texts through the morning had been informative, but only up to a point. Mavis and Althea had indeed managed to get hold of the chief inspector, and he had, apparently, understood why Annie had done what she'd done. He'd even promised to speak to someone in Swansea about her situation. Then she'd heard no more, so had no idea what might befall her whenever an officer chose to grace her with their presence.

As she'd sat on a bus that drove along some impossibly narrow, winding roads, then along the magnificent sea front to reach the center of Swansea, she'd tried, relatively unsuccessfully, to speak to Tudor; he'd been out in the woods surrounding Anwen-by-Wye with Gertie and Rosie, where the reception was abysmal, so they'd ended up agreeing to talk that night, when he'd shut the pub, which seemed like a very long way off. Not even Carol had been able to chat; too busy with her search for missing pickle jars and trying to placate Albert – who seemed, at the time Annie had been on the phone, to be practicing screaming for Wales.

The only person she'd been able to have a sensible conversation with had been Christine, who'd listened attentively, had told Annie with certainty that she was sure everything would turn out just fine, and reassured her she'd have stuck to her cover story too, had she been in the same situation. But none of that had really helped because – while Annie liked Christine a great deal, and even admired her spirit in many ways – she was convinced that, quite often, Christine saw life as a game she was playing, and the higher the stakes were, the greater her excitement.

Annie didn't find her current circumstances to be at all exciting. If she ended up with something on her record, because of her lies, what would that mean to her ability to continue being a private investigator? And if she couldn't do that – what *would* she do? She couldn't go back to the City of London to work, she'd burned her bridges there. Her parents would be devastated if she had to move in with them – which would most certainly be on the cards if she had no income. Not that they wouldn't have her, of course – in fact, Eustelle would probably be beside herself with glee to have her only child under her roof again, though Annie had moved out aged seventeen and had been independent since then. As both her parents had taught her, self reliance was an absolute necessity.

Annie's knee struck the underside of the table with a thump just as the door opened and a woman entered. The first thing Annie noticed about her was that above her expensively-cut navy trouser suit, her mouth was smiling, but her eye's weren't. Annie slammed her hands onto her thighs, hoping that would help her gain control over her wayward limbs, because she didn't want those flinty eyes to spot that she was nervous.

The woman sat opposite Annie. She placed a notepad on the table, and hooked her bobbed, steel-gray hair behind her ear – which reminded Annie of Mavis's similar habit. She wondered if this woman would be like her colleague in any other ways, but realized – as soon as he began to speak – that this woman was Welsh, not Scottish.

'I'm Detective Chief Inspector Carys Llewellyn.'

Annie smiled. 'Annie…Parker,' she said timidly.

'So I understand. Not *Porter*, as you told our officers last night, at the home of Mr Frank Turnbull.'

Annie nodded. 'Yes…about that…'

The detective held up her hand, and Annie clamped her mouth shut, thereby allowing the woman to say, 'I've been brought up to speed, thank you. While I was walking my dog this morning, in fact. That brother of mine likes to make my life a misery every chance he gets.'

Annie put two and two together. 'Chief Inspector Carwen James is your brother? And you're a detective chief inspector here, in Swansea?' The woman nodded. 'Seems you two have the entire policing thing sorted across most of Wales between you, in that case,' observed Annie with what she hoped was a winning smile; she was trying to at least crack the ice she sensed ran in the senior detective's veins, and felt that commenting upon siblings being named Carwen and Carys would be a bit too personal.

Carys Llewellyn's smile grew slowly, but surely. 'To listen to him, he has the upper hand, due to the much larger geographic area covered by his oversight, and – of course – we wear very different hats, him being policing and me being detecting.'

Annie nodded; she didn't want to push her luck too far but felt she had to take her chance to speak. 'I'm grateful he phoned you about what I'd done. Is it…is the fact that I hung in there with my false name all cleared up now, Detective Chief Inspector?' She had to know.

The detective nodded, slowly. 'It has been, insofar as I've accepted the facts as they were presented to me. But my big brother didn't just tell me about you – he told me a bit about the nature of the case you were working on, too. And that got me interested…so, instead of just doing my brother a favor by talking to uniform about who you are, and why you'd given a false name, I came into the office and told them to fill me in. And that got me even more interested.'

Annie shifted in her seat and noticed that DCI Llewellyn's eyes were glinting. 'In't this all a bit beneath a DCI?' Annie dared. 'Accidental death. An elderly man with dementia taking a tumble. Not what I'd have thought someone at your level would get involved with…and on a Sunday afternoon, no less.'

Leaning back in her seat, the woman sitting opposite Annie nodded slowly, and Annie began to wonder if she did everything slowly…or if she was a naturally deliberate person. Then she opened her notepad, pulled a pen from the pocket inside her suit jacket and said, 'I've got the basics, but I want you to brief me. Tell me everything you know about Frank Turnbull, Jeanette Summers…and Turnbull's daughters, your clients. And please arrange to let me have copies of all the files you have pertaining to the case as soon as possible.'

Annie squared her shoulders. 'Oh, I don't know about that. I mean, the background research my colleagues and I did, as well as all the original information received from our clients, would be confidential. I'm not sure I can just hand it all over to you.'

Slowly – deliberately – DCI Carys Llewellyn tilted her head, and allowed a shark-like smile to all but split her face. 'Oh come now, I'm sure Annie *Parker* wouldn't want any sort of a blot on her copy book that might mean the enquiries agency she works for wouldn't be able to hire her out to clients who prefer their PIs to have a clean record, would she?'

The comparisons between the sometimes obnoxiously unctuous Chief Inspector Carwen James and his sister hit Annie in the face; he was a relatively rural creature, and a bit of a social climber, who liked to have a duke and a dowager on his side – whereas his sister had a distinctly urban edge to her; sharper, and possibly more deadly.

And now Annie was facing a moral, ethical, and professional dilemma: should she do as she was being asked, and share what she had a feeling Mavis would shout from the rooftops was confidential information; or should she save her career by telling DCI Llewellyn what she knew – thereby possibly better helping her clients, ultimately, to achieve their goal of truly understanding what Jeanette Summers had been up to, and whether their father had really been giving his girlfriend his permission to sell off their inheritance?

She shrugged and said, 'Okay then – I can't send the files till I get back to my laptop, but I can give you most of the background now.'

Annie spoke as the DCI took notes, in shorthand, it appeared, or possibly just the most appalling scrawl. Occasionally, the detective held up her hand and asked Annie a supplementary question, but she didn't interrupt often, and Annie felt she did a good job of talking through the facts of the case, as she understood them. She made sure she mentioned what Turnbull's two daughters had told her about specific items being offered for sale online, even listing the pieces of their late mother's jewelry that she could recall without her notes –

which turned out to be quite a few. She also spoke about the assessment of his net worth Carol and she had been able to piece together – with their clients' input – and a broad timeline of the period over which the suspicions of the sisters had grown.

In closing she said, 'I didn't lie, or change any facts when I spoke to the officers last night, except for my name and address. Honest. So what they got from me then would be a full and truthful account of the occurrences of last evening, on top of what I've just told you by way of background.'

Llewellyn nodded. 'Good. Thanks. Now – anything else? Any thoughts or ideas that aren't factual, but are…well, let's say are based on your experience or intuition?'

Annie weighed her response. 'Yeah – Jeanette Summers is a heavy drinker; I spotted that right off. And she's been laying in on a bit too thick locally about how hard she's had it caring for Frank Turnbull; in my experience, the people who put a lot into looking after a loved one don't go on and on about it at the pub to the extent that a reasonably new barman knows all about it. She's also been outright lying, saying the daughters haven't been trying to stay in touch with their father; I believe my clients on that front…they'd been stymied by her in all their attempts to do as much as talk to him recently, and Jeanette sent Tina packing the last time she turned up at the house unannounced – which was the last straw, and sent them to your lot with their concerns, before they turned to us.'

The DCI took a note. 'Yes, I'm aware that official approaches were made prior to your company's services being retained. Which is another reason why there's not as much push-back against someone at my level taking a look into this as there might have been. Since you spoke to Mrs Tina Rees this morning – to use her married name, though I understand why you refer to your clients as the Turnbull sisters – she's been in touch with us, to make known her concerns about Jeanette Summers, and has left us in no doubt that she views her father's death as suspicious. Appropriate steps have been taken to begin both an investigation into how the original complaint against Ms Summers was handled internally, and I have set a few wheels in motion concerning the demise of Mr Turnbull. So, anything else you feel you can add?'

'Well, I've got a question, to start with: why was I the one who even ended up telling her he was dead? Tina, I mean. Why hadn't one of your lot done it? I've got to be honest, it caught me off guard...I thought she'd have known before I talked to her, see? It was...well, I bet your lot get trained how to do it, but I just had to do the best I could. And I keep going over and over it in my mind. I don't think I did a very good job of it. And that'll plague me, I know it. So – why didn't she already know?'

DCI Carys Llewellyn's lips became a thin line. 'It's another aspect of this case we're looking into,' was her terse reply. 'It's a matter that's being scrutinized internally; not something the public will ever hear about...though, of course, we always aim to improve our service to the community when given the opportunity to learn from...missteps.' She sighed, then added, 'I believe the family will receive an official communication about the matter, at some point.'

Annie nibbled her lip as the DCI slowly tapped her pen on the edge of the table, her expression grim, and knew she had to come clean. She cleared her throat. 'Look, I'll admit I was shocked by finding the poor bloke like I did, and I didn't enjoy having to tell his daughter he was dead. I'm feeling guilty about it, to be honest. I know he wasn't in my care, or nothing like that, but his daughters had asked us to look into his situation...so, you know...I'm feeling it. And it's good to see that the police are taking it so seriously, because – yeah – the Turnbull sisters had raised the alarm, and I can't understand why no one would have told them he was dead.'

Annie paused as she considered her words carefully, then added, 'There *is* something that won't be in the police accounts about last night, though I don't know if it'll help at all.' She slapped what she hoped was a winsome smile on her face. 'I...er...I had to go to the loo before I left the place, and I couldn't help but look into the bedroom of the deceased.' She hoped she'd made her curiosity sound innocent.

A wry chuckle preceded DCI Llewellyn's prompt. 'And...?'

'Well, I don't know what to make of it, but your people should have a look under his bed…there were little bits of silver and plastic under there. I did think mice, but I've got to admit, the more I consider it, the less likely that seems.'

DCI Llewellyn's pen hovered in mid air, then she placed it beside her pad. She leaned forward. 'Tell me more.'

Annie shrugged. 'Well, I can't – I don't know what it was. It was just there. Between the bed and the bedside table. The side with the window, not the door.'

'Now that's very interesting, Annie, because we sent a forensics team to the house a couple of hours ago…what with me wanting to be thorough and all that, you understand?'

Annie nodded, though she wasn't sure exactly what 'thorough' meant, in the circumstances. 'So what did your lot make of it?' She was keen to know.

The detective's brow furrowed. 'Nothing, because there was nothing there. Nothing under the bed, in the bed, or anywhere else in the bedroom, or the entire house, that could match the description you just gave me.'

Annie tried to not sound too triumphant when she said, 'Just as well I took photos, and snagged a sample then, eh?'

Carys Llewellyn's smile split her face much faster than previously. 'Annie Parker, it seems you're exactly the sort of woman my brother said you were.'

'Really? And what's that then? Gobby and bossy?'

'Detail orientated, and highly professional.'

Annie glowed.

CHAPTER TWENTY-EIGHT

Carol was at her wits' end, so decided to make the most of the dry spell to take Albert out for a walk. She suspected the Anwen-by-Wye green was wet enough for the ducks to be happily wading about on the grass, but, failing that, she'd take her son to see them splashing on the duck pond. Suitably dressed for the weather – which meant several layers for both herself and her son – Carol set off, all but certain she wouldn't bump into anyone.

The bounce of her walk seemed to keep Albert quiet on her chest, and Carol decided to stroll along the lane that headed toward Chellingworth Hall, to get a better idea of the lay of the land behind Sharon's shop. It wasn't as though she hadn't taken the route many times before, but she'd never really given her full attention to any possible access points to Sharon's back garden.

By bobbing about she managed to make out the rear of the shop through an overgrown hedgerow; despite an unusually hot and dry summer, the autumn had been mild and moist, and it looked as though the greenery had made the most of its chance to sprout in the past six weeks or so. Trying her best to not discombobulate Albert, she stood on tiptoes, then bent down, as she moved along the section that bounded Sharon's garden. She spotted a sort of hole in the base of the undergrowth that could have accommodated – what? – a large dog? There wasn't exactly a path there, but Carol suspected that something had been using the pass-through to come and go. But had the void been created over one night by someone laden with jars of pickles, or over a longer period of time by an innocent creature? That was the question.

She wandered back and forth along the stretch of hedge. The rain meant there were no tracks on the lane itself, but she reckoned she'd found a way for someone to access the now-empty shed, as long as the person was prepared to push through some pretty thick, though not prickly, greenery. She examined the branches for signs of breakages, and found some, though only up to shoulder height. She reasoned that was because the higher growth was less lush, more pliable, and easier to push aside. She pulled out her phone and took photographs of everything she'd noted, then attended to her suddenly grizzling son, soothing him with smiles and her silly faces, the ones she knew usually delighted him.

With Albert pacified, Carol wandered a little further along the lane before deciding that the blue-black clouds overhead looked a bit too threatening for her to continue. Just as she'd started to head home her phone rang. She debated whether she should answer it, but saw it was Althea's number so took the call.

'Hello Althea, how are you?'

Carol knew that the dowager struggled to get her mobile phone in the best place for her voice to be clearly heard, so waited patiently as Althea began her conversation as not much more than a mumble, then repositioned the phone so that Carol could actually hear what she was saying.

All Carol caught was Althea saying, '...so she's in bed until further notice.' Her tummy flipped. 'Who's in bed, Althea? I didn't hear what you said in the beginning.'

'Stephanie, dear. She fell when she was on her way up to the upper floors, yesterday. Didn't Mavis tell you?'

'No...I've been a bit busy. Sorry. How is she? Stephanie, I mean?'

Althea sounded cautious. 'Well, you can't be too careful, of course, but she's not in hospital, which is good. I remember you took a nasty spill when you were having Albert, and they kept you in, but he was just fine, and I'm sure Stephanie will be too. Just a bit of a bump on her shoulder, that's all. But Henry's insisting she stays in bed for the day, to be on the safe side. Which is why I wondered if you could help, you see.'

'Help with what, exactly? Mavis hasn't told me what you're all doing up at the Hall – is that what you need help with?'

'I hate to ask, but, yes. You'd have to come here though – or maybe Mavis has some ideas about how you could help from your home. I don't know. I just thought I'd give you a quick ring to butter you up before Mavis phones you...because she can be a bit...you know…sometimes, and that's not what we need now. We need all hands to the pumps if we're going to weather this one. So I'll let her give you the specifics, but please consider it. Bye.'

Carol stared at her phone, and pushed it into her pocket, only to have it ring almost immediately. Suspecting it would be Mavis herself, Carol didn't check the number on the screen. 'Yes, Mavis, what is it you want, and will you please tell me what on earth you're all doing up there at the Hall?'

Stephanie sounded taken aback. 'It's me, Stephanie. Are you alright, Carol. You sound a bit…you know, um…distracted.'

Carol bounced Albert as she replied, 'Sorry, I didn't mean to bite your head off. I thought you were Mavis. Though I shouldn't be biting her head off either. Anyway – Althea just told me you had a fall yesterday…are you and the baby alright?'

Stephanie chuckled. 'You know what it's like to be a pregnant woman who falls, don't you? So I can tell you that the doctor gave me and the baby a clean bill of health, but no one seems to want to hear that. Henry's got me being held as a prisoner in my own bed until such time as he thinks I'm capable of walking downstairs. They wanted to phone an ambulance, for goodness' sake. Tell me Carol, does it ever stop? The fussing, I mean.'

Carol sighed. 'Stephanie, I'll say this to you as a woman who's been a mother for about six months, to one who will shortly become one: take the fussing, take the sleep, take the rest…take every bit of it that you can. Because it'll all stop, and you'll wish there were a dozen people at your beck and call to help you out at two in the morning, when you're fit to sleep on your feet.'

There was a pause before Stephanie replied, 'Should I really consider Henry's suggestion that we retain a nanny, do you think?' Carol thought the duchess sounded horrified at the prospect. 'I've been pushing back against the whole thing…but, if what you say is true…' She didn't finish her thought.

'Tell you what, Stephanie, if you make sure that Henry does his fair share, you'll be fine. We usually are – but David's away at the moment so it's a bit full on. But, listen, now that I know you're alright – you phoned me…so, what can I do for you?'

Stephanie sounded more focused when she replied, 'I think Mavis is going to ask you to get involved with this thing we're all doing up at the Hall, but please understand you can say no. It's not really urgent – except to Henry. It can wait – I'm sure the telly people won't be airing anything in the immediate future, I'm also pretty sure they'd have to seek some sort of permission from the family – unless all they do is trawl the public record, of course.'

Carol cursed silently, then said, 'Why won't anyone tell me what is going on? I have no opinion because I have no data. Please give me information.' She tried to not sound as frustrated as she was.

'Oh heck, Henry's here. I'll phone you later.' Stephanie disconnected.

Carol swore under her breath at the phone. 'Right, let's get you home then, shall we?' Albert smiled and gurgled his agreement, then Carol's phone rang again. This time she didn't answer it. 'That's what voicemail is for, isn't it? Yes it is, oh yes it is,' she said aloud to her son, in her coo-cooing voice. And bounced him all the way back to her home.

She was burping Albert over her shoulder when the next call came in, so she ignored that too, then, when he was in his swing again, she felt she had to answer Mavis's third attempt to reach her, but she did it with a heavy heart.

By the time the call ended at least she knew more about the frantic activity up at Chellingworth Hall, and sort of sympathized with why the Twysts wanted to do what they were doing, but she immediately felt the weight of their expectations that she'd be the person who could – magically, it seemed – find all the information available in the public domain about the thirteenth Duke of Chellingworth – and preferably within a couple of days. She'd told Mavis she'd do what she could, but that Albert had to come first, because he didn't seem to be as happy as she'd like him to be – just as her son decided to give his lungs a good old airing out, proving her point. She was relieved that she didn't manage to catch the platitude about inconsolable babies that Mavis delivered as her parting shot, then she picked up Albert to soothe him; he was crying as though he had personal knowledge that the world was going to end in three minutes.

Carol was wiping his tears, trying to distract him with a stuffed toy, and pulling faces to make him laugh as her phone pinged and pinged with several incoming texts, which she promised herself she wouldn't read – then she did, and was cross with herself for allowing her attention to be divided between work and her son.

But it was when Annie phoned that she really lost it. Which she knew was unfair on Annie – but she also knew that as her friend of many years, Annie would understand. As it turned out, Annie said all the right things to comfort her, and Carol felt a million times better when that call ended. Which was something for which she was extremely grateful.

As she lay on the sofa that evening, with something mind-numbing on the TV, Albert bundled beside her, and Bunty on the antimacassar above her head, Carol chatted to her son about nothing, and several somethings, which included asking him the critical questions: 'So, if someone managed to get all those jars out of the shed in Sharon's back garden in the dead of night, and through that little gap in the hedge, how did they actually transport it? I mean, jars are heavy, right? And they're breakable. So how did someone – anyone – do it? And then, how did they get them away from the place? If someone had used a car or a van at that time of night – and with there being that many glass jars to shift, I bet it was a van – then why didn't anyone hear it? I know most people sleep overlooking the green, like your mam and dad do, but a van would have had to drive from the lane and around at least part of the green to get out of the village. Unless they drove along the lane to the Hall…but that wouldn't help because the gates are locked at night, aren't they, Albert?'

Her son didn't answer, because he was asleep. And soon Carol was too.

CHAPTER TWENTY-NINE

By the time Annie left Swansea Police headquarters, the thick cloud cover and persistent rain meant that it was already gloomy, even though it was only half two, and she had to squeeze herself under a narrow overhanging portico to keep dry as she waited for the taxi that had been arranged to deliver her back to her seaside flat.

Once there, she luxuriated in a hot shower for ten minutes; for some reason she felt chilled to the bone, and a bit woozy, so she hoped that warming herself through would help her feel a bit more normal. Finally settled on the sofa with a mug of hot chocolate beside her, Annie phoned Carol hoping she'd be able to have a bit of a heart to heart, rather than just a work-based talk, because the guilt she felt about the death of Frank Turnbull had increased during the drive in the taxi, to the extent she was worried that the entire episode was – somehow – her fault.

'How you doin', Car?' she opened, hoping that would steer the conversation toward the personal rather than the professional.

'Annie, I've told you over and over again, my name is Carol, not flippin' Car, and my son's name is Albert, not Bertie, or Bertipoos…or any one of the other annoying things you call him. And I'm married to David. Not Dave. Got it!?'

Annie pulled a face at her phone then said, 'Gordon Bennett, what's got into you? You alright, doll?'

Silence.

'Carol? You still there?'

'Yes. Sorry. I haven't had a good day. Shouldn't take it out on you. Sorry.'

Annie had really hoped she'd be able to talk about how finding a man dead – a man into whose welfare she'd been enquiring – was making her feel, but she could hear that Carol sounded exhausted. 'No probs, doll. So, come on then, tell me all about it. I'm a good listener, me.'

Annie reckoned Carol was trying to swallow a sob, then her friend all but exploded with: 'Oh Annie, I'm just not coping well with David away. I'm at the end of my tether. I don't think I'm cut out to be a working mum. How do they do it, the single mums? I'm so tired all the time; with David not being here to take any of the strain, I'm just not getting the sleep I need to be able to function properly. I can't wait for him to get back…and, after that, he and I are going to have to have a sit down and a proper talk about whether I'm going to carry on with the WISE work, because I think I might need to just take it a bit easier than I have been. I've got Mavis and Christine, and Sharon and Marjorie, pulling me in all directions. I know I'm supposed to be the calm, information-gathering center of the whole operation, but I don't feel very calm or especially centered at the moment. And there goes Albert…again. I don't know what's wrong with him – he won't shut up. I've got an appointment with the doctor for him tomorrow – I'm worried there's something really amiss.'

Knowing very well it was best for her to not comment upon Albert at all – because that would only result in Carol referring to Annie's lack of experience in the motherhood department – Annie thought it best to respond by saying, 'Good idea to get him in to see the doc, Carol. Could Mave or Chrissy wait a bit for whatever it is they've asked you for? And what about Sharon? Is that the business with the pickles? Surely that's not as important as Bert…*Albert's* health, right? Can't you put her off a bit too? Get yourself rested, a bit more calm. Dave'll be back tomorrow night, won't he?'

Annie waited patiently as Carol had a bit of a cry, then managed a sniffly, 'He will – but I thought I could manage on my own, Annie.'

Annie's heart melted. 'Oh Car, that's the thing, see? You don't have to do it on your own. You and Dave are a team – always supporting each other, much better together than apart. It's not a bad thing to rely on your spouse for emotional and practical support…don't think that. And it's not that you're not up to it – who would be? It's so much to try to manage, and juggle. I bet the single mums you think of as superwomen would like the sort of relationship you have with

Dave…who wouldn't? Come on, doll, you can get through this. And there's no shame in feeling the way you do, neither. You and Dave's a team – and you're down a team member at the moment, so all of this is to be expected. Besides…it's probably just teething stuff, you know.'

'Teething?' Carol snapped.

Annie sighed – why had she mentioned anything about Albert's health or development? 'Well, I know I in't got any of me own kids, but that would be about right, wouldn't it? Teething at his age?' Had she backtracked enough, she wondered.

'I am *so* stupid! What sort of a mother am I? Why didn't I think about teething? It's so obvious. I've been worried that he hadn't started yet...but it didn't occur to me that he could be, and that it could bother him this much. Oh Annie, thank you. What would I do without you? You're right – that's probably all it is. At least I won't sound like a complete idiot when I talk to the doctor in the morning…thanks for that. Aww, poor dab…are your gums hurting you?'

Annie could picture Carol bending over Albert, with her wide, warm smile, her loving arms reaching to embrace him, and felt sadly isolated. But she didn't want to add to Carol's burdens, and didn't think her chum was in the right frame of mind to have a heart to heart about how guilty Annie was feeling. Instead she said, 'Well look, I'll get out of your hair, and I hope you and Albert have a better night tonight. Good luck at the doctor's tomorrow. You'll let me know what they say, won't you?'

Carol promised she would, sounding rather distracted, then added, 'Was there something you wanted, Annie, or were you just phoning for a chat? How's it all going there? Alright?'

Annie toyed with several possible responses, but plumped for, 'Yeah – nothing I can't sort on me own. Bye for now – talk soon. Give Bertie a snuggle from me.' She disconnected before Carol could comment further.

Annie wondered about trying Mavis next; not because she expected Mavis to be sympathetic to her plight – she knew well enough that

Mavis always snapped into her no-nonsense so-called bedside manner when emotional responses would have been the norm for others – but she knew she had to update someone at the agency, and wanted Mavis to know she was planning on sending a detailed report later that evening. But then she thought better of it; why not just put the time into writing up her notes properly? Then she could email them to both Mavis and Carol and she'd be done with it for the night. So that was what she did, sending the email by just gone ten. She also sent a text to Tudor, asking after Gertie, but he didn't reply, so she eventually went to bed in a bad mood.

CHAPTER THIRTY

As he gazed at his wife, seated at his right hand at the dinner table, Henry was terribly concerned that Stephanie looked paler than he'd have liked. True, even his own ruddy complexion had faded since the summer, but Stephanie had a touch of waxiness about her skin he didn't like the look of.

'Please stop staring at me, Henry,' whispered his wife. 'You're giving me a complex.'

Henry nodded with embarrassment and tucked into his cauliflower and stilton soup with gusto. He noticed that his mother appeared to be ignoring her soup, Clementine had already finished hers, and Mavis…well, he could never quite tell whether Mavis was enjoying her food, or if she treated it merely as fuel, enjoyment being an indulgence she was not allowed.

Although all suitably dressed, the group around the table appeared lacklustre, except for Clementine, who was positively – and irritatingly – bubbly. And sporting what Henry thought of as the most unflattering shade of puce he'd seen in a long time.

Althea's comment of: 'He lived quite a sad life, didn't he?' suited the mood.

'Who did, Mother?' Henry was nonplussed by the way the dowager frequently began a conversation at what seemed to him to be the midway point.

Althea sounded wistful. 'The fourteenth. So sad that he had to give everything up to come here to take on the seat.'

Clementine asked, 'Is that like you, the way you gave everything up, Mother?'

Althea smiled. 'Oh no. That was quite different. To start with, I'd not managed to build a career for myself as a dancer when I met your father, and I'd have given up even more than I could ever have achieved in that world to be with him. I came to Chellingworth more than willingly, though, to be fair to him, Chelly did try to warn me that I'd be taking on an entire raft of responsibilities when I married him. I thought I understood what he meant at the time; it took me a good number of years to realize I didn't…but, by then, I had the both of you, so I was always able to offset the challenges of being a duchess with the delights of being a mother. So, no – I didn't have to walk away from a glittering career in the way Harold did.'

Mavis added, 'Aye, those entries he made in the family history were illuminating.'

'Quite,' replied Althea, softly. 'How fascinating that he'd been corresponding with the likes of Liszt, Rossini, and Verdi. Imagine that. And to have entered the Royal Academy of Music aged twelve – he must have been a prodigy. Feted when he performed, in demand by the Queen herself. Amazing. I don't mind admitting I had no idea he'd really "done" anything before he'd acceded to the seat. And that his son gave up his naval career to follow his father – that was quite something. Though I dare say being on a ship in the 1800s would be something he might have been glad to see the back of.'

Henry felt a little aggrieved. 'I, too, understand what it's like to have to give up one's planned career to assume unexpected responsibility.'

Stephanie cooed, 'Of course you do, dear. We all recognize that you sacrificed your career as an artist for the seat, don't we?'

Henry was gratified to see that everyone nodded. 'Duty to one's family is always paramount,' he said, sitting upright, and meaning it.

'It is that,' replied Mavis, 'and I'm pleased to see it being brought to life, here, at Chellingworth. I'm sure we'll manage to find something concrete to be able to clear up all this business about Fred. We've done quite well with the fourteenth and fifteenth dukes – all we need to do is work our way backwards a bit.'

With the solemn nature of their undertaking having been highlighted by Mavis, a dour silence ensued.

'Buck up,' fizzed Clementine eventually, 'we didn't find the desk today, but we might tomorrow. There are still lots of places to look.'

'Aye, you're right,' replied Mavis; Henry thought she sounded unconvinced. 'Tomorrow's another day, we'll all be fresher, and we can start the week in a businesslike fashion.'

Althea observed, 'The beef is rather tough, don't you think, Henry? It's unlike Cook to present us with beef that's tougher than butter.' Henry noted that his mother had eaten very little – for her.

'Would you like a fresh serving?' Stephanie asked.

'No thank you, dear, I'm not terribly hungry.' Althea's voice was quiet.

Maybe that's because you ate half a Victoria sponge for tea, flitted though Henry's mind as a possible response, but he wisely held his tongue, and enjoyed his own meal.

Sitting back from her dinner, Althea asked her daughter, 'No What's-his-name this weekend, dear?'

'We've spilt up.'

Henry noted that his sister didn't sound at all heartbroken. 'Sorry to hear it, Clemmie,' he replied. 'He seemed like such a...'

'Steadying influence?' Clementine shot a venomous look in her brother's direction. 'He was, and I'm sure another woman will find that just wonderful, but what had begun as a beautiful meeting of the minds ended up making me feel stifled. He couldn't cope with my artistic flair, and nature. There was no future in it.'

Althea sounded curious, rather than suggesting condemnation, when she asked, 'But hadn't you been together for just a couple of months?'

'Long enough,' replied Clementine, placing her cutlery on her empty plate.

'I see you're no longer a vegetarian either.' Henry couldn't help himself. 'You managed to polish off that beef without too much trouble.'

His sister shrugged. 'I found myself lacking energy. And, as Vince says, there's nothing like red meat for energy.'

Henry noticed that his mother sounded tired when she enquired, 'And who's Vince, dear?'

Clementine sat very upright. 'He's the portraitist I mentioned to you during the harvest supper, Henry. Incredibly talented, and so busy. We've seen quite a bit of each other since I mentioned that you might like to commission him. You won't be sorry, Henry.'

Althea whispered, 'Of course, Vince Blanche – how could I have forgotten that?'

Henry had finished his meal. 'I haven't agreed that I shall, Clemmie. It's not as though you've ever shown me any of his work, so how could I possibly decide?'

His sibling beamed. 'I have photographs on my phone that I could show you. After dinner?'

Henry wasn't having any of it. 'I'm not going to make a decision about who should capture my likeness for posterity by judging their work on a tiny little screen. I'd like to see something this chap has done in the flesh, so to speak. The portrait will be the same size as father's – I'd like to see at least a few things he's done on that scale, in person.'

Stephanie said, 'Good point, Henry.'

The duke's spine straightened. 'Exactly.'

His wife continued, 'We should arrange that, before the baby comes. And what was it that had you all running about the Hall all afternoon, by the way? I feel as though I've missed out on a great deal…about which my dear husband has chosen to tell me nothing.'

Clementine clapped her hands with excitement. 'We've been on a treasure hunt – for an old desk, that none of us can find. There might be secret compartments, and they might hold the key to this family's reputation. Isn't it exciting!'

Stephanie turned to her husband. 'So you think Harold hid the report he commissioned into Fred's crimes in some old desk? What set you off in that direction? I thought you believed the report might be found in Harold's rooms – that was where we were going yesterday, after all.'

'No, the desk isn't in Harold's rooms,' replied Clementine, which annoyed Henry a great deal. 'Christine and I looked there first. And it's not in the music room either, despite the trumpet.'

Stephanie looked puzzled. 'Pardon?'

This time Henry managed to speak before his sister. 'Harold's portrait shows some torn sheet music and an abandoned trumpet,' he explained, 'which made some people think the desk might be in the music room…which I knew it wasn't.' He glanced toward his sister, who poked the tip of her tongue in his direction.

'Clemmie, please make at least some attempt to act your age,' chided Althea.

Her daughter snapped, 'He started it.'

Althea tutted.

Stephanie pressed, 'Do you mean you're trying to locate the desk in the portrait of Harold, the fourteenth duke? The one with the lovely clock on it? I always thought it odd that Harold was painted with that clock showing ten past two, it almost looked as though one hand were missing, but I dare say we'll never know why he did that.'

Henry looked taken aback. 'Ten past two? Ah, I see. But you mean that you know where the desk is? Where is it?'

Stephanie had everyone's attention when she replied, 'It's in the small barn. I found it in one of the upper rooms to which it had somehow made its way. The clock, too, still – oddly – set at ten past two, I noticed. I thought the desk might make a good changing table for the baby, but it needed some restoration. I had it brought down a couple of weeks ago, though I don't think they've started work on it yet. But it was quite empty.'

Althea was on full alert, which always alarmed Henry. She snapped, 'What about the secret drawers?'

Stephanie sounded puzzled. 'What secret drawers? I didn't see any. Though the back of the desk was rather badly damaged – damp, or possibly even water, I think. That's why it's in the small barn, for it to be worked on.'

Althea was almost wriggling with excitement. 'Damaged or not, I bet there *are* some secret drawers, or maybe hidden compartments.'

Henry was concerned that his mother's tone was so insistent. 'I tell you what, it's far too late to do anything about it tonight, but why don't we go to the barn in the morning and examine the desk then,' he suggested. Quite sensibly, he thought.

Althea spluttered, 'Henry, where's your sense of adventure? The drive to rescue the family's reputation?'

Henry could tell that his mother was going to be annoying until she'd personally examined the wretched desk.

'Exactly, Henry,' said his sister, most irritatingly.

Fortunately for Henry, his wife came to his rescue. 'I understand your keenness to examine the desk, Althea, but think of the practicalities; more or less everyone's gone for the day, and the barns are really the dominion of the craftspeople who are only here during the week in any case. Why don't we wait? We'd have the help we need on a Monday morning that we'll be lacking on a Sunday night, so I'll make sure the piece is accessible for us to take a good look at it in the morning. Leave it to me.'

'Yes, dear,' said Henry, relieved. He did his best to stare at everyone at the table in such a way that they understood that was to be an end to the matter.

'Now then, shall we all withdraw for coffee?' He rose as he spoke, leaving absolutely no one in any possible doubt about his intentions.

CHAPTER THIRTY-ONE

Christine had reasoned it was better to let the Twysts enjoy a family dinner without her company, so made her intention to dine alone clear when she left Chellingworth Hall after tea. She needed a shower; a fruitless couple of hours hunting about in disused rooms lifting innumerable dust sheets in an attempt to locate the wretched desk – that she was beginning to think had become firewood many decades earlier – had left her feeling grubby.

Finally refreshed, and having pulled together a meal that consisted of left-over pasta followed by a whole tub of dark chocolate ice-cream, she found she couldn't settle. She refocused her efforts to track down Natalie Smith online – to no avail – and found herself unable to concentrate on a book, magazine, or even the radio.

She purposely didn't phone Alexander, because she wouldn't give him the satisfaction of letting on that she was worried about him. But she was. And she was desperately unhappy about the impact his shutdown had had upon her; that was how she'd categorized the way he'd reacted when they'd been sitting in the car at the foot of the steps into Chellingworth Hall. The Alexander she'd thought she knew had disappeared in an instant, to be replaced by a cold, calculating person, without a shred of mercy in his soul, and that...that scared her.

She finally plodded down the stairs to the office below, in an attempt to loosen her limbs, as much as anything, then flopped onto the sofa there, and managed to become engrossed in the photographs of strange, deep-sea creatures in a copy of *National Geographic*. Annoyingly, she eventually realized that Alexander had dropped the magazine on the coffee table when he'd arrived on Friday morning, so even that became tainted, in her mind. As she dumped it back where she'd found it, she had a thought: both his scarf and umbrella were no longer on the stand beside the door. That meant he'd come back to the barn before heading off to who knew where. Of course he had a key to the place, and the security code for the alarm, but it hadn't occurred to her that he might have returned after he'd abandoned her at the Hall. She ran upstairs; yes, his overnight bag had gone. How could she not have noticed that? She felt strange as she pictured him moving around her apartment, gathering together his belongings, with that anger, and deadness, she'd seen in his eyes.

Christine stomped around her little sitting room for a few minutes, then decided to turn on the television, hoping to find something soothing to distract her; it was still far too early to even try to sleep. She didn't watch much TV, so had to hunt about for the remote control. Eventually she found it half submerged between the sofa's cushion and arm, along with a small spiral notepad, that fitted in the palm of her hand. She recognised it as Alexander's, and snorted with irritation; he had one of the most capable smart phones available, yet still liked his little pad with his cryptic notes and codes, a throwback to the days when he'd been a highly-regarded lackey for the underworld bosses in Brixton, no doubt.

Christine fizzed with anger as she flicked through the pages, all covered with strange words, abbreviations, and sets of numbers, none of which meant anything to her, but which still made her feel uneasy. After all, she reasoned, why would a person with nothing to hide need to use such codes and hieroglyphs? The pad was blank from about two-thirds of the way through, but it was clear that a page had been ripped out, because the edge of it had clung to the tiny metal loops. She could see a depression on the next page, and her natural curiosity kicked in – accompanied by the knowledge possessed by most readers, like her, of the Nancy Drew and Secret Seven books.

Christine got up and hunted about in every drawer, then ran down to the office, where she found what she'd been looking for – a pencil, and a soft-graphite one at that. A few moments later she was looking at what she'd managed to make visible on the indented page by rubbing ever so gently with the pencil: RR MARBELLA.

Of course, she didn't *know* why Alexander had written the name of a seaside town on Spain's Costa del Sol on his pad, nor when he'd done so, but she couldn't help herself wondering…did RR mean

Ronnie Right? She reasoned it could. Then she further reasoned that the man might have fled to Spain. Suddenly a cog rolled into place, and she grabbed her mobile phone.

She checked the time; yes, dinner at Chellingworth Hall could reasonably be expected to have finished, so she texted Stephanie.

Are your Mum and Dad at their home in Marbella at the moment? Would it be okay if I phoned or texted them with a question I have about the area? Hope it's okay to ask! If yes, could you send me their number/s please? Thanks, Cx

It was around eleven when she received an answer from the duchess, which included her mother's mobile number, and a suggestion that texting would be better than phoning, and that earlier in the day was the best time to catch her. Christine set an alarm for seven the next morning.

CHAPTER THIRTY-TWO

It was almost midnight when Annie woke up with a headache, and it was when she was standing in the kitchenette, mopping around the sink where she'd splashed water from the glass she'd poured to be able to take some painkillers, that two thoughts popped into her head almost simultaneously: it dawned on her that she hadn't mentioned the patch of wet carpet in Frank Turnbull's bedroom to DCI Llewellyn, and the little shards of silver foil she'd just peeled off the back of the blister-packed painkillers reminded her of the bits she'd found under the dead man's bed.

Feeling somewhat elated, yet still annoyed about her thumping head, Annie ambled back to the spacious, comfortable bedroom, and hoped sleep would find her, meaning she'd be up with a bounce in her step in the morning, and ready to share her information and insights with the police. However, not only did sleep not find her, but she couldn't even find a comfy way to arrange her body in what was a perfectly acceptable queen-sized bed.

She was cross she'd given all the scraps she'd picked up off Frank Turnbull's bedroom floor to the DCI, then sat up with a smile as she realized she still had all the pictures she'd taken. Plumping her pillows, Annie grabbed her phone from her bedside table and peered at the photos. There was one where – if she enlarged it as much as she could – she could just make out some printing on the silver foil. 'Co-cod' was all she could read, and none of the other photos helped at all.

She started an online search for pharmaceuticals that began with 'co-cod' and almost immediately found herself on the NHS website reading about something called co-codamol – and it didn't sound good. She suspected she might not sleep again at all that night.

MONDAY 24ᵀᴴ OCTOBER

CHAPTER THIRTY-THREE

'Can't I speak to DCI Llewellyn on the phone, now?' Annie was annoyed by how calm the person on the line sounded. She'd had three mugs of coffee, and was almost vibrating. 'It's important,' she added, believing in her bones it was. 'I was with her yesterday, and she asked me to tell her anything I could about Frank Turnbull's death – and I've got something more to tell her. Are you sure she can't be disturbed? Just for a minute?'

The irritating person asked her to hold on, then returned to the line. 'Could you come in to see her in an hour?'

'At headquarters again?'

'Yes.' The soothing tone made Annie's over-caffeinated blood boil.

'Alright, I'll be there, then,' she replied, and swore loudly once she'd disconnected. Annie immediately phoned for a taxi. She didn't have time to faff about on buses. The costs she was incurring on this case were continuing to mount up, but she was being highly professional, and keeping all her receipts in one pocket in her handbag; Mavis would be proud.

Upon her arrival at the building that lacked any character at all, and looked like every other boring, anonymous office block, a uniformed officer led Annie to a room that differed from the one she'd been in the day before in that it had a fake pot plant in the corner, and a window. She ignored the plant and stared out of the window, at a wall. She'd counted every brick three times before DCI Carys Llewellyn joined her.

The woman's trouser suit was charcoal, rather than navy, but, otherwise, she looked almost exactly as she had the day before – though Annie noted that the circles beneath her eyes were a little darker, and her highlighted hair had less of a sheen to it.

The DCI took the seat opposite Annie's. 'Sorry to keep you waiting. It's been…busy. Now, what can I do for you? I understand you have some information for me?'

It was clear to Annie that this meeting was going to be all business, so she spoke her piece. 'I checked the photos I took of the stuff I found under Turnbull's bed, and I believe it was the remnants of packaging from co-codamol tablets. I believe Jeanette Summers carelessly discarded some packaging under the bed at some point, then she must have cleared it all up before your lot got there yesterday morning. Now, I've done a bit of digging around online, and it looks to me as though those tablets could give a person who's been taking them for a long period of time many of the side-effects that Jeanette was bandying about as evidence that Frank was infirm and had dementia. I know I sent you the photos, and maybe you can get someone to look at them too. Or maybe there's a bit of the silver packaging that has the whole name on it in the sample I gave you. Anyway, I thought I should tell you, in person. I can show you the photo on my phone that's got the best image, if you like.'

The DCI sighed. 'Thank you. Our team has matched your discoveries, and we have similar suspicions. We also now have evidence that Jeanette disposed of an amount of such remnants early yesterday morning, on the beach below the Turnbull house. A witness phoned about some suspicious activity that she considered to be littering, and an officer in the area was able to retrieve some of the pieces of packaging. The witness also took photographs of Jeanette scattering the pieces, so we've got that, at least. We're fortunate that the slivers of silver caught the witness's eye.'

Annie relaxed in her seat a little. 'And had she really been giving them to Turnbull? Did you find any of the stuff in his system?'

Carys Llewellyn shook her head slowly. 'The toxicology report isn't available yet, though we know from his doctor that he'd been prescribed such a medication some time ago, after he'd suffered a fall. In her statement to the attending officers on the night of Frank Turnbull's demise, Jeanette voluntarily claimed she'd given him one pill earlier that day, because he was in pain – which might cover her for that.'

Annie felt uneasy. 'Did he...was he...?'

The woman sitting opposite her answered her unasked question. 'The findings of the post-mortem confirm his cause of death – a broken neck – as consistent with him falling down the stairs, as were a couple of broken ribs. But there were no other specific injuries that might confirm that he was...helped to fall. His GP has confirmed, however, that a recent cognitive investigation led him to a diagnosis of dementia. That, when taken together with his physical deterioration – including a marked lack of coordination, a decline in his fine motor skills, and general compromised mobility – might explain why he left his bedroom, then fell to his death. However, Mr Turnbull had not yet been assessed for dementia by a specialist; he'd missed two appointments, it appears. Miss Summers was the person with whom the arrangements for those appointments were made, rather than the specialists' office being in direct communication with the deceased; not an unusual circumstance, for them, it seems – they are quite used to having to connect through carers. We suspect she had no intention of presenting Mr Turnbull for that assessment, and that she had, as you suggested, been giving a constant and high dosage of co-codamol to Mr Turnbull without his knowledge, which – as you have discovered – our experts tell us could have produced the physical and cognitive effects witnessed by Mr Turnbull's GP.'

'Have you got her?' Annie leaned forward, eager to know.

'The last known sighting of Miss Summers in the vicinity was when she was observed dumping the evidence on the beach yesterday morning, and we are currently on the lookout for her.'

Annie nodded. 'Thanks for that. It sounds like...well, that she had a plan. That it was coming to a head. But why are you telling me all this? Isn't this, you know, police stuff? Confidential.' She added quickly, 'I won't tell anyone, of course.'

'It is, and I would appreciate your discretion. However, I saw how...responsible you felt for this tragedy when we met yesterday, and I hope that what I've been able to tell you will help with those emotions. If anything can.' The DCI nibbled her lip. 'It's more of a challenge to have to deal with the nagging belief that you could have done something to prevent a death than most people imagine, or know. I understand that feeling only too well, my career having presented me with many instances where I've been left wondering if I could have done more...or if I could have done something differently, to allow for a better outcome. And when a death is the outcome, the constant replaying of the situation can become draining. I don't believe you could have done anything differently that would have led to a better outcome, Annie. That's what I want you to know. Following up on Mr Turnbull's daughters' complaints, we now believe that Jeanette Summers targeted him, established a relationship with him, and has been manipulating him while controlling him with powerful pharmaceuticals since she moved into his home.'

Unbidden, the image of Annie's parents rose before her; they were older than in real life, and much more frail. She empathized deeply with what she suspected the Turnbull sisters must have felt when they began to worry about how their father's new girlfriend was shutting them out of his life. 'It's evil,' she whispered, 'just evil.'

Carys Llewellyn nodded. 'We'll find her, and we've got a lot more to go on now than we did this time yesterday.'

'Good. And thanks.' Annie smiled, sadly.

'You're welcome.' Llewellyn shifted in her seat, sitting back a little. 'You know, I had a bit of a chat with my brother about you last night.' The detective's eyes narrowed. 'You're held in high regard within your adopted community of Anwen-by-Wye, aren't you?'

Annie was gobsmacked. 'Am I? I thought they just put up with me, to be honest. I'm not known for being backwards in coming forwards, and I do like to speak my mind. Then there's my general inability to remain upright if there's the slightest chance to trip over my own feet and, well – let's be honest, there's no hiding it is there? – I stick out like a sore thumb there...because I'm English, which, from what I've experienced personally, outweighs me being Black, in a Welsh village.'

Carys Llewellyn threw back her head and laughed. 'Yeah, he said you were funny, too. But a bit down on yourself.'

'Oi, I'm not sure I like being talked about behind my back.' Annie was a bit miffed.

The DCI smoothed down her jacket. 'Sorry, but this is a serious case, as you know, Annie, and I always use every avenue to help my investigations. You see, the thing that makes you especially interesting for me in this instance – other than that you're you, and the circumstances of your being in Swansea at all – is the other critical fact we learned from the post-mortem. And it's why I wanted a proper chat to Carwen about you; it wasn't just idle gossip between siblings, I needed him to give me a considered character reference.'

'Why? What else did the post-mortem tell you?' Annie stuck out her chin, defiantly.

The DCI looked grim. 'Time of death. It looks as though Frank Turnbull died no more than thirty minutes before you discovered his body, which tallies with what you said in your statement about his skin not feeling noticeably cool to the touch when you felt for a pulse. Which, in turn, means that Jeanette Summers couldn't possibly have pushed him down those stairs.'

Annie felt simultaneously deflated, and on her guard. 'You're right, she couldn't have done it. Because she was with me for an hour before we found him. So I'm her alibi, right?'

'Indeed you are, Annie. Indeed you are.'

CHAPTER THIRTY-FOUR

It had been agreed that the group working on The Case of the Disgraced Duke – a title which had been decided by Mavis in place of Althea's original suggestion, The Case of Frightful Freddie – would meet at ten in the library. It had also been agreed, over coffee the night before, that this was the time by which Stephanie would have made arrangements for the Sheraton desk to have been brought there, from the small barn, for them to examine. Everyone accepted this would be a more comfortable arrangement for the dowager.

Mavis and Althea enjoyed their usual early, light breakfast at the Dower House, then prepared themselves for the day ahead, and met in the sitting room at a quarter to ten in readiness for Ian Cottesloe to drive them to Chellingworth Hall.

Ian arrived promptly enough, but then took ten minutes to convince Althea that the Gilbern was not going to be useable until it had been sent away to be worked on for some time by a mechanic who specialized in restoring such vehicles. Mavis was impressed by the way he handled the situation. She was also relieved when Althea declared herself satisfied with the arrangements Ian had made, and agreed to be driven in the Land Rover for the foreseeable future.

It wasn't until Althea attempted to enter the vehicle that Mavis realized how very much her friend's mobility had decreased, especially when it came to lifting her leg high enough to get in. Ian remedied the immediate problem by fetching a small step, which was then stowed in the rear to allow for Althea's disembarkation. However, Mavis decided she'd have to have a talk with Althea as soon as they were alone.

Mavis knew that Althea had sustained injuries of various sorts, at various times, because the dowager had ridden horses for most of the past fifty years. However, it had only been a few weeks earlier that she'd witnessed Althea getting into the Land Rover with no apparent problem whatsoever. She needed to find out what had changed. Althea had said nothing about any particular problems, or new aches and pains, and Mavis – even with all her nursing experience – hadn't spotted anything untoward.

The drive to the Hall was swift, and silent. Upon their arrival, Althea puzzled Mavis when she thanked Ian and added, 'Had it not been for the rain I should have enjoyed the walk, but this weather changes so very much for a person.'

Having been greeted by Edward, Mavis and Althea joined Henry, Stephanie, Val, and Clementine in the library.

'Gosh, we're quite a crowd,' remarked Althea.

'No Christine this morning, I'm afraid,' noted Mavis. 'She's got something she needs to take care of, of a personal nature.'

Althea rolled her eyes. 'Ah, young love,' she sighed, as she settled into a comfortable seat beside the now-famous desk.

It was in a sorry state; the glory with which it had once displayed its beautiful lines had long since passed, and its back – as Stephanie had warned – was much the worse for wear.

'You see,' opened the duchess, 'with it being this bad already, I thought that a little work could at least restore it to usefulness. And that top is a good size for changing nappies, isn't it, Henry?'

Mavis noticed that Henry looked horrified at the mere thought of a dirty nappy, and wondered how he'd live up to what were clearly high expectations on the part of his wife.

'Indeed,' he said, 'though I doubt it's what the designer had in mind.'

'But so much better than something one could purchase these days,' added Stephanie, glowing.

'I dare say they'll have to take the back off in any case,' observed Althea, 'so why not just rip it off and be done with it? Then we could see all the innards at once.'

'Oh, I'm not sure that's appropriate, Mother,' snapped Henry. 'It's a priceless piece.'

His mother replied tartly, 'With a back panel that's warped and all but hanging off? Priceless? Well, alright then, maybe not rip it off, but isn't there someone on the estate with the skills to be able to remove it without causing further damage?'

'That's why Glyn is waiting outside,' said Stephanie. 'He was the one I asked to do the work needed to bring this piece to a condition where it could be used. He said he would replace the back, repair the leg – you see there, it's splitting – and would work on the finish of the piece too. I asked him to bring his tools here today, and that's also why the piece is standing on a dust sheet. Do we agree that I should ask him to remove the back?'

A general nodding of heads was followed by Henry whispering, 'But no one's to say why we're having him do it – word would be around the village in a flash.'

Mavis watched with amusement as a young man entered the library, and took in the surprising group sitting about on the edges of their chairs. They all watched him work. His discomfort grew with every move he made.

Henry was bobbing about trying to see what the man was doing exactly. 'Is the task too difficult?'

Glyn faced the duke, blushing. 'Not difficult, Your Grace, it's just that I'm not really used to an audience, you see.'

Althea chuckled, 'So, Glyn, you'll not be applying for a job on that telly thing where folks turn up with stuff they've had in an attic, or a garage, for years – completely ignoring it – until just after someone dies, and then they can't get it fixed fast enough, because "so-and-so would be so proud to see me do it". I've always thought the so-and-so in question would have been a good deal more proud if the person had hauled it out of said attic, dusted it off, and got it fixed before they died, so they could have enjoyed it too.'

Mavis couldn't let that pass. 'That's a rather jaundiced view. We'll speak more when we're alone about how very much we really enjoy watching that programme together.' She smiled at Glyn, not prepared to chastise the dowager further in front of a member of the Hall's staff, but becoming quite concerned about why on earth her friend was being so uncharacteristically snitty about…well, everything, it seemed.

Glyn returned Mavis's smile, then grinned broadly when he managed to achieve his tricky goal of being able to step away from the desk having removed its entire back panel.

He looked at the piece in his hands, and at the open back of the desk. 'Such fine work,' he said, in reverential tones.

'Indeed,' snapped Henry, in what Mavis felt was verging on an overly dismissive tone, 'just leave it there, on the floor, and we'll manage without you from here on, thank you…Glyn.'

'Of course, Your Grace,' said Glyn, and he left, looking utterly bemused. Mavis could only imagine the conversations he was about to have with his colleagues.

Any lack of mobility on Althea's part seemed to magically disappear as she leapt from her seat and managed to poke her face into the back of the desk before anyone else had a chance.

'Mother!' Henry and Clementine chorused.

'Look, look – I can see it. There's a drawer on the inside that isn't on the outside…look!' Althea was almost hopping with glee. She stuck her small hand inside the desk and started waggling it about.

'Don't push it, or pull it,' said Mavis, sharply. 'I did a bit of research last night, and it seems you have to push on the outside to find the secret parts of these pieces, because of some sort of release arrangement inside. The general rule, I believe, is that you should push instead of pulling.'

Clementine looked annoyed. 'That's not terribly helpful, is it? I mean, where exactly does one push?'

'Maybe try the veneer inlays,' offered Val timidly.

Mavis had noticed that Val Jenkins had been rather quiet since she'd arrived – not that Althea had been giving anyone much a chance to talk. As she considered Val's situation, Mavis recalled it had taken a little time for her to become used to speaking in the company of folk with titles herself, though Althea's warm initial welcome, and her own manner – honed at innumerable bedsides – meant she'd found it maybe easier than most. She knew of the friendship between Val and Stephanie that had existed before Stephanie had married Henry and had become a duchess, but wondered how comfortable Val would be with not just a duke and dowager to deal with as well, but now also Stephanie's sister-in-law, who was, herself, something of a force of nature.

Everyone poked at the piece, with Althea being the one who eventually squeaked triumphantly, 'Look, I did it!'

A shallow, narrow drawer had emerged from what appeared to be an unbroken panel of wood. And inside was something long, round, and tied with a red leather strip. Mavis could hardly believe it – it was an honest to goodness scroll.

Val spoke with surprising authority. 'Everybody stop.' Everyone did, and stared at her. She blushed, then cleared her throat and said, 'I know I'm not the member of my family renowned for restoring rare books, but I've seen my father work enough over the years to be aware that this document could be in an extremely fragile state – especially given the moisture damage sustained by the panel Glyn removed. I suggest we find a pair of tongs, or something like that – which will spread the pressure on the material when we lift it – then we can take it out of the drawer and examine its condition on the table over there.'

Edward was summoned, and he returned not five minutes later with a variety of implements he'd 'borrowed' from the kitchen. He'd been assured they were all scrupulously clean. Mavis imagined Cook Davies could be more than trusted on that count, and it was only a matter of moments later that Val had removed the scroll and declared the paper to be sound.

The document turned out to not be one long scroll, but a sheaf of rolled papers. Unfortunately, they'd been that way for so long that Val spent the next achingly long twenty minutes separating the sheets and laying them individually on hastily cleared tabletops, their corners held down by slim volumes that had been plucked from the shelves in the room. There were nineteen pages, the signatures at the end of what was – indeed – clearly a report, covered the entirety of the final one, with the fourteenth duke's flourish and seal at the bottom.

'So this is definitely what we've all been looking for,' said Clementine, sounding awed. 'Excellent.'

'I believe so,' said her brother, sounding less entranced. 'But it looks like we'll have the devil of a time reading it – that handwriting is appalling.'

Mavis stepped forward. 'May I?' She leaned over the first sheet, trying to not breath on it. 'Leave it to me – I've seen worse; some of the doctors' notes I've had to read over the years have allowed me to become more than a wee bit adept at this sort of thing. I suggest I read it quietly and tell you all the highlights. Agreed?'

Everyone nodded.

Mavis accepted a chair with a good, straight back that Henry placed beside the desk, as well as a pair of white gloves that Val suggested would be a sensible precaution. Everyone else settled themselves as Mavis began to read.

'Aye, well…no surprises to start with: it talks about the report being prepared by one Thomas Mercer, and a Robert Davies on behalf of the fourteenth duke, and how it comes about as a result of an intensive and extensive period of research on their parts. There's a lot of stuff about the credentials of Mercer and Davies, which is neither here nor there, because – as I dare say we all agree – he who pays the piper names the tune, and we already know the fourteenth was dead set against Fred, due to his wrecked musical career. It's clear the pair were hand-picked by Harold to do the job.'

Stephanie sounded glum when she asked, 'Do you think they'd really only search out dirt about Fred, because Harold wanted them to? Then that's what becomes the official record. That might not be good for the family.'

'Aye, mebbe,' said Mavis her gloved fingers running along the lines of scrawl as she continued to read. 'The investigation took six months and many witnesses were interviewed,' she continued. 'It seems they had to pay those they interviewed for their time.'

Althea piped up, 'You're always talking about how you need good records to be able to send invoices to your clients; I wonder if the fourteenth duke made them provide receipts too.' She twinkled at her friend, then clamped her lips closed.

Mavis glanced at the dowager and said pointedly, 'Moving on then…here we are, something that looks like an actual fact – though it took them four pages to get to it. It states that two men were brought from China by Fred, one a "man who knew of exotic plants, being an accomplished gardener", and the other was his brother. They were installed at Chellingworth Hall by Fred – much against his mother's wishes – in 1841.' Mavis paused, her lips and fingers moving, then she added, 'Then there's a load of terrible things said about the men which I've no intention of reading. I don't hold with folk who say "it was the norm back then" to believe such dreadful things about people who were different from themselves…so let's leave it at that. Suffice it to say, there was a great deal of animosity directed toward the two men from China, and toward Fred for bringing them here.'

'Weren't Britain and China at war at that time?' Val seemed surprised that she'd spoken aloud.

Mavis looked up, momentarily. 'That's as maybe, but there's still no call for some of this…tripe. Anyway, something we might accept as being relevant is the noting here that both brothers were involved to a greater or lesser extent in designing and overseeing the work done to create the new gardens, but that they both disappeared soon afterwards. Now, hang on there…this is interesting. Let me read…yes. It says here that the thirteenth duke never spoke of the men again, and that he did something the authors of the report emphasize as being highly suspicious: he ordered everyone off the estate for an entire day – which sent the whole area into a lather.'

Althea sounded surprised when she said, 'Everyone? Good gracious.'

Henry harrumphed. 'Sounds a bit peculiar, I must say.'

His mother replied, 'And terribly awkward for all concerned. Can you imagine how that must have impacted the estate, Henry? All those animals left un-milked and unfed, people unable to tend to their crops and so forth; don't forget, back then the estate operated quite differently than it does today. What a to do there must have been – I can quite understand the upheaval that must have caused.'

Stephanie mused, 'I wonder why he did that…if he had nothing to hide. Was this immediately after the two men disappeared, Mavis? Does the report make that clear?'

Mavis's lips moved silently, then she sighed. 'I cannae say. The words used in the report don't state categorically when this happened, but they imply that the disappearance and the evacuation of the estate happened almost simultaneously…though that interpretation might be what the authors wanted us to think. They were thorough in gathering statements about the impact the closure had, but aren't as keen to give dates. What they do say is that there was another change here at the Hall – that when everyone returned to the Hall and Estate, Fred gave orders for all the planting in the almost-finished gardens to be overhauled.'

Henry asked, 'Just the things that had died, or major changes?'

Mavis nodded. 'It seems a major change. According to this, the gardens were "almost completed" but that "all the planting was altered, to align with new plans". It says that, when the updated planting was completed, which happened in a relatively short space of time, using many workers from far afield, Fred "took to his chambers, and his life ended shortly thereafter".'

Henry sounded triumphant. 'So the report doesn't claim murder, nor suicide? How wonderful.'

'Hang on,' snapped Mavis, 'I've no' finished, yet. The report goes on to say that Fred refused to ever explain the disappearance of the two men from China, not even when the dowager begged him to do so. It's also stated here that he would fine anyone who mentioned the men, and would banish them from the Chellingworth Estate thereafter. He even challenged a visiting duke to a duel when he mentioned it…though the duke left after being threatened with a poker, claiming Fred had lost his mind.'

'That could be the root of the rumor about Fred being ostracized,' suggested Stephanie. 'I can't imagine it's pleasant to be chased off by a poker-wielding man whether he's a duke or not.'

Althea mused, 'It's certainly an odd way to behave. Maybe Fred was a bit gaga, after all.'

'No mention of such in this report,' replied Mavis. 'It ends with an amount of innuendo. All in all, while it doesn't make any specific claims, it seems to be a bit of a hatchet job, to me. Though maybe we can accept some of what pass for facts in it as containing a grain of truth.'

'I'm not sure if that's a good or bad thing,' said Henry looking at his wife, who shrugged.

CHAPTER THIRTY-FIVE

Annie Parker was sitting where she had been for the past half an hour – on a rather uncomfortable chair in the reception area of Swansea Police headquarters waiting for a taxi. She couldn't help but see Mrs Tina Rees – Tina Turnbull, as she thought of her – arriving. Annie stood to greet her client, wondering how the poor woman would react when she set eyes on the private investigator who'd not been able to save her father.

'Have they found her?' Tina looked as though she hadn't slept much; her eyes were red-rimmed, her hair lank. 'Have they found that wicked woman yet?' She grabbed Annie with surprising strength.

'I don't think so. I was with DCI Llewellyn a little while ago and she said they're doing all they can to track her down.' Annie felt dreadful that she couldn't give her client better news.

Hoping the bereaved woman might have a bit of moral support in her time of need, she added, 'Is Tanya joining you?'

Tina's eyes filled with tears. 'No. She's in hospital. Had to be rushed to A & E last evening, from here. They think she's had a heart attack. The shock, on top of all the stress, I'm sure of it. Stuck in Morriston Hospital, she is. Her husband had to leave the kids so he could get to the hospital last night. The kids'll be fine – they're both old enough to look after themselves – but I'm glad I've seen you, because I was going to phone you anyway. Do you think you could move out of the flat today? My brother-in-law could stay there, then. Me too, to save us both all the driving. I've brought everything I need with me for myself – and some extra bits for Tanya too, to be going on with. Her husband's gone back home again to get her own stuff from their house, because they said at the hospital that she might be in for a while. At least until they can be sure what happened, exactly, and how serious it is. It would make a big difference if we could both be down in Langland, see? I'm sure you understand. They won't let us stay at Dad's house yet. I wish they would, because then I could have a good look around the place to see what's there, and what that Jeanette's got rid of, or taken. They've said maybe they'll take me there tomorrow, but they haven't "released the scene" yet. Besides, there's no point in you staying any more, is there, because there's nothing left to investigate. Not now that Dad's...gone.'

Annie was taken aback, but gathered her wits quickly. 'Of course I can move out, Tina. I'm just waiting for a taxi to go back there now.' She checked her watch. 'If I'm quick, I could pack everything away and leave it nice and tidy for you, then come back here with the keys, if you like. Or what about the bloke I got them from in the first place? The one who lives on the top floor. I could give them to him, instead, if you don't know how long you'll be here. Or is there a manager in the building?'

Tina looked panicked. 'I don't know about a manager...the person who owns the flat didn't tell me about that, he just said that friend of his had a spare set of keys and to get them from him, but I agreed the date I did mainly because his friend was going away on holiday. Halkidiki, he said. I remember that.' She looked puzzled. 'Why would I remember that?'

Annie's mind raced. If only she'd managed to get her driving licence, getting about the place would be so much easier, but every lesson she'd taken had been a disaster, to the extent the instructor had suggested that maybe not everyone was born to be a driver.

She had a flash of inspiration. 'Do you know the Seaview Hotel?'

'Of course, it's been there forever.'

'How about I leave the keys behind the bar there? I'm sure they'd hang onto them for you, so you could pick them up from there whenever it suits. There's no flat number on them or anything, and I won't tell them that, so they'd be anonymous.'

Tina looked as though she might cry with relief. 'Yes, that'll work. Thanks. When do you think you could be out?'

Annie felt the pressure of the situation. 'By half five this afternoon. At the latest. There's a washer-dryer in the kitchen; I'll run the sheets and towels through that, so everything will be fresh for you. I noticed that the sofa in the sitting room pulls out into a spare bed, and there was extra bedding in the hall cupboard…how about I make that up too? So it's ready for your brother-in-law. Alright?'

Tina hugged Annie so tightly she thought she might run out of air. Pulling back, the distraught woman gasped, 'I can't thank you enough. Everything you've done…finding him, telling me…being there. And the DCI told me you'd been really helpful…it was you who found all those bits from the poison she was feeding him…you're wonderful. Thank you.'

Annie shuffled with embarrassment, thinking to herself, *I wish I'd been so wonderful that your father was still alive*, then felt the familiar heat crawling up her neck to the top of her head. *Not now*, she thought, waiting for the inevitable thudding, rushing, lava-hot wave to wash through her body.

Annie always felt a bit wobbly when she had a hot flash, so looked around for a chair, and as her eyes swam just a little – the way they always did – she saw a woman with a wet umbrella enter the reception area and create a little puddle of water on the floor as she stood, wondering where she should go.

'The wet carpet! I never told her about the wet carpet!'

Tina looked puzzled. 'What are you talking about?'

Annie stared into the woman's bloodshot eyes. 'I've got to tell them about the wet patch on the carpet in your father's bedroom. That must be it! It wasn't me being great at my job that made Jeanette invite me to meet her for a drink, then join her back at the house that night – she set me up to be her alibi. She made a big song and dance about the whole thing. Inviting me to go to the house with her at the top of her voice, checking the time with the barman before we left, going on and on about how long she'd been away from your father, away from the house. It was a plan, Tina…a way to make sure everyone would know she couldn't have been the one to drag him out of bed and set him tumbling down the stairs. I get that now. And the wet patch on the carpet means someone else was in your father's bedroom that night…someone who'd come in from the rain, and who dripped all over the floor beside his bed. Jeanette had an accomplice, Tina – that's what it means.'

Tina looked horrified. 'You mean she…she really planned to…oh no! Dad!'

Annie felt dreadful, and tried to rein in the excitement she was feeling about the breakthrough she knew she'd just had, because Tina was falling apart in front of her eyes. She reached out and held the woman, allowing her to sob onto her shoulder.

Annie whispered, 'Come on, we've both got to see DCI Llewellyn, now.'

CHAPTER THIRTY-SIX

'Luncheon is served, Your Graces,' announced Edward evenly, 'and I have been asked to communicate to Her Grace' – he nodded toward Stephanie – 'that her mother has been attempting to reach her on her mobile phone for some time, and would be grateful for some form of communication.' Edward's face managed to convey absolutely no emotion as he spoke.

Stephanie replied, 'Thank you, Edward. I'll phone her after lunch.'

Henry responded, 'Why not now? She must be worried about your fall.'

Stephanie tensed – Henry could see her shoulders hunch. 'Did you tell my mother that I'd fallen?'

Henry could see she wasn't happy. He stood, in an attempt to show he was in control. 'I did not, because you expressly told me not to. But I might have, inadvertently, mentioned that you were back to your usual self following the fall. Your mother's been sending me texts since early this morning, and I fear I slipped up. It might be easier if you kept your phone with you, dear, instead of leaving it in the bedroom.'

Stephanie also rose. 'You're the one who keeps telling me I have to take care of myself, keep an eye on my blood pressure and so forth. Well, for your information, it always goes through the roof when Mum phones me. I know she's lovely really, but she does go on so about…well, nothing of any consequence, which is what annoys me so much. I swear I know every single ailment of each person she's so much as chatted to at a bar – and I'll never meet any of them, yet she insists upon talking to me about them as though they're family members I've known since childhood. It's annoying. So that's why I don't have my phone with me all the time, Henry, because – now that I don't have a full-time job – she feels she can chat to me whenever she likes.'

Henry led the way to the dining room, feeling more than a little guilty. Stephanie said she'd join the group when she could, and excused herself to go to her room.

Lunch began as a strangely subdued affair, not least because the dowager refused to eat anything, except for fruit – which was so rare an event as to be noteworthy in itself. Henry also couldn't fathom what was going on between her and Mavis. He acknowledged he was not always the most astute of people, but even he could sense a tension between the two women; Mavis had been what he judged to be over-solicitous of his mother for the entire morning. Short of asking what was going on he suspected he wouldn't be told – and he had absolutely no intention of raising the topic, especially since there were more pressing matters to discuss, namely, the contents of the report that had been commissioned by Harold, the fourteenth duke, about his predecessor's actions.

When the main dish had been served – a lightly poached salmon fillet atop a bed of greens – Henry said, 'We'll need no more help, thank you, Edward,' keen that not even his scrupulously discreet butler should overhear the conversation he hoped would follow. Once they were alone, he added, 'Maybe now would be a good time for us to review what Mavis read aloud to us.'

Clementine whined, 'Why spoil a perfectly good lunch, brother dear?'

Althea's tone was grim when she added, 'Why discuss it at all? The report made it all perfectly clear. Two men vanished, Fred covered it up. He must have had something to hide. Sending everyone off the estate sounds…well, decidedly fishy, if you ask me.'

Mavis stepped up. 'Now come along, it wasnae that bad. Let's no' forget the way Harold felt about Fred. He was bound to have less than charitable thoughts about the man who'd left him in the lurch, so to speak. And we can at least feel more comfortable now that Fred didnae kill himself, after all; the tone of the report was such that if Fred had killed himself, that would not have been left out of it.'

Althea piped up, 'Which is also borne out by the records at St David's Church; no hint there either that he was a suicide. Which –

overall – is not something that would bother me about the man. I mean, for a person to take their own life they must be, or must feel they are, in a terribly dark place. That aspect would have been a tragedy, rather than a scandal, but it's not the case. I think the report and the church records prove that.'

Mavis agreed. 'And to die unexpectedly, leaving the title to pass to a cousin, is not something a person has any control over – so let's all at least acknowledge that Fred didn't run away from his responsibilities.'

Althea replied tartly, 'I'm not so sure about that, Mavis; he should have seen to it that he had an heir. That's a part of the overall responsibility of a duke – to ensure the line continues. Had he married and that marriage had not borne fruit, that might have been a different matter. Chelly married me not long after he was widowed to ensure that more than one child was born to the line, and, with Devereaux having fallen victim to measles as he did, it's a very good thing that Chelly took his responsibility so seriously. As do you, Henry. I only hope your firstborn is a boy, and that Stephanie has it in her to produce a spare too.'

Henry's heart fell when he saw the expression on his wife's face; she'd entered the dining room in time to hear Althea's last pronouncement, and he could see she was clenching her fists as she took her seat at the table.

He noticed that his wife's voice wasn't as steady as usual when she observed, 'I assume we're having a private conversation, without attendance at the table. I'll follow Althea's lead, and allow fruit to suffice.'

She started hacking into an apple with what Henry judged to be an undue amount of ferocity. When the apple was well and truly sliced, Stephanie added, 'I don't know why everyone's looking so glum, that report was nothing but an unpleasant puff piece – full of innuendo and hearsay. There were few facts in it. I should know – back in my days in corporate PR I had to write several pieces like that – not sailing too close the wind, legally speaking, but stirring up enough mud to allow some of it to stick.' She sighed heavily.

'I'd agree,' replied Mavis. 'At least now I suppose we know which two persons disappeared, and maybe we can understand why rumors surfaced about his having killed them.'

Althea added, 'You mentioned a contemporaneous cartoon in *Punch* magazine, Henry, about which Chelly never spoke to me. Do you happen to know if a copy of the cartoon exists here, at the Hall?'

'Not that I'm aware, Mother.'

'You see,' Althea leaned forward, 'it seems extraordinary to me that Fred would have been in China at all during the period when the report suggests he brought the gardener in question, and his brother, to Chellingworth. As Val mentioned, Britain and China were at war at the time; the first Opium War ran from 1839 to 1842, so quite what he'd have been doing there at that time, I cannot imagine. He certainly wasn't attached to any fighting force that we know of. That wasn't mentioned at all. Maybe he was a spy. Oh, I say...that sounds juicy.'

Mavis tutted. 'Don't go getting ahead of yourself, Althea. The report didnae suggest that at all. Though I'm impressed by the accuracy of your dates, I don't think Fred was a spy behind enemy lines. His portrait shows him in the gardens at Chellingworth, and we know he spent his time here – after whatever the incident was that led to the disappearance of the Chinese gardener and his brother – creating large parts of the gardens as they appear today...though I've no idea if they still exist in the way he planned, planted, or envisaged them when he made all those changes.'

'We'll never know,' said Henry, then added, 'but I'm inclined to agree with you, Stephanie, the report is nothing more than hogwash. I believe we could show it to Barry Walton, the TV producer, and he'd see there was nothing to the rumors.'

'Oh, I wouldn't be so sure about that,' said Val.

Clementine asked, 'What do you mean?'

Val had finished her lunch, so sat back and said, 'I'm no expert, but I took a long, hard look at different styles of documentaries and factual programming, before Barry and I agreed on the eventual format for *The Curious Cook*. And there's a particular style of programming that is quite popular when dealing with past events where the full truth is still not known, or where there are conflicting interpretations, or views. Things like why and how the pyramids were built – you know, were they "just" to memorialize pharaohs, or were they really designed by aliens? That sort of thing.'

Henry shifted in his chair. 'I don't understand. Fred was...what, an alien? Balderdash. Is that what you're saying they'd try to make people believe?'

Val squared her shoulders. 'Let me tell you how the situation regarding Fred could be dealt with using this specific technique: the hypothesis is put forward by a host with a trustworthy face, in liquid tones, that Fred killed two men – and got away with it. Then he set himself up here at Chellingworth using underpaid and overworked labor to create indulgent gardens, then killed himself, finally overcome by guilt. Each shocking aspect is explored by the host, and this report is exhibit A...with the hearsay and rumors contained within it being used to maybe initially rebut the hypothesis, but with question marks being raised about its veracity. The entire TV presentation is about the scandal, and all the viewer is left with at the end of it is a series of pointed questions that are – essentially – left unanswered, but which lead to an inevitable conclusion...that being whatever the producer tells the scriptwriter they want it to be. You see it used all the time in instances like "Were the pyramids designed and even built by aliens using alien technology – because how could man create such wonders, so long ago, that still puzzle us today?" – that sort of thing.'

Henry shrugged, 'The pyramids *are* incredible structures...and it *is* baffling how they managed to create them, I suppose...'

'Henry, not the point,' snapped Stephanie. 'Val's right – this report is a load of old codswallop, but it did the trick then, and it could revitalize conversations about Fred's murderous reputation now. We need more than this "hogwash" as you so aptly called it, Henry. It's a good start, because at least it tells us what Harold thought...but I think we need to try to find some original writings by Fred, or other records from his time, that might throw more light on who on earth this gardener was, and why Fred brought him back from China in the first place – let alone working out why Fred even went there. It certainly wasn't to walk the Great Wall, because, as Althea pointed out, the relationship between Britain and China at that time was…well, they were at war with each other, so I'm guessing that "poor" would be understating it dreadfully.'

Val said, 'I'm afraid I can't come back to help tomorrow, I'm needed elsewhere. In fact, I should really leave after lunch. Sorry. I hope that's okay. I could help again from Friday, if that's any use.'

Stephanie replied, 'Of course, you need to do what you need to do – it's been lovely having you around so much, and you've been such a big help. Thanks, Val. But I hope we've got it all cleared up before then. Unless it's not something we're ever able to really work out.'

Althea rose. 'We must. It's imperative. The reputation of the family name depends upon it, doesn't it, Henry?'

Henry's heart was heavy when he replied, 'Yes, Mother.'

CHAPTER THIRTY-SEVEN

Annie wondered where all the rain was coming from. At least the weather matched her mood. She was sick of the rain, and sick of the days being so short, and sick of feeling so useless. She could have kicked herself for not checking the times of trains from Swansea, because if she had, she'd have known the last one that could get her close enough to Anwen-by-Wye to get her home that night departed at six thirty p.m., but she hadn't found that out until it had been too late to make it. So now she was waiting at the Seaview Hotel for Christine to come and collect her, as though she were a small, incapable child. She'd felt such a fool phoning to ask for a lift, but she'd decided it was best to ask Christine, rather than Tudor, because he had a pub to run, after all, and Christine was only faffing about at Chellingworth Hall on something to do with an ancestor of the family having topped a couple of blokes before eventually topping himself, which she couldn't imagine was at all urgent.

She stared into her G & T as though comfort might be found floating beside the meager slice of lemon. It wasn't.

'Terrible news, isn't it?'

Annie looked up to see the young barman hovering beside her, both his hands full of used glasses.

'Yeah, he was a lovely man, by all accounts,' she replied.

'Who was?' The barman looked confused.

'Frank Turnbull. The man who died.' Annie felt her own brow furrow.

The barman's expression cleared. 'Ah yes, him. No, I meant about Jeanette.'

Annie's back straightened. 'What about her?'

'First her boyfriend dies, then her father's taken ill and she has to rush off to look after him. Mind you, knowing what she went through up on the hill there, I dare say she'll be the right person to tend to a poorly parent.' He looked as sage as his youth would allow.

Annie's investigative senses tingled. 'Did you see her before she…left?' She reckoned it was worth asking.

The youth rested one handful of glasses on his hip. 'I did, as a matter of fact. I was coming here to start my early shift yesterday morning; I've got lectures at Swansea Uni all week, so I do lates Mondays to Fridays, then earlies at the weekend, see? I saw her coming up from the beach. Looked a bit rough, she did – which I suppose is only to be expected. She told me she was off then.'

Annie told her heart to stop beating so quickly. 'Did she say where she was going, exactly?'

The ceiling was thoroughly inspected by the young man as he answered. 'She just said "home", and I don't know where that is. I mean, you can tell by her accent she's from the Valleys, but not far up, I wouldn't have thought.'

Annie replied, 'I'm good at spotting which part of London a person's from by their accent – is it the same for you?' She leaned forward and half-whispered, 'I gotta be honest, being English means a lot of you sound the same to me…sorry.' She beamed a winning smile as though it were a cherry on top of an ice-cream treat.

The barman laughed and winked. 'Well, I won't say anything, if you don't, but yes, there's a big difference in a person's accent if they come from here' – he leaned down to whisper – 'which is dead posh' – he stood straight again – 'or from Swansea proper, like me, or out by Baglan – Port Talbot way, or up the Valleys. And if they're from Llanelli, well, sometimes I can't understand them myself!' He laughed at his joke. 'No, no, I'm only kidding – I can understand them well enough.'

Annie gave what he'd said some thought. 'But Port Talbot's one of the places on Swansea Bay, in't it? It can't be more than ten miles away. If the variations are obvious – to you – for such small areas, how far up the Welsh Valleys exactly do you think her accent places Jeanette? And which valley? Even I know there's a load of 'em.'

The look of concentration on the young man's face made Annie want to smile. 'Well, yes, there's lots of valleys, but I'd say she was Tawe Valley.'

'Is that where Pontardawe is?' Annie reckoned it was worth a punt.
'Yeah, out that way.'

Annie felt elated. 'Ta. I'll try to track her down. We got on, see? By the way, what's your name, so I can tell her you were sorry to see her go?'

He smiled. 'Me? I'm Aled.'

Annie looked as surprised as she felt. 'Really? I know another Aled who helps out in a pub where I live – in a little village in Powys called Anwen-by-Wye.'

It was the barman's turn to look surprised. 'You live in a village in Powys? I though you'd come here straight out of Eastenders.'

Annie laughed as she said, 'Well, I haven't been there quite a year yet, and before that I was in London…yeah, the East End. Well spotted. Though I have to say those actors they've got on Eastenders? Well, it sounds like they're from all over the South East, not the East End proper. But there, maybe there just in't enough of us real Cockneys who want to be actors on the telly for them to be able to get enough of us.'

Aled rolled his eyes. 'Oh, don't get me started on that one. It's only recently there've been any people on TV with Welsh accents at all – except the Welsh news, you know. Anyway, now it seems they can't get enough of them, so they're giving the Welsh character parts to all sorts. Half of their accents sound so terrible it sets my teeth on edge, and my mam can't cope at all. Turns it off as soon as they open their mouths she does. Especially if they're from north Wales when they're supposed to be from the south. Swears about it too, sometimes, she does – and it takes some doing to make my mam swear. Chapel, she is.'

Annie could tell that Aled might have stood chatting to her for the entire evening, had he not been called back to his serving duties by his manager. She was grateful for his insights, but equally relieved to see the back of him. She pulled out her phone and punched in the numbers she'd been told would get her straight through to DCI Llewellyn's team.

A few minutes later – after a couple of 'Hold on, please' episodes – she heard a now-familiar voice on the line. 'Yes, Annie, what can I do for you?'

'Well, I think it's more what I can do for you, DCI Llewellyn, actually.' Annie tried to not sound too pleased with herself.

'And that is?'

'I've just been having a chat with a young bloke, named Aled, who works in the Seaview Hotel. He saw Jeanette Summers yesterday morning, and she told him she was going off to look after her father, at "home", where he'd been taken ill. Now I've got to say I don't think she's run off to look after a poorly parent…no, I don't believe for one minute that's the case. However, Aled did tell me something else that's interesting: he thinks Jeanette's accent places her as coming from the Valleys, and Jeanette herself mentioned to me that she had a friend in Pontardawe who lived with an elderly gentleman, who had died recently – an accident at a local gorge, which I have to say sounds a lot fishier now than when she told me about it. I haven't got an address, but she said his name was Finch. That could be a lead, right? Pontardawe? Finch? And he's dead…though I've got to be honest and say I don't *know* if there was any funny business in that case…but…oh…hang on a minute. Of course! Not Chandler, but Highsmith.'

DCI Llewellyn sounded puzzled when she replied, 'Pardon?'

Annie was almost vibrating as she waved to Christine, who had just arrived. 'The book by Patricia Highsmith – two blokes meet on a train, and one killer does the other one's dirty work, so they'll each have an alibi. Though, of course, the second bloke doesn't want to go through with it, just the first one. You know the story I mean.'

The deliberate reply on the phone was: 'I understand, yes. Thanks, Annie. Let us look into this. If you get any other…insights…let me know? Again, my brother was quite right – he told me you could get blood out of a stone when it came to gathering information with your great conversational skills. Talk soon.'

Christine Wilson-Smythe was scanning her surroundings with a polite smile on her face. 'You can't beat an out-of-season seaside hotel bar for its pervasive atmosphere of abandonment and gloominess, can you? Who knew that so many ships in bottles even existed?' She nodded at what Annie had thought of as an impressive display, even if it could do with a bit of a dusting.

'Right, I'll get this down me neck' – Annie picked up her glass – 'then we should both pop to the loo before we go, because I want to get back home as quick as we can, so no stopping on the way for us.'

Christine pulled her phone from her handbag. 'Okay. No arguments from me, on either score.'

Annie noticed her friend's brow crinkling, and couldn't resist asking, 'Expecting a text? Mr Bright, by any chance?' She winked.

A shadow of concern passed across Christine's face, then she smiled. 'He's got a few things he's a bit busy with at the moment. I'm sure he'll be in touch when he can be.'

The women both stood. 'I thought he was in Anwen, and up at Chellingworth Hall, with you. Carol said he was.'

'He was, but he had to go back to London, unexpectedly. I'm sure he'll be fine.'

Annie reckoned Christine's expression meant she was sure of no such thing, so she decided to be the best friend she could be by saying, 'The loos are over there. I'll just say bye-bye to Aled on our way out, then you can tell me all about what I've missed while I've been here, and I can fill you in on the sadly tragic Case of the Suspicious Sisters, too.'

Annie handed her empty glass to Aled. Christine still looked distracted as she said, 'Good, yes. We're all over The Case of the Disgraced Duke, so maybe you can lend a hand when we get back – it's taking a lot more reading and collating – and hunting about in dark, forgotten corners – than we'd thought.'

'Excellent – tit for tat it is then, all the way home,' said Annie, ignoring the fact that Christine was pulling a face at the phrase.

CHAPTER THIRTY-EIGHT

Albert Hill was sleeping like the baby he was, and Carol was snoring, open-mouthed in a chair beside his cot, with Bunty purring on her lap. She'd left her son alone several times earlier in the day, but, this time, she'd been too tired to even walk downstairs, so she'd settled into the nursing chair for five minutes…and woke with a start, confused to see her husband standing over her.

Carol shot to her feet – with Bunty making a safe landing, then hightailing it out of the nursery – and wrapped both arms around him. 'Oh, David, how wonderful to see you,' she whispered into his ear. 'You're home. At last. Safe. I missed you a lot. Come on, let's not disturb Albert…I'll make you a cup of tea downstairs.'

David nodded. 'Alright, I'll be down in a bit. I just want to look at him sleeping for a few minutes.'

Carol pottered about, clearing surfaces – quietly – and boiling the kettle. By the time David joined her at the kitchen table, there were mugs and a pot, all ready to go.

He popped the baby monitor between them and said, 'He looks alright. Did the doctor say anything else about what we could expect with the teething? You know, other than what you told me on the phone already.'

Carol shook her head. 'No. She directed me to some online sources she reckons are good, and, of course, I've done a bit of my own research; it seems it's different for every child, and that's about it. It's painful when teeth erupt, of course, but children react in different ways. Albert grizzles, then screams, and he can't be soothed, it seems. And now I understand why one of his cheeks has been a bit more pink than the other one. I was such an idiot to not spot the signs – but at least the slightly elevated temperature he's got is normal, so that's good. I picked up a watermelon in the supermarket in Builth when I was there, because the doctor mentioned that giving him that to suck and chew on might help, though I have to get all the seeds out, of course, and the woman who helped me in the chemist suggested a teething ring we can put in the fridge. I tried that in the car, coming home – without chilling it, of course – because Tom Jones wasn't working and the traffic was a nightmare…I'd forgotten it was half term for the local schools this week.'

'So, no gin, then? Rubbed on his gums.' David grinned, and Carol all but melted.

'Oh God, I love you David Hill,' she said, giggling, and grabbed his hand across the table. 'I've been a real mess without you…and that's not right.'

David poured his tea, then his wife's. 'I'm sorry, but you know I had to go; keeping the work flowing in as a freelancer means I have to make sure my name's firmly lodged in the minds of potential clients. And they liked it – it was good. Went down well. But I was a mess away from you, too. I kept wondering how you'd do the presentation; you were so good at them when you were my boss, back in the London days. In fact, you were good at everything you did.'

Carol saw tears drip onto her hand before she knew she was crying, then dissolved for a few moments, while David ran around finding paper tissues and shoving them under her nose, so she could blow. Carol was relieved he didn't ask what was wrong; instead he held her as she cried, which was such a good feeling that she pulled herself together more quickly than she'd thought she would, and was finally able to form a sentence.

'I don't recognize the person I've been since you left for Brighton,' she began. 'I've felt as though I have no control over anything at all. I mean, just look at the place – the whole house looks as though a bomb's gone off…there's washing in every room, dishes in the sink, the bathroom looks as though I've been housing a cantankerous octopus in there for days…and I…I…I think I've ruined the coat Mam and Dad gave me for Christmas.' Her tears returned, with force.

This time, David gently lifted her chin so she could see him as he smiled and said, 'None of that matters at all. You're safe. Albert's safe. We're all together. That's it – *that's* all that matters. All the rest is just stuff. And, by the way, if you mean that plum-colored coat they gave you a few years ago…well, maybe it's better ruined, because I never thought it flattered you as much as it could have done.'

Carol felt shocked. 'You said I looked lovely in it.' Carol could tell from her husband's expression that he realized he'd put his foot in it. She smiled. 'You're right – it's all just stuff, and not even the coat matters. Thanks for the reality check. I needed to hear it. I'm being pathetic.'

'Don't say that, love. You're not being pathetic – you've had a stressful few days, Albert's been worrying you, and you've had a ton of work to do. It's okay to feel as though things are getting away from you for a bit.'

Carol sipped her tea, hoping for comfort. 'I know. And I also know I'm capable of coping. Usually. And that's why the past few days have…well, unnerved me. Because I've really wondered if I'm trying to do too much, which means I'm not doing anything as well as I could. I phoned Mavis this morning and said I wouldn't be doing any work today, not even after the appointment with the doctor. She said she was fine with it, that I was entitled to a day off today because of everything I did through Friday night and on Saturday. But…I…I feel as though I've let Albert down – that's what's really got to me.'

David smiled sympathetically. 'He was acting up, you didn't know why, you got the doctor to check him over – and now we know he's in fine form, and just going though a natural, if painful, process. You've been the perfect mother. And, by the sounds of it, you've been a spectacularly productive member of your business team too. So I really don't think you've let yourself down on any front at all. Now, how about we take our tea into the sitting room and have a snuggle on the sofa? I'll find something on the telly that won't challenge more than three brain cells, and you…*we*…can get an early night. I'll take the first wake-up call from our son. And I promise I won't give him even the tiniest drop of gin. Alright?'

CHAPTER THIRTY-NINE

When she told Christine to drop her outside her thatched cottage overlooking the green in Anwen-by-Wye, Annie had done so knowing that – before she did anything else – she'd need the loo. Once she was ready, she headed to the Lamb and Flag, to collect Gertie. Yes, it was late, but she knew Tudor wouldn't mind her knocking at the back door that led up to his flat; besides, if he'd read her texts he'd know to expect her. Not that he'd replied...again. Annie tucked her annoyance at Tudor's lack of communicativeness away as she stood, waiting for him to open up.

When he did, the ancient door screeched open, as it usually did, and Gertie bounded out to greet her. Despite Annie and Tudor both telling her to 'get down', Gertie did all she could to get up close to Annie's face, which Annie eventually brought within her reach, to be able to be licked and snuggled.

'You'd think I'd been away for months, not days,' said Annie, finally standing up and petting Gertie's writhing back.

'A few days is a long time for a dog,' observed Tudor, 'and for me. How did it all go?'

Annie dared, 'I've told you in me texts. Thought you'd have replied to at least one of 'em.'

Tudor pulled his mobile phone out of his pocket; it was in a sorry state. 'Dropped it in the duck pond, and Rosie kindly retrieved it for me. No damage to Rosie, I'm pleased to say, but the phone's had it. I'm off to Brecon tomorrow to get a new one – haven't had time to do it before.'

Annie felt inexplicably relieved. 'Aww...sorry to hear it, Tude – I don't know how I'd survive without mine. Mind you, I do a lot of work stuff on it.'

'How do you think the delivery blokes keep in touch?' Tudor sighed. 'I've not known if I'm coming or going the past couple of days – nor if they've been coming, neither.'

They shared a chuckle. 'Fancy a cuppa? Or the bar could be open for a G & T if you fancy one.' Tudor winked. 'I won't tell anyone, if you don't.'

Annie gave the idea at least two milliseconds of thought. 'Go on then, but just one, mind you. I've got to be up at the Hall in the morning – it seems everyone with a title needs me to lend a hand with…something…up there.'

'Come on in then, and let me ply you with booze until you tell me more – because the way you hesitated just then makes me think something's afoot.'

Annie and Gertie followed Tudor inside, and Rosie joined them all. Tudor turned on a couple of lights, but left the pub largely in the dark, which lent a conspiratorial air to the proceedings as they sat at the bar – both on the customers' side – and settled with a drink each.

'So,' said Tudor, mugging an earnest expression, 'tell me all about it. You can start with the Swansea operation, if you like, then move on to what's going on that's got all the titled lot in a tizzy.'

Annie filled him in on all the facts pertaining to the case in Swansea, and he reacted exactly as she'd hoped he would; he was sympathetic, and impressed, at all the right points in her story. When she concluded, 'So I'm hoping to hear from DCI Llewellyn that they've nabbed Jeanette Summers soon,' he smiled.

'You're a strong woman, Annie,' said Tudor. 'I'm not sure I'd have been able to deal with what you did the way you have.' He grabbed Annie's hand and began to shake it vigorously. 'I'm proud to know you, Miss Holmes,' he said, then squeezed her hand, before letting it fall back into her lap.

'Thanks,' she said, feeling a bit odd. 'Thanks…' Annie could sense the feeling of guilt she was grappling with climb up her throat, as though it were a creature, desperate to emerge and be recognized. She forced it back to its hiding place, believing the sight of it would send Tudor running. Yes, she trusted him – but she needed to keep this terrible secret inside her, trapped, until she'd been able to properly examine it herself.

Tudor appeared to be oblivious to Annie's turmoil as he reached forward and hugged her. Annie remained on her stool, rigid, focused on her internal battles. Tudor pulled back, looking puzzled.

Annie was still grappling with allowing herself to seek solace in another human being, and felt she'd had just about enough of it for one night. Desperate to distract herself, and Tudor, from her emotional state, she said cavalierly, 'I'm still a bit puzzled about Turnbull, to be honest.'

'How so?'

Annie was grateful that Tudor mirrored her change of mood. She petted Gertie, maybe a little too vigorously. 'Well, for all that I reckon she and a mate worked it out between them to kill the poor bloke, I still don't know why Jeanette would have done it. I mean, she was onto a winner there. Trouble is, I had a bit of a look around, but I don't know much about how valuable stuff is. And this is me being honest here – despite the fact that me and Eustelle could give them experts on the *Antiques Roadshow* a run for their money…we've been watching it together, on the phone, forever, we have, and between us we always gets the valuations right.'

'I bet you do,' said Tudor, attending to Rosie, who seemed to think she was allowed to chew on Gertie's tail.

'Well, that aside, I would have thought the goose could have laid a few more golden eggs yet, if you know what I mean. She hadn't cleared out his house, not by a long chalk, and…well, there's always the house itself. I mean, maybe she's managed to get him to write a will leaving it all to her, instead of his kids – not that I mentioned that possibility to my client, of course – but, even so, I'm having a hard time working out why she'd have done it – or had it done – now.'

Tudor looked thoughtful; genuinely thoughtful, judged Annie, and she was grateful for it.

He said, 'There must be a time-sensitive element you're unaware of – that the police are unaware of. Maybe this Jeanette really did need to get away at a given time – or maybe she and her accomplice agreed a time for the deed to be done, and she hadn't managed to get everything out of the house she'd have liked to?'

'Maybe…but I'm not going to work that one out tonight, am I? Ta for the drink, Tude, but I think it's time for me and Gert to get back to my place so I can hit the sack.'

'Walk you home?'

'Nah, I'm good, thanks, Tude.'

'Fancy a spot of dinner tomorrow night? Upstairs, not down here. I could rustle up a shepherd's pie.' Tudor winked. 'I know it's your kryptonite.'

Annie chuckled. 'Go on then – I'll come here about six, then we'll see how we go, alright?'

'It's a date,' called Tudor as he waved Annie and Gertie off, struggling to hold Rosie back.

'It is that,' replied Annie, smiling. As she looked back, Tudor was still waving.

TUESDAY 25TH OCTOBER

CHAPTER FORTY

Carol had slept like a log. She didn't remember getting up at all during the night, so – when she did wake, and her bladder forced her to surrender the duvet – she checked on Albert, who was looking angelic in his cot; he was awake, and happily munching his fingers. She saw to her own needs, then his, then – telling David what she'd done, and that she'd be back in half an hour – she left her husband and son happily dozing on the big bed. In the kitchen, she petted Bunty, who was luxuriating on the kitchen floor in front of the Aga, pulled on her wellies and mac, and let herself out of the house.

It still wasn't quite light, though the clear sky suggested the day would be bright, if chilly. Carol loved seeing the village asleep – or, at least, just waking up. It had a rhythm to it that brought her comfort. Sharon would open up the shop in a few minutes, to be ready for all those who had their own morning rituals; cats – who, unlike Bunty, were allowed to roam – were making their way back to households where they knew they'd be fed, having got up to who could guess what through the night; neighbors were leaving for work in cars of all sorts, and a couple of young lads were pulling a cart on four fat little wheels around the green. As they passed, Carol could see that the cart was half-filled with stones.

Clothed in the rural child's autumnal uniform of wellies, jeans, and waterproof jackets, both boys were ruddy-faced, and quite wet and grubby.

'Did you take those from the wading area beside the duck pond?' Carol reckoned that must have been where such smooth stones had come from.

'No, we've been all round the village, picking them up from the side of the road,' said the taller of the boys, staring up at her, and speaking in Welsh.

'What's it got to do with you anyway?' The shorter boy also answered in Welsh, and defiantly stuck out his chin.

Carol didn't want a fight, she wanted a bit of peace and quiet, but she reckoned the boys had replied to her in Welsh rather than English because they were being cheeky, and thought she wouldn't understand them. She did, and continued her exchange with them in Welsh, just to show them they weren't going to be able to get one over on her.

'Are you the Hughes boys?' Your mum's Mrs Hughes who teaches at the infants' school, isn't she?' Carol was sure she was right – she'd seen the boys – albeit looking a good deal better turned out – at church with their parents.

'Might be,' replied the shorter of the two.

'Owain and Rhys,' said Carol firmly. 'Which of you is which?' She couldn't recall.

'I'm Owain,' said the taller of the two sullenly, then he rallied with a cocky, 'No one will miss the stones from the pond...the ducks certainly won't. They're ducks.'

'We used to have ducks. They're really stupid,' volunteered the shorter brother, who had to be Rhys.

'Why do you want stones at all?' Carol was puzzled.

'*Coelcerth,*' replied Owain, 'for *Nos Galan Gaeaf.*'

'Are you doing that at school?' Carol was even more puzzled; she'd grown up in Wales, born of Welsh parentage going back forever – indeed, she couldn't be more Welsh – but she'd never heard of people actually celebrating the ancient festival of *Nos Galan Gaeaf,* instead of Halloween. She imagined it must be part of some sort of school project.

'They're doing it up at the Hall this year,' exclaimed Rhys, as though Carol was the most stupid person on the face of the planet. 'Haven't you heard? The vicar's lost it, calling it heathen, but the old one who isn't a duchess any more is getting her way. As usual, says Dad.'

Carol knew that, in centuries past, people would write their names on stones and place them into a bonfire on the night of October thirty-first; indeed, she'd taken an entire course on Welsh history, which included traditions dating back thousands of years, when she'd studied at university. She'd have to talk to Althea about her plans, and wondered why she hadn't heard about them until now.

'So, if you need those stones for *Coelcerth*, where are you taking them now? Are they for the whole village to use, on the night?' Carol was trying to work out why two boys would be pinching stones from the duck pond before most people were up and about.

'We'll make them available to people, at a fair price,' said Rhys proudly. 'Want one? Nice and flat, and they're clean. Just let it dry out properly before you go trying to write on it. Since you're our first customer, how about two for five quid?'

Carol laughed. 'Highly enterprising, boys, but no thanks. I think we've got a few we can find in our back garden, thanks. So go on, get yourselves home, you'll be late for school.'

'Half term,' replied Owain, who was struggling to get the cart moving on his own.

'Off all week,' added Rhys, who sounded as though he couldn't be happier about it.

'I'll look out for you when it's time for penny for the guy, then, before Guy Fawkes' night, shall I?' Carol suspected they'd make the most of any money-making opportunities available to them.

'Yeah, once *Nos Galan Gaeaf*'s out of the way, we'll be on the green with our guy.'

'And your cart?' Carol laughed.

'Always our cart,' called Rhys, as the boys pulled together. They disappeared around the corner that led to the close at the side of the church.

Carol ambled along in the same general direction, and saw the boys unload their prized cargo, forming a pile beneath a tree in the lovely garden that surrounded their large home. As she looked up she was inspired; Albert would love a treehouse! The one the Hughes boys had was incredible – it was large, sturdy, had a proper roof, a good, stout ladder, and there was a large bucket on a rope hanging over a balustraded balcony on one side of it. The flag on top sported a dragon with an eye patch – which gave her a piratical air; Carol had always thought of the dragon on the Welsh flag as being female, with one paw raised in defence of her family.

As she made her way around the green, she waved to Sharon – who was pulling the awning out to protect the vegetable display, and to Tudor – who was being dragged around the green for a walk by Rosie. Carol wondered where Gertie was, then wondered if Annie was back from the coast already. Being out of touch with everyone for just one day apparently meant Carol had no idea what was going on with her friends, or the entire village, and she couldn't have that. With a spring in her step, and a determination borne of a many hours of restorative sleep, she headed for her home, and her family; she'd talk to David about a tree house over breakfast.

CHAPTER FORTY-ONE

It didn't escape Mavis's notice that Althea was late for breakfast; she believed the dowager had avoided her the previous evening, and hoped she wasn't going to try to do the same again. In fact, she'd already formulated a strategy to make sure she had enough private time with Althea to broach the subject of her mobility; she'd suggest the pair walked over to the Hall for the planned gathering there by ten – the sun was out, and, although it wasn't exactly warm, it certainly promised to be a dry day.

Let her get out of that one without the subject having to be tackled, Mavis thought to herself as she poured a second cup of tea.

'Good morning, dear, I hope you slept well,' said Althea as she joined her companion at the breakfast table.

'Good heavens, what are you wearing?' Mavis was annoyed with herself that she'd sounded so alarmed; she'd trained herself to not react overtly to the dowager's bizarre wardrobe choices, believing it only made the woman select even more peculiar get-ups.

'They're jodhpurs, dear.'

'I can see that. Though I've never seen such vividly mustard-colored ones before. I mean what are you wearing them with?'

'A perfectly serviceable sweater.'

Mavis stared at Althea. 'Serviceable, maybe, but it's…it's hideous, and huge. Are those supposed to be chrysanthemums? Purple ones? And why on earth did you buy one that was so…well, it's quite large. You look as though you're being eaten by some sort of ravenous plant.'

'I thought we might walk to the Hall this morning; it's a lovely day. The jodhpurs will keep my legs warmer than a skirt or slacks would, and the sweater will be cozy under my winter coat.' The dowager smiled sweetly and poured herself a cup of tea.

Althea had pre-empted Mavis's plan, and Mavis wasn't having any of it. 'So you'll be up to it then? The walk.' Mavis was determined she'd get the woman to talk about her mobility.

'Indeed. It'll make a pleasant change – the weather's been so dreadful…we really should take the chance to have a good walk while we can, before the rain comes back.' Althea crunched into a piece of toast with what Mavis judged to be a sense of triumph.

'There's nothing for it but for me to ask you outright then. You couldn't get into the Land Rover yesterday…why is that?'

'Oh, just a passing thing, nothing to worry about, dear.' Althea buried her face in her teacup and started to hum, which annoyed Mavis intensely.

Placing her cup in the exact centre of the indentation in her saucer, Mavis said, 'I've been a nurse for too long for that to wash, Althea Twyst. I'm well aware you've used a walking stick for some time to address a slight weakness in your knee. I also know you've sustained injuries over the years that have healed, and that you have a touch of arthritis in several joints. But seeing you unable to get into that vehicle – something you've been able to do with no trouble at all until just over a week ago – is something we need to talk about. What is it? Your hip? Painful when you try to raise your knee above a certain level? Giving you a sense of it cracking, or jamming, when you walk, maybe?'

Mavis noticed the cup shake a little in Althea's small hand, then watched as her friend put it down.

'You're very perceptive, and you're right,' said the dowager quietly. 'I had some X-rays taken a few months back, and was told to expect the symptoms you've just described as part of the general degeneration of my right hip. They've arrived more rapidly than I'd expected or hoped.' She looked at Mavis, who spotted the defiance in her friend's expression. 'But it's nothing I can't push through. A brisk walk will sort it out. I've been ferried about in cars for too long; the rain has made it unpleasant to be out and about, but I believe that today I'll be able to get the exercise I so badly need.'

Mavis considered her response, then replied, 'I'm not your nurse, I'm your friend, and I – mebbe more than most – know that many people choose to keep the details of their physical condition from their friends and loved ones. You have every right to do so; the confidentiality that exists between doctors and their patients is critical. But, as a friend, *and* as a medical professional, I have to tell you that a hip that is wearing out will not be made any better by you trying to exercise more than is comfortable for you. Yes, you need to keep mobile, and yes, walking a short distance, gradually building it up, can be good for your hip pain. But maybe walking from here to the Hall might be a bit much, straight off the bat.'

Althea pouted. 'I could try to make it. It's not that far.'

'It's the better part of a mile, up hill and down dale,' replied Mavis, more snappishly than she'd meant. 'Let's work up to it, by taking gentle strolls about the place, when the weather allows.'

Silence followed, into which Althea eventually threw: 'The doctor said cycling would be good, but I honestly don't think I'm up to that, all round. She also mentioned swimming…but where would I swim?'

Mavis smiled. 'There are leisure centers in Builth Wells and Brecon…but maybe not?'

'Not,' replied Althea. 'I can't be seen to be…I don't want people to see me…in a swimming costume. I couldn't do it, Mavis. I'm old. Wrinkled. A terrible sight. Besides, I'm me – Althea Twyst, once the duchess of Chellingworth, now its dowager. I do prize givings, attend ceremonies of all sorts – I don't splash about in public swimming pools. It's not that I'm being a snob about it – it's just that…well, who wants to be handed a prize for the best apple crumble in the area by a woman they know to be a haggard, desiccated old thing who can barely stay afloat? The only reason I mean anything in this community is because of my title, and the way I represent it. And that means being different. I have to be different, because if I'm not, then why does my presence mean anything?'

Mavis sighed. 'Ach, my dear, sweet woman. Can you no' see that folks would be pleased to receive a prize from you just because you're a woman they know for her good works?'

Althea stood, and grasped the tabletop with both hands. Mavis was a little taken aback to see that her friend was shaking, and – for once – deadly serious.

'Mavis, this is all new to you, I understand that. But when I talk to Henry about duty, and when I talk to the Reverend Roberts about tradition, and when I mention to Stephanie that there are paths we have followed within this family for generations, I am not doing so because of snobbery, or out of hubris. Yes, I gave up the life I'd expected to live to become Chelly's duchess, and I was being truthful when I said I loved him so much I'd have given up anything to be with him. But the only way I was ever able to accept leaving what I did, was to fully embrace what I took on. Henry blathers on about the burden of the title – but he's had a much easier time of it than his father ever did. The estate and the Hall are on much firmer ground financially now than they ever were before, thanks to a blossoming of interest in the public of seeing how the one percent lives…of witnessing how we've been stewards of the land, and – in our case – particularly of this area of Wales. It's no small feat, Mavis, and I – and Henry, and Stephanie, and the children they will have – we're all part of a construct that holds itself up for ridicule while it also plays an important role. Those responsibilities, those duties are things upon which I shall not turn my back. I need to function properly to be able to do my duty, and my duty is to push into the future that which has meaning from the past. I shall persevere.'

Mavis allowed what her friend had said to sink in, then waited while Althea calmed down a little. Eventually the dowager retook her seat, with a noticeable wince.

'This is no' just about a public swimming pool, then.' Mavis knew it wasn't.

Althea put her head in her hands. 'I'm old, Mavis. I'm worried I haven't prepared my children well enough for what's ahead of them. You've seen them – they're like infants when they're together…I feel I should have done more. And, with the little time that's left to me, I shall do all I can. Which means I shall make my own decision about when I have my hip replacement surgery. Just because she's got a stethoscope, it doesn't mean that specialist knows everything, nor controls everything. I won't be going into hospital until I'm good and ready.'

'No matter how painful that hip becomes?'

'I can take it. I'm a strong woman. Always have been. Like this little chap – getting on a bit, but determined to keep going.' Althea petted McFli, who seemed to think she required some ankle licks.

'Strength comes in different forms,' said Mavis, pouring more tea. 'And one type of strength is accepting what's best for you, even when you're a wee bit afraid. I know you don't care for hospitals – who does? Not even I relish the idea of being in them, unless I have to be. But I wonder if that feeling is impacting your thinking. It's no' unusual for older patients to worry they'll go into a hospital and no' come out again. Is that on your mind, dear?'

Althea sat very upright. 'Nonsense.'

'Ah,' replied Mavis. 'I see.'

Althea shrank into her massive sweater. 'Don't you think we could at least try to walk to the Hall? I'll let Henry know we'll be delayed. We could take it slowly, and there are lots of benches dotted about the place for me to take breaks.'

Mavis chuckled. 'Like a bairn negotiating for a later bedtime, you are. Very well then.'

'Thank you.' Althea smiled sweetly.

CHAPTER FORTY-TWO

Christine had set up everything she might need at her desk in the office, and steeled herself for her phone conversation with Sheila Timbers, Stephanie's mother. They'd already exchanged several texts while Sheila had been indulging at the local spa the previous day, and had agreed to finally speak at ten. She dialled the number and waited. Christine hoped the woman was a little less scattered than her texts suggested.

'Sheila Timbers, at your service. I have to say, it's very exciting to think I'll be contributing to one of your "enquiries". So pleased my baby's alright after her tumble. How is everyone? That lovely man of yours, for example? And Carol's Albert – we're planning on coming over when the baby is born, so we'll get to meet him then, I suppose. Two babies to meet at once – though one of them will be our first grandchild, which is wonderful.'

Christine wasn't sure how to untangle the jumble of comments that had been hurled at her, so decided for a businesslike reply. 'Yes, Stephanie seems fine, which is good. Everyone else is fine too. And thanks for agreeing to help me out. I'm sure I can count on your discretion.'

She hoped she could, but somehow doubted it. When she'd met Sheila, in the chaotic run-up to Stephanie and Henry's wedding, she'd thought of her as a somewhat timid woman, but had discovered – through various conversations about her with Stephanie through the intervening months – that Sheila was much more chatty than she'd imagined, if only she was in her own comfort zone.

Christine looked out of the office at the pale blue sky and weak sunlight, and pictured Sheila in the much better weather on the Spanish coast. She sighed inwardly – she wouldn't mind a bit of proper sun herself.

'I know how to keep mum when needed,' replied Sheila, sounding confident. 'So, how can I help the women of the WISE Enquiries Agency? Oh – it's just like a film.'

Christine dragged her thoughts away from iced drinks with little umbrellas in them and replied, 'It's a simple background investigation, nothing to be alarmed about. I'm trying to find out all I can about a man by the name of Ronald, or Ronnie, Right. I believe he has links with Marbella, and I know that's where you and John live. I also know it's not a tiny place, but wondered if you'd ever heard of him. So, does the name ring a bell?'

Peals of laughter rang out across the miles between them. 'Well, if being at a party with him and his lovely wife last night counts as "hearing of him", then, yes, we have. Him and John go way back; he was one of John's customers, when John still had the lumber businesses, you know?'

Christine wondered if Sheila had the right man in mind. How could she? Alexander had been more than clear about Ronnie Right having left his wife and children in London. 'The Ronnie Right I'm interested in runs a roofing business in London. He left his…I wasn't aware he had a wife in Spain. Maybe you're talking about a different Ronnie Right.'

Silence. 'I'm sure he was a roofer – but hang on a minute.'

Christine hung on, and could hear Sheila Timbers calling to her husband. 'John…Ronnie Right was a roofer, wasn't he?'

John's echoing reply was: 'Just sold up. Always was, yeah. Why?'

'Nothing.' Sheila returned her attention to Christine. 'Yes, our Ronnie was a roofer, John says he's just sold up, but I knew that because that's what the party was for. Big celebration. Finally able to retire. His wife's been here for a couple of years, but he hasn't had much of a chance to enjoy the place. Like I said, she's been here all the time, seeing to everything while they've been having it done up, and now they can enjoy their golden years in it together. It's just above us, up the hill a bit. Better view than we've got. Nice place, I suppose, but very modern-looking. Like white boxes, all joined together. Not my cup of tea, but each to their own, I suppose.'

'And you know his wife?'

More laughter. 'Well, truth be told they aren't married, though she goes by Right. Danielle. Nice girl. I say girl – she's a bit older than

Stephanie, maybe even early forties, but there's a few years between her and Ronnie. I helped her choose some of the furniture for the place. She's put up with all the building work without a word of complaint, and now it's all over – and just in time, like I said. The last contractors finished about a fortnight ago, and there's Ronnie all retired this week. Perfect, for them both.'

Christine was making notes as she worked out how best to take things forward. 'And you've met Ronnie before last night?' She needed to be sure.

'Oh good grief, yes. Loads of times. I know he hasn't been here much, but he's been here often, if you see what I mean. Flying visits. That's what it's like in the construction business – there's always someone who needs something doing urgently. John knew that, and it was why he was one of the first lumber places to be open seven days a week. And that paid off nicely. Ronnie's been coming and going since they bought the place.'

Christine tried for more information. 'I wonder, could you describe him, please?'

Sheila's reply was curious. 'Too funny – we were talking about that last night. He's changed a lot since I first met him, see? Then? Well, he was a bit of a little barrel, to be honest. But he's dropped such a lot of weight, and he's been going to the gym. Had those veneers done on his teeth, too – though I think they're a bit too white to be, well, you know…they don't appear natural. Looks quite different overall now, he does. Puts John to shame.'

'And I love you too.' John Timbers had obviously come close enough to his wife for Christine to hear him clearly.

'Hello to John,' she said.

'Christine says hello…and John says hello back.'

'No children?' Christine was digging as deep as she dared.

'Aww, no. Such a shame. I think they'd make great parents. I know they're a bit lovey-dovey, but that's not a bad thing. They didn't meet until…well, until she was a bit old to start a family. He'd been too busy, I suppose. Him and John didn't really mix on the social side of things back in London, but I dare say Ronnie was up to his neck in it.

John tells me roofing's a very competitive part of the industry.' She giggled. 'He also tells me most of the blokes who work on roofs are bonkers, but that's John for you. So – is this helping? What a turn up for the books that we actually know him, eh?'

'It is,' said Christine, while thinking, *I've got to make the most of this opportunity.*

Sheila added, 'I could give you his mobile number, if you like – or Danielle's. I don't think they've got a phone at the house – a lot of us don't. I mean, we're out by the pool now – much easier to just have my mobile by my side than have to worry if someone's phoning the house, isn't it?'

'Of course. And, yes, both numbers would be useful. And – I don't suppose you know their address, do you?'

Sheila reeled off two long phone numbers, then said, 'I haven't got their address here in my phone.' She laughed, 'I could take you there, but no. Hang on. John – do you know Ronnie and Danielle's address? Thanks, love. And will you bring me my white cardi, please? Yes, the thin one, thanks. Aww, I'm so lucky, Christine – that husband of mine treats me like a princess.'

Christine noted the address John Timbers called out to his wife, and thought about how lovely it would be to be able to sit beside a pool, even with a thin cardigan being necessary.

'Anything else?' Sheila sounded a little too enthusiastic for Christine's liking. 'Why do you want to know about Ronnie anyway?'

'He's been mentioned as a reference for someone we're doing a background search on,' lied Christine. 'We just wanted to be sure he was...you know, a reliable referee.'

'Salt of the earth, says John, so I think you can take it that anyone he's supporting will be up to – whatever it is he says they can do. Sort of person to never let you down, is Ronnie, I'd say. Not if what Danielle says about him is anything to go by.'

Christine dared to ask her next question. 'Not that it's part of anything I'm investigating, but do you know why they aren't married?'

Sheila sighed. 'Well, I do know that, actually, though it's not common knowledge: Ronnie was married once, when he was very young...too young, he reckons. Catholic girl, from your neck of the woods...Ireland. Won't hear of a divorce. They weren't together long, two minutes in the whole scheme of things, but he's kept her in a nice place all these years, and Danielle says she doesn't begrudge her too much – there's enough money to go around. Mind you, she's been making noises recently about just how much he's paying this woman that Danielle thinks should be theirs, by rights...especially now he's sold the business.'

'I don't suppose you know who he's sold it to, do you?'

Sheila didn't hesitate. 'Well no, that hasn't come up. But then it wouldn't. Just glad to be shot of it all, he said. Best to be here with no responsibilities; he can relax and enjoy life, now.'

'Thanks, Sheila. Enjoy it all yourself.' Christine gave in. 'It's a nice day there, by the sound of it. Outside, in the sun, are you?'

'Well, it's not as warm as I'd like, but, there, the summer's gone now. Not that it's cold and wet like it has been for you – Stephanie was telling me about the weather you've been having. We're off to Barbados next month. We don't usually go until Christmas, but that's around when Steph's expecting the baby to be born, so we'll have our time in the sun, then come to stay at Chellingworth Hall through Christmas and into the New Year. She's said she'll be glad to have me around for a bit when she's a new mum – and I'm going to enjoy being a grandma...though I'm not too sure how it'll feel to be called one. Ha! But, there – I'll let you get on now. Hope I've helped. Give my lovely girl a hug from her mum and dad when you see her? Bye.'

'Bye, Sheila, and thanks. Regards to John.'

Christine sat in the silence of the office and gave what she'd just learned some thought. Ronnie Right had a secret life – in Spain – that didn't involve his wife and five children at all. And he'd been living it for at least a couple of years. She now had the man's address, and knew Alexander had dispatched someone to Spain to find him and harm him. But, if she shared her knowledge with Alexander, she'd be supporting his planned punishment of the man who'd let him down.

She didn't know what to do for the best – or even what 'the best' meant.

While she was sitting there having an internal debate, her mobile phone rang. It was Stephanie.

'Hello, Christine. Did you mange to get hold of my mum?'

'Thanks, I did. She sends her love. Sounds excited about the baby – and she and your dad are pleased you're okay after your fall.'

Stephanie laughed. 'Oh yes, Mum's excited alright. I don't think she'll be knitting any baby bootees any time soon, but I dare say she'll pick up something with a designer label on it while she and Dad are in Barbados. Which I'll have to hide when they're not here, because Henry's not into that sort of thing. Was she able to help?'

Christine decided to dive in, taking Stephanie into her confidence; she explained the entire situation.

'Oh gracious, that sounds…complicated. And I think it's just as well you didn't tell Mum – she means well, but she's not the best at keeping quiet about things. So, tell me…what on earth makes you think Alexander has sent someone off to kneecap this Ronnie Right? I can't see Alexander either asking for that sort of thing to be done, or even condoning it.'

Christine explained what she'd overheard Alexander saying.

Stephanie didn't respond immediately, then said, 'Hmm…well, I can't say that sounds to me as though he's telling someone to cripple a man – which is how you've interpreted it. What if he just meant that someone should try to talk some sense into this Ronnie person – to stop him from walking away from his family. I mean…I don't know exactly what you heard, and I didn't hear the tone in his voice at the time, but, to be honest, Christine, the Alexander Bright I've met isn't going to go around ordering people to inflict wounding and maiming. But there, what do I know? I can't even predict how my own husband is going to react to anything I say or do, let alone imply I understand another woman's partner. But…maybe have a think about how much you trust Alexander. Ask yourself what sort of a person he really is.'

Christine thanked Stephanie.

Stephanie added, 'I understand from Edward that Annie's just arrived here at the Hall. I'm running late – again. Are you going to join us today to help with The Case of the Disgraced Duke?'

'Yes, but not right now. This has to come first – I hope you understand.'

'I do. I'll get word to Annie, and we'll see you later. Maybe for lunch?'

'I'll try. I'll text you.'

'Bye, Christine – and good luck. Trust your heart and your head – they're both worth listening to.'

'Thanks, Stephanie. And let's keep this between ourselves, alright?'

'Mum's the word…oh, sometimes I make myself laugh.'

CHAPTER FORTY-THREE

'What's that clattering? Are you alright? What on earth is going on?' David Hill walked into the dining room to find his wife with her bottom in the air, and her head under the table.

Carol emerged with a thump and a bump. 'Albert threw his stuffed tortoise under here – somehow. He's got a surprising amount of strength in those little arms.'

'Future rugby player, you reckon?' David smiled.

'Albert Hill playing for Wales? Now that would be something, wouldn't it?' She paused, her hands on her hips. 'Gosh, how proud the parents of those players must be. I've only just now really got that.'

'There are other sports,' said David impishly. 'Cricket – he might be a brilliant bowler.'

'For Glamorgan? He might.' She winked. 'Right, I've got it – now I need to get myself settled. I'm due to talk to Annie, Mavis, and Christine when they all meet up at the Hall to work on this duke thing – and they're going to allocate me some jobs I can do here for the day. Look, it's five to ten now…come on, help me clear a spot, will you? Or else maybe you can hold Albert while I get my laptop set up, and the camera aligned.' She lifted her son from his playpen, and David wrapped him in his arms.

'What was that? Did I hear screaming outside?' Carol stopped fiddling with her laptop.

David peered through the curtains, bouncing Albert. 'There's definitely something going on over there.'

'Where?' Carol joined him, yanked open the net curtains, and took in the scene outside.

Across the green, on the corner where she now knew the Hughes family lived, a woman was screaming her head off, and another woman was running across the green toward her; Sharon was racing from the vegetable racks outside her shop, abandoning a pile of oranges on the ground; Tudor and Rosie were rushing to the screaming figure, with Rosie taking the lead.

David asked his infant son, 'What do you think's going on out there, then, eh, Albert, my boy?'

Carol was heading for the kitchen. 'I'm going to find out – and to see if I can help. You stay here with him. I've got my phone if I need to make any calls. I'll keep you in the loop.'

Carol grabbed a lumpen old cardigan she'd thrown onto the back of a kitchen chair, stubbed her feet into her boots, and was off, her phone in her pocket. She raced across the green, glad she'd worn her wellies, and realized that Tudor Evans had already phoned 999. The two wailing women had disappeared toward the Hughes's house, with Sharon in tow, and she could see Marjorie Pritchard stomping in her general direction.

She listened as Tudor barked into his phone, 'Ambulance. Number One, St. David's Close, Anwen-by-Wye. Three boys, all vomiting blood. I'm not sure…about ten or eleven years old? Within the past five minutes. I'll take this phone to one of the mothers, you can speak to her yourself, please hold on.' He ran off, pink in the face, Rosie yapping at his heels as though this was all a great game.

Carol followed, hoping Marjorie wouldn't catch up with her.

The scene in the Hughes's garden was chaotic. Mrs Hughes – whose first name Carol suddenly recalled was Sarah – was holding the head of her son Rhys, who was retching onto the grass beneath his tree house. His brother, Owain, was on his back on the grass, holding his stomach, and rolling about, groaning. Another boy was being rocked in her arms by a woman Carol assumed was his mother. She approached, and could see the evidence of what Tudor had told the emergency services operator – the boys had been vomiting blood.

Anxious that Owain didn't remain without comfort, she went to his side, his mother nodding her thanks as she continued to focus her attention on Rhys, and the phone Tudor had handed her.

Carol spoke sympathetically to the writhing Owain. 'Where does it hurt? Do you need to throw up some more?' She felt her own gag reflex start to kick in; she'd never been good in situations where vomit was involved. Her heart sank when she saw blood smeared across Owain's face, and on his arm. Had the boys consumed some sort of caustic substance? The prospect was horrifying. What on earth had they done?

Carol reached out to Owain, who groaned, rolled onto his side, and threw up some more. Carol's immediate reaction was to recoil in disgust, which she knew didn't bode well for her future as Albert's mother. She forced herself to get within inches of the poor boy, to comfort him, saw what was in the grass, and gagged…then forced herself to look again.

Of course. The wagon, the gap in the hedge behind Sharon's shop, the enterprising nature of the Hughes boys, the bucket on the rope to the tree house; it all made sense!

She turned and shouted, 'Have you three boys been stuffing yourselves with pickled beetroot? Come on – own up to it. I know you pinched all those jars from the shed behind Sharon's shop. They're all hidden up there in your tree house, aren't they? Have you been helping yourself to them?'

Sarah Hughes looked shocked, then stared at her son in her arms. 'Is she right? Have you all been guzzling jars of pickled beetroot? Making yourselves sick. Is that what this is?'

Rhys pushed his face into his mother's chest, and Owain groaned louder beside Carol.

The third boy looked up at his mother and croaked, 'Sorry, Mam…I didn't mean to. We had a dare about who could eat the most beetroot, see…' He began to cry, and Carol saw his mother's expression change from anguish, to shock, to relief, to anger – all within about four seconds.

Sarah Hughes stared angrily from one of her sons to the other. 'You stupid boys – look what you've done to yourselves. I was worried sick – I thought you were both dying. Well, you can explain yourselves when the ambulance arrives. And what exactly were you doing going around stealing stuff? Stealing? That's a terrible thing to do.' She was on her feet, her son Rhys now left to sit on the grass holding his tummy, looking guilty.

'Come on then,' shouted Sarah Hughes, her hands on her hips. 'Why on earth would you do something so wicked? I've a good mind to phone the police about this. You cannot, and will not, be allowed to go around stealing things. Sharon's been worried sick about it, haven't you, Sharon?' Sarah nodded toward Sharon, who looked non-plussed. 'We all have been – thinking someone's been sneaking around the village stealing things. And it was you two, all along. You wicked boys. Well, that's it! No video games at all for about a year, I should think. And if you reckon for one minute that you'll be allowed to go on the trip to Tenby that those pickles were going to raise the money for, well, you've got another think coming.'

'Good,' shouted Rhys, using all his strength. 'We hate Tenby. Tenby's stupid. Boring. That's why we took the stuff – because we don't want to go to blinkin' Tenby.'

'Yeah, Tenby's stupid,' called Owain, then rolled over and threw up some more.

Sharon made her way over to Carol, who now felt more comfortable standing back from Owain and letting him take care of himself – as his mother was doing with his brother.

'What a to-do, eh?' Sharon wasn't smiling, but looking resigned. 'I'm glad they're alright really, though I can't imagine it's very pleasant for them at the moment – nor will it be even when they've recovered. Sarah won't let them get away with this, I shouldn't have thought. Look at her, she's tamping mad. Anyway – thanks for putting two and two together. With any luck, there's still a lot of what they stole up there, in their tree house. I dare say their mother will start by having them bring it all down again, which won't be a bad thing, 'cos I can't see myself getting up there to fetch it. Good for you for solving it all, Carol,'

Carol smiled. 'You're welcome…and there ends The Case of the Purloined Preserves. Thank goodness.'

'Yeah, thank goodness indeed – though I'm not sure goodness had much to do with it – so, thank *you*, Carol.'

Carol suggested, 'Maybe you should give Llinos Trevelyan a call later on – let her know what's happened? Though – you know –

maybe talk to Sarah before you do. I dare say you could keep the boys' names out of it, if you wanted.'

'That's the mother's decision, I should say,' replied Sharon.

Carol sighed as she realized that maybe teething problems were the least of her worries in terms of the responsibilities of motherhood that lay ahead of her in years to come.

CHAPTER FORTY-FOUR

Alexander Bright was sitting in a dingy pub in a part of south London where gentrification was something that happened to other areas. To make matters worse, he was waiting to meet someone he really didn't want to see at all. The person in question was a roofing contractor who'd gone out of business a couple of years earlier; like so many others who played the system, this particular character had taken on a huge contract for a developer, had accepted payment for the work, then had delayed and delayed, finally finishing late, with a shoddy end product. Of course, the company this particular cowboy had owned at the time had 'gone into liquidation', so there was no way for the developer to recoup his losses. That had led to the entire development project going bankrupt, which was when Alexander had stepped in. Yes, the people who lived in the flats Alexander had invested in to allow them to be completed had benefitted in the long run – because the original developer had planned to sell at exorbitant prices – but, still…this chap? He was the sort of unreliable scum Alexander usually avoided like the plague, but he was a good mate of Ronnie Right's, and Alexander was hoping he might be able to help him find Ronnie – who'd gone to ground somewhere in Spain, probably near Marbella, according to industry whispers.

Alexander wasn't surprised that the man was late; when his phone rang, he checked to see who was phoning, in case it was his contact, with some lame excuse for not showing. It was Christine. He hesitated. He couldn't bear the idea of them arguing on the phone, let alone with him sitting where he was while they did it. He almost let the call go to voicemail, but answered at the last moment.

'Christine,' he said, and left it at that.

'Alexander.'

He waited. 'You rang me,' he prompted.

'I've found Ronnie Right.'

Alexander was gobsmacked. 'How did you…I mean, good. Great. And…are you going to tell me where he is? Or do you still think I'm going to have the man crippled?'

He heard a sigh. 'I've been thinking about what I overheard. And I've been thinking about what I know, and feel, about you, as a person. And I've concluded that – despite what I heard – you aren't the sort of man who would seek to hurt another person. Unless you were flying across a room to knock him down and take away his gun – which you did when you saved my life. Which is quite acceptable, by the way. But, no, other than that, I don't believe you'd initiate violence. So, yes, I'll tell you.'

Alexander left his mineral water on the table, got up, and headed to his car. With no need to see the creep he'd planned to meet, he slid into his beloved Aston Martin as he listened to Christine tell him about Ronnie Right's life in Marbella. He noted all the relevant details.

'Thanks. Thanks for this. Not just getting the information, but for what giving it to me represents…for both of us. It hurt me that you thought I'd be capable of…you know. Look, Christine…we've both unintentionally wounded the trust we had in each other. I'm prepared to put whatever it takes into rebuilding that trust. Are you?' He didn't see any point beating about the bush; Christine meant the world to him, and he felt she deserved the truth.

'I am.'

Alexander thumped the steering wheel triumphantly. 'Good. I look forward to it. And, in other news…I'll share some information with you that you might find useful. Natalie Smith is about five foot six tall, brunette – though I'd say dyed, not natural – she's got brown eyes, originally comes from Newcastle, and is a designer and printer of bespoke wallpapers, hence her being an habitual visitor to the V & A. Her company is called "Walls by Smith". And, by the way, she's quite delightful. I ran into the happy couple – yes, they're getting married next month, and, yes, we're invited – last evening. And, no, I don't think she's on the make – she's as nutty about him as he is about her…though, please, feel free to dig away.'

Alexander couldn't decide if Christine's answer of: 'we will' meant she'd do some digging herself, of if she'd discuss the matter with her colleagues.

'I'd better use the information you've given me about Ronnie, before his wife endures much more, don't you think?'

Christine replied, 'It's all about his family, for you, isn't it?'

Alexander smiled, and wondered if she knew that was what he was doing. 'It always is, for me, Christine. And I did tell you that. But, look, let me get on now? We can talk about this when I come back to Wales. You'll be there for the rest of the week, right?'

'Probably; I'm not planning on coming back to London at least until we've sorted out all this business about the thirteenth duke. Speaking of which, I was supposed to be up at the Hall by ten – I'm late. I'd better go. I…I do love you, Alexander. And I do trust you.'

'I know, and I love and trust you too. So let's start living what that means. I'll see you soon.'

He ended the call, and dialled again. 'Hi, Jerry, it's me. Yes, I've got an address in Marbella for Right. Grab a pen – I'm not texting it to you. And when you get there, you leave him in absolutely no doubt about the fact his wife and kids come first. He's shacked up with someone named Danielle – no idea if she knows about his real life back here, so tread carefully there…she might be as much in the dark as his missus is. I want him talking to his wife and kids, on a video call, while you're there. No lies allowed. Full disclosure. Those kids need to know they aren't the reason he walked out. If we can't stop him walking – and the way he's been planning this escape for years means that's not likely – then the least we can do is set up his family here for the best possible future, with the least possible trauma. I'll get over to his wife's place now, so I'm there to help pick up the pieces at this end. Go!'

CHAPTER FORTY-FIVE

Annie always thought it quite amazing that she was able to just knock at the door of Chellingworth Hall, knowing she'd get a warm welcome.

'Good morning, Edward, am I the first to arrive? I hope it's alright that I brought Gertie – I expect Althea will bring McFli, so they can play together while we all get on with whatever it is we're supposed to be doing.'

Edward stood back to allow Annie and Gertie to enter and said, 'His Grace is with Mr Fernley, in the estate office. Her Grace will be down from her rooms presently, and I believe the library is the "headquarters" for the group's meetings. Her Grace the Dowager has sent word that she and Mrs MacDonald will be delayed. As will Miss Wilson-Smythe, I'm afraid. Would you like to wait in the library?'

Annie was torn; she didn't fancy having to entertain Gertie until who knew when, on her own, in a library full of priceless books. 'Me and Gert will take a turn around the gardens. I'll keep an eye out for Mavis and Althea, and I'll come in when they do, okay?'

'As you please,' replied Edward, and he opened the door again for Annie to leave.

With Gertie leading the way, Annie headed off toward the walled garden, which she knew Mavis and Althea would have to walk past if they were coming up from the Dower House. She was pleased to have the sun on her face; even if it wasn't really warm, it was a lovely feeling. The air was fresh, the light mellow, and she could smell woodsmoke in the air. It was a perfect late-autumn day, and she knew how lucky she was to be able to enjoy it.

As she approached the beautiful Victorian red-brick walls, she spotted Ivor, tending a small bonfire. She waved, and he waved back, smiling. Annie wandered over for a chat – she liked Ivor, though his accent was sometimes a bit of a challenge for her; his first language was Welsh, and he'd told her he'd learned to speak English in his teens because it had been made clear to him, in no uncertain terms, that he'd not do as well in the world beyond the small village where he'd been raised if he didn't. He'd been at Chellingworth for decades, and still communicated with several members of his gardening staff in Welsh, because they, too, preferred their mother tongue. All of which meant his accent hadn't softened as much as some – Carol's for example, who'd knocked the edges off hers when she'd lived and worked in London.

'Lovely day for it,' quipped Annie as Ivor bent down to play about with Gertie.

'Gorgeous, isn't she,' he observed.

'She is – though she can be a right pain when she wants to be, too,' replied Annie indulgently. 'I've been away for a few days, and – despite the fact she was all over me at first – she's been sulking this morning. Trying to teach me a lesson, I suppose.'

'I've had them all my life, dogs. Like kids they are. I would say "especially at this age", but they don't change. Miss us, they do – as much as we miss them. But, there, it's the unconditional love you can't beat, isn't it?'

'You're right.' Annie gestured toward the fire. 'Weeds?'

Ivor nodded. 'And diseased wood. All got to be burned. Nothing for it. And with the weather we've been having, I've got to take my chance while it's dry. Mind you, there'll be words from her over at the Dower House, I dare say. Can't steer clear of the gardens these days, she can't. Never interested until two minutes ago. Now she's an expert all of a sudden. I don't know where she gets it all. Telly, I suppose. They should have a warning on a lot of them programmes – just so you don't think you know everything in half an hour it's taken me fifty years to learn.' Ivor sucked his tombstone teeth, and rolled on the balls of his feet – much the way the duke did, thought Annie.

'You just out for a walk with this one?' Ivor enquired.

Annie chuckled. 'Well, no. We were all supposed to be meeting at the Hall at ten to have a chat about the thirteenth duke. But everyone else is going to be late, so I thought I'd stretch my legs. Hers too. She might have a nap a bit later, then.'

'The thirteenth, eh? He built this lot, you know. And planned and planted the hedged gardens, and the beds beyond. As far as I know – up until the dowager got interested – he was the last one here who was really bothered with the gardens at all.'

'I didn't know that,' said Annie. 'That must take some doing. You know, to be able to plan it all – see it in your mind's eye as it will be one day…when all the trees and shrubs have grown in.'

'It's a talent,' replied Ivor.

Annie was quick to reply, 'You must have it yourself, Ivor. You couldn't do what you do as well as you do it, if you didn't. This place always looks magnificent.' She meant it, and knew it never hurt to compliment a person on a job well done; it didn't happen enough in life, to her way of thinking.

Ivor beamed, showing even fewer teeth than Annie recalled him having. 'Thank you very much. Means a great deal that does. Mind you, I'll be honest and admit we still use a lot of the plans the thirteenth duke drew up. Left a lot of documentation, did that one – and the head gardener before me was keen to impress upon me the rule that we should only change the planting if something had died…not just for the fun of it. The thirteenth did a good enough job that the way it looks nowadays is largely down to him.'

Annie knew the group researching The Case of the Disgraced Duke had reached the point where they were trying to find out more about the man himself, so she dared to ask her next question: 'I don't suppose I could have a look at the plans, could I? Are they…well, to hand, you know?'

Ivor looked Annie up and down. 'All in the potting shed, over there, they are. Been there forever. And all his other bits and pieces too. Working documents. But, yes, I don't see why you can't have a look at them.'

Annie was delighted. 'Thanks, Ivor. If I could borrow them just for a couple of days, that would be fantastic – we're doing a sort of project about the thirteenth, see, and they'd be really useful. Give us an insight into the man.'

'Come with me then – this fire's on its way out, now, so we can leave it to its own devices. But I'll get a couple of the lads to give you a hand. All kept in metal boxes, they are, so they'd be a bit heavy for you – especially since you've got her to control as well.'

'You're a gentleman and a scholar, Ivor,' said Annie, urging Gertie to let go of a root she was thrashing to death.

'Don't tell my wife that,' said Ivor with a wink, 'or she won't expect me to nip off to the Lamb and Flag for a pint every now and then.'

CHAPTER FORTY-SIX

Carol had told David all about the nature of the kerfuffle across the green, and they'd toasted Carol's success at closing a case – that the agency had never even really opened – with a pot of tea. Having missed her appointed time for her video call with her agency colleagues, Carol phoned Christine to find out what was happening, to discover that she, too, had missed the meeting.

Christine asked, 'Carol, I wonder if you can help with a little something – personal thing. Please?' Carol always wanted to laugh when Christine put on her poor, pathetic, pleading voice. She sounded like a little Irish girl, begging for sweeties – nothing like the posh City professional Carol had first met years earlier. As she sat at her dining-room table with her son at her feet, Carol felt as though that life had happened to a different person.

Smiling at her son, Carol replied, 'Fill me in, and I'll do what I can – but if "real" work comes up, it takes precedence, okay?'

'Always – though I can't imagine this'll take you long. Natalie Smith. Walls by Smith…need everything you can find. Personal. Financial. The lot. I'll text you all the facts I have. Thanks.'

'And this is because…?' Carol liked to know why she was doing whatever it was she was doing.

'Hmm…Alexander thinks she's on the level, I fear she's on the take. She's involved with Bill Coggins, someone Alexander really cares about, and they're in business together, of course. He…well, okay then, *I'm* a bit worried that this woman might be after Bill's money – of which he has none…though he's saying he wants to buy Alexander out, so that's a bit of a puzzle…anyway…that's why. I'm keeping my fingers crossed, Carol. Whatever you can – as soon as poss…you know?'

'Well, that's all as clear as mud, then,' said Carol. 'All over it, Chris…oh, in fact, I've just opened her company's website. Have you seen these wallpapers? The murals she's created? My word…there's one here that would be perfect for Albert's room. Okay, I'll get back to you soon. I'll text to tell you there's an email, okay? Bye.'

'Bye.'

Carol found herself disappearing down a rabbit hole she hadn't expected, amazed by how reasonable some of the wallpapers, and special murals, were, considering…

She pulled herself together; with no idea when she'd be required to lend a hand to the issue of the thirteenth duke, she decided to focus on what Christine had asked – and spent the next hour or so completely immersed in the life of one Natalie Smith, who turned out to be quite a woman – in more ways than one.

CHAPTER FORTY-SEVEN

With everyone having been so badly delayed in arriving at Chellingworth Hall, instructions had been sent to Cook Davies to push back luncheon. When the group finally convened in the library, there was a great deal of excitement as the metal boxes that had been delivered by two of the gardeners were opened, and their contents examined.

'You've found gold, Annie,' exclaimed Althea, as Henry lifted volume after volume out of the boxes that had been placed on the floor, and put them onto the dust-sheet-covered tables.

'Good heavens, it looks as though these have been handled by someone with exceptionally dirty hands,' said Henry, clearly appalled by the state of some of the books.

'They're working garden plans and planting details, Henry,' replied his mother. 'Of course they're going to get dirty. That's the point. They're being used to make the magical landscape we see beyond these windows.'

'Even so – one might have imagined they could have been copied, and saved,' said Henry.

Stephanie responded, 'Maybe we can arrange for that to be the case going forward. I'll speak to Val about her father maybe doing some restoration work on these originals, then they can be held here, in the library. How about that?'

'Capital.' Henry felt that was a good idea.

Christine suggested, 'Let's divvy it all up, and each focus on one thing – how about that?'

Mavis nodded. 'Aye – divide and conquer. Good idea. And what good work by you, Annie, in tracking all these down. I know we need to talk about the situation in Swansea, but let's put this ahead of that for now. No news, I suppose?'

Annie shook her head. 'Nothing yet. It might take them some time to track down Jeanette Summers – if they ever do. But I trust DCI Llewellyn to let me know.'

Althea chipped in, 'And she's nothing like her brother, you say, Annie? Good – just one of that sort is quite enough.'

Henry, his wife, his sister, Christine, and Annie each took a volume of what they had discovered were the thirteenth duke's journals – while Althea and Mavis plumped for the large bound volumes which contained the pull-out plans for the gardens.

Some time later, Edward entered a completely silent library to announce luncheon, which was accepted as an irritating interruption to some fascinating reading by those present.

After they'd all been served, Mavis suggested, 'While we're all here, why don't we share what we've discovered so far. I must admit I'm finding the details of just how much work was involved in creating the walled garden, and the other areas he designed and planted, to be fascinating. The number of people involved in digging, moving earth, building walls…it's quite something, isn't it, Althea?'

The dowager paused, her eyes eventually lifting from the glistening Cumberland sausage on her plate. 'It is – and I have to say, what appeared in the report written for the fourteenth duke is borne out to some extent; a good number of the workers were not local. Though, to be fair to Fred, I can see why that might be the case; the population in these parts was small at the time, and most were farmers who needed to tend to their own livelihoods. It's no wonder the man had to import labor. So…well there's that, I suppose.'

Clementine sighed. 'I have to be honest and say that I'm not surprised he managed to fit records of what he did over so many years into the slim volume I read; his life was incredibly boring. And he talks about plants. A lot. There's a whole page about him trying to save a monkey puzzle tree that was gifted to the twelfth duke by some copper baron from Swansea. We have several monkey puzzle trees, so I assume he was successful. But – generally boring. Fred, the early years, snooze-fest. Except for when he writes about his mother.' Clementine giggled. 'It seems she was a bit overbearing…he writes about all her rules, and – despite the fact he was known as the Batchelor Duke – it's clear his mother put a great deal of effort into bringing what she thought of as "suitable" young women to

Chellingworth to try to get him to marry. He talks about that a fair bit – but it seems he preferred his plants, and didn't at all understand her sense of urgency.'

Althea tutted, loudly.

Henry expounded, 'The volume I read was anything but boring, and his mother receives no mention, which is hardly surprising, since it deals with his expedition to China. It read like a real action thriller. To be honest, it boggles the mind that Kew Gardens would commission anyone to hunt about in China for rare plants when a war was raging between our two countries. From what he writes, he found himself in some very sticky situations, essentially behind enemy lines. There's a great deal of detail about hiding out in some dreadful places, all the time having to drag plants about with him. Bizarre.'

Stephanie added, 'It sounds as though the volume I'm reading follows Henry's. I can quite understand why he'd have done his best to help Chen Li, the man who hid him from the Chinese forces, and his brother Chen Fang. Of course, Fred was incredibly fortunate to meet two men who spoke some English – though it appears that Chen Li was already known to the people at Kew as being knowledgeable about local plants, and where to find them, and that Fred was told how to make contact with him. So that makes sense – in a way. It also appears that Fred himself had spent some time studying the Chinese culture before he accepted the undertaking from Kew. But imagine the risk they all took, with Fred getting them onto a ship to bring them back to England – and then he brought them here to Wales. The volume I read spoke of that, and of the struggle to save the plants he was bringing back for Kew. Extraordinary, really.'

Annie said, 'The journal I'm reading talks about how the two Chens – which is how the journal refers to them – worked with Fred to plan and execute the garden designs for Chellingworth. I wonder how they fitted in around here; I mean, it's a bit weird for me, and I'm only English…well, Black and English, but for two Chinese blokes, coming here directly from China, in the middle of a war, back in the 1800s? Gordon Bennett, that must have been difficult. I wonder if they ever left the estate…and how they got on with the workers here. It doesn't say much about that. It's clear that Fred and Li – which is how he refers to Chen Li – spent a great deal of time together. Which makes sense if Chen Li was the real plant expert, and maybe Chen Fang came along…well, because it was too dangerous for him to stay in China, I suppose.'

Christine pushed away her empty plate. 'I'm reading his final journal, I believe. Now, we all know that the fourteenth's report mentioned two Chinese men disappearing, and we believe that somehow morphed, through various local rumors, into two men being killed and buried on the estate somewhere. But there's nothing in Fred's journal about anyone disappearing. Though it's notable that neither Chen brother is mentioned in the volume I have. Indeed, a great deal of it revolves around the changing of the garden designs – especially in terms of the planting. Fred seems to have been obsessive in that respect. If you say a lot of workers were needed to create the initial gardens, I don't know how many were used to tear it up and replant it. And I haven't seen any explanation for why he did that. He also mentions that he is determined to have the work completed by a deadline – though his journal doesn't mention when that is, nor the reason for it.'

Henry leaned on the table, steepled his fingers, and said, 'Interesting.'

'Henry, elbows,' snapped his mother.

Henry removed his elbows and hid his hands on his lap.

Mavis asked, 'Does the journal you have run all the way to the time of his death, Christine?'

Christine replied, 'I haven't finished yet, but I have to admit I'm keen to do so. I can miss afters, so would you mind if I just grabbed an apple and went back to work?'

'Me too,' said Annie.

Althea piped up, 'And I have an idea about the plants…the planting as it finally ended up, that is. The names are ringing bells with me. The Victorians gave special meanings to plants, you see.

And he was specific about the new plantings; the amended plants feature *yellow* acacia, *yellow* tulips, *purple* hyacinths, *red* carnations, *white* lilies, and weeping willows, amongst others. Yes, very specific…and there was the cudweed he was holding in his portrait too. But for me to be certain about what I suspect, I'll need to send for something to be brought here from the Dower House, though, to be honest, I'd much rather do this at home. You've all seen how Ivor's been using the book with all the plans in it in the garden, and it's very sweet of Stephanie to say she'll try to find out if the book can be restored, but I'm quite sure that Mavis and I could be trusted with it overnight, wouldn't you all agree?'

A consensus was reached that Althea and Mavis would return to the Dower House with the volumes of plans and plant lists, while the rest of the group returned to the library to continue their reading.

When Annie's phone rang some time later, it startled everyone. 'I'll pop outside into the Great Hall to take it. It's our client – Tina,' she added, nodding at Christine.

Henry resettled himself, doing his best to race to the end of his volume, while Stephanie wandered the shelves having finished hers. Clementine had taken herself off somewhere 'to check something', though Henry had commented upon her departure that he was in no doubt she'd disappeared because she was bored.

When Annie joined the group again, Christine looked up. 'News from Swansea?'

Annie nodded, took a seat beside her colleague, and whispered, 'Tina says the police have checked Frank Turnbull's finances; Jeanette Summers emptied his bank account through the fortnight before his death. And it turns out she has a habit of running up gambling debts. Tina's in a terrible state. Her sister's still under observation in hospital. It's…not good. Though, I suppose, that might explain why Jeanette planned for Frank to die when he did…she'd already managed to get her hands on what she wanted – all his cash.'

'Have you finished, Christine?' Henry sounded tetchy. 'Does he die at the end of that one?' He paused, then added, 'Silly question – but you know what I mean.'

Christine smiled. 'Yes, I do know what you mean, Henry, but no, I haven't finished it yet, and I've just received a text which means I need to take a break. It's Carol, telling me she's just sent me an urgent report I've been waiting for. Excuse me for a moment – I'll step outside to attend to it.'

The group had whittled itself down to Henry, Stephanie, and Annie – who all exchanged a hunted look.

'We're not really getting anywhere with this lot, are we?' Annie had put into words what the duke and duchess were feeling.

'Sadly, no.' Stephanie sounded resigned.

At that moment Clementine bounded into the library. 'I think I've cracked it. Me – would you believe it! And I'm not even a professional investigator.' She grinned at Annie in such a winning way, that Annie punched the air and cheered.

'What? What have you found, Clemmie?' Henry sounded a little annoyed, and unconvinced that his sister had managed a breakthrough.

'Henry, you must remember the Chinese room, up on the third floor. In the east wing – at the end of the corridor. We used to go there when we were children, to play.' He brother looked at her blankly. 'Oh, come on, Henry. Remember we used to go there to dress up in those fancy embroidered robes? The room with the wall paintings? The flying and swooping cranes? Nothing?'

Henry sounded surprised when he replied, 'Why yes, I do, now you come to mention it. Good heavens, I haven't so much as walked along that corridor in…well, a great number of years. What about it?'

'I tell you what, instead of me telling you, let me show you. Come on – bring the lump with you, Stephanie, and I don't mean your baby bump.' She giggled. 'You too, Annie…and Christine should come too. She was out in the Great Hall concentrating on something on her phone. Let's pick her up on the way.'

When Christine burst into the library everyone could see that she was – for some unknown reason – absolutely delighted about something or other.

She bubbled, 'There's something I must tell you about, Stephanie, Henry. A wonderful company, "Walls by Smith", run by a wonderful woman, Natalie Smith. She designs and prints the most gorgeous murals and special wallpapers – and I'm sure there'd be something on her website that would suit the new nursery you're planning…there's an especially lovely one with birds in flight. And she could do with your support, because she's putting a great deal of the money she's made from her talents and entrepreneurship into a venture by which she'll be backing her future husband's family business, which they've been running since the 1700s. And she's pregnant too. And Alexander and I have been invited to the wedding. What do you think about that, then?'

No one knew quite what to make of Christine's excitement – and she clearly wasn't going to explain herself.

Clementine's response was: 'Come on, come with us. We're off up to the third floor. I believe I've solved it all, you see. Found the missing pieces, that make sense of the whole thing. Which is so exciting…and even more so, because there's something of a theme running through all this.'

Henry sighed. 'I'll escort you, dear.' He took his wife's arm. 'Lead the way, sister, dear…lead the way. And try not to be too irritating, please.'

Clementine skipped out of the room. 'No way I'm not going to gloat, Henry – I've cracked it! You can thank me later.'

MONDAY 31ST OCTOBER

CHAPTER FORTY-EIGHT

Barry Walton was happy with the way the filming of the completed plasterwork project at Chellingworth Hall had gone. To begin with, the whole restoration was ahead of schedule; they'd had a problem-free set up on the scaffolding, a good, clean shoot, and an excellent standard of work by the craftspeople involved that would look good in the final cut: a satisfying day's work. Now all he had to do was escape before that blessed dowager hunted him down; she'd been lurking about the place all day and kept sneaking up on him whenever he wasn't on his guard. She'd invited him to stay for tea half a dozen times, but he wanted to get back to London before the weather broke. It had been a glorious day, but high winds were forecast overnight, and he didn't want to be stuck on the M25 in that.

He'd almost managed it; the rest of the team had packed up and left, but there was some problem locating the coat that had been whisked away from him by the butler upon his arrival. He was finally pulling it on in the Great Hall when the dowager and the woman who always seemed to be at her side – a paid companion? – approached him, beaming with what he took to be a malevolent air.

'Mr Walton, how fortuitous that you're still here. We're just about to take tea in the library. I must insist that you join us.' Barry was amazed by how quickly the small woman managed to get about on her cane, and it took no more than an instant for her to slip her arm through his and add, 'How kind of you to escort me.' And they were on their way, his coat still hanging off one arm.

When he entered the library, it looked quite different to the last time he'd set foot in the place, and there wasn't as much as a crumb of cake to be seen, let alone any actual tea. He sensed danger.

A row of tables was arranged at one end, covered with books. To either side of the tables sat an alarming array of people: the duke, the duchess, Christine Wilson-Smythe, and Val Jenkins – all of whom he recognized – had been joined by a skinny, intense-looking, pale woman with vivid blue hair, a rounded, smiling woman with floppy blonde curls, and a Black woman who he could tell was tall, even though she was sitting down. He had no idea who they were, or why they were staring at him with such smug expressions. The dowager and her companion took the only two empty seats beside the tables, and he had no choice but to hover next to the only unused chair that was slap-bang in the middle of the room. He felt as though he were facing a firing squad.

'Please sit,' said the duchess graciously. Was she being friendly? Or menacing?

Barry perched, and waited. He read the silence as ominous, and smiled nervously at Val, hoping for a friendly greeting in return. He didn't get one.

The duke addressed him. 'When you last visited us, you mentioned the thirteenth Duke of Chellingworth, and his colorful, and questionable, background.'

Barry's heart sank. He'd been regretting bringing up the topic ever since he'd done so, because he was toying with the idea of featuring Chellingworth's thirteenth duke as one in a series about historical scandals that had flown under the radar, which would allow him to focus on current political and governmental issues and injustices, under the guise of telling historical tales. Now…this. The family was clearly up in arms about it. Oh well, he'd dealt with worse in the past; he'd sit and take a telling off, then get on with digging dirt for himself.

'I did,' he replied simply. *Best to leave it at that,* he thought.

The duchess spoke next. 'As I have no doubt you noticed at the time, what you said about the thirteenth duke was news to me.' Barry felt a nod was appropriate. 'And my concerns were listened to by my husband. Thus, we have spent the intervening period doing our best to ferret out the truth about the…rumors…you mentioned at the time.'

Oh no, thought Barry, *they're going to bleat on about how one of their ancestors could never have done something so heinous. Right – sit quietly and take it.* 'How fascinating,' he said. 'It must have been quite an undertaking.' He nodded toward the books displayed on the tables.

'Aye, indeed it was.' The companion was speaking.

Odd, thought Barry.

She continued, 'I've been given the honor of making the introductions today, so allow me to do that.'

Even odder.

The companion stood and marched across the room.

She's used to marching…and getting her way, judging by the way she holds herself.

'You know His Grace the Duke, and Her Grace the Duchess, of course – them being your hosts while you're here at Chellingworth – and we all know of your connection with Val Jenkins, our local television celebrity. Her Grace the Dowager was also present for your last visit to us, as was the Right Honourable Miss Christine Wilson-Smythe; she's the daughter of the Viscount Loch Carraghie and Ballinclare, by the way.'

Barry felt compelled to nod as the woman mentioned each person. He wasn't surprised to find that Christine had a titled father – though the fact it was an Irish one made things more interesting. But, frankly, why someone had to be gifted with both good looks as well as a title, he didn't know.

He didn't have time to dwell on the inequities of life, because the Scotswoman was marching around in front of him again, and she scared him a bit, so he gave her his full attention.

'The other thing you might not know about Christine is that she is one of four women who set up the WISE Enquiries Agency a few years back, which now operates out of a delightfully converted barn on the Chellingworth Estate.'

Barry couldn't help himself. 'There's a detective agency here? Out in the wilds? Why? Is there much detecting needed…in these parts?' He couldn't imagine there was. Chellingworth was located in the back of beyond, with nothing much for miles around but a mildly picturesque village – with a relatively decent pub, to be fair – and a load of scraggy old sheep dotted about on the hillsides.

The woman approached him, which was alarming. 'It's a long story as to why we're here, but we've no' been slacking since we arrived.'

Barry picked up on the 'we' and began to feel even more uneasy. He replied with a raising of his eyebrows and left it at that.

'First, please allow me to introduce you to Lady Clementine, the duke's sister.' The woman with blue hair smiled at Barry and wiggled the tips of her fingers in his direction. 'This is Mrs Carol Hill, our finance, computing, and technical expert, who joined us from the City of London.'

Barry didn't think that the round woman with floppy blonde curls, and wearing a shapeless floral frock, looked like much of a City type, nor a techno-whiz – more the madly mumsy type, to his mind – but he smiled.

'And I am Mrs Mavis MacDonald, most recently the matron overseeing the care of the residents at the Battersea Barracks.'

Makes sense, thought Barry. *Army nurse, tough as old nails.*

'And lastly, but by no means least, this is Miss Annie Parker. Now you might think there's no' much for four professional enquiry agents to be doing "in these parts", Mr Walton, but I'm able to tell you that in recent weeks alone we've successfully dealt with The Case of the Aggressive Acquisition, The Case of the Roofer who Relinquished his Responsibilities, The Case of the Antiquarian and the Artist, The Case of the Purloined Preserves, *and* The Case of the Suspicious Sisters. To her enormous credit, we received word just yesterday that Miss Parker's most recent efforts in Swansea have led to the arrest of a woman suspected of having arranged to have her partner killed, and the apprehension of two other persons of interest in what the police are describing as an organized group of women who made their livelihood by targeting elderly gentlemen, fleecing them, then ensuring their deaths happened at the most opportune moment, while all providing alibis for each other. Solving it means that Annie's been instrumental in bringing several killers to face justice in the past few months.'

Barry looked at Annie with fresh eyes. *She doesn't look the type*, he thought. *More the sort you'd be happy to natter with over a drink or two.* Then he wondered if what he'd always considered to be his ability to assess a person's character at first sight was letting him down.

He felt as though his comment of 'Impressive' was expected. *A duke, his mother, his wife and sister, plus four private investigators and a TV chef: what an odd collection of people. And they've all got that look in their eyes – like I'm what they're having for tea. Here we go, Barry – brace yourself.*

'And what have you discovered about the thirteenth duke?' He thought he owed them a handy segue.

The dowager stood – reaching her full five feet – and balanced precariously on her walking stick. 'A great deal, young man, and we've even put it all together very neatly for you – with supporting evidence.' She waggled her cane toward the tables, then sat down again, which Barry thought was just as well because she looked as though she might topple over otherwise.

The duchess stood next, looking cool, calm, and in control. Barry noted her sleek hair, her aquiline features highlighted by a little make-up, and her overall air of composure. *She used to do the PR for this place – look out Barry, puff piece on its way.*

'This has been a real team effort, Barry, which is why we're all here. Our valued additional member, Mr Alexander Bright, will be joining us later; I'm afraid he's been delayed a little on his way down from London.'

Barry tried to look disinterested. *Alexander Bright? Handsome as the devil, and a rakish reputation to match. Used to be seen on the society pages, but not so much in the past year or so. Must be with the Wilson-Smythe girl now…oh…fascinating, and noted.*

The duchess continued, 'We won't be bothering you with all the exact references, but suffice it to say that everything I'm about to tell you can be proven by referencing the works you see displayed here today. We have found the original of the report commissioned by Harold, the fourteenth duke, as well as the personal journals kept by Frederick, the thirteenth. We also have the plans of the gardens here at Chellingworth that were created by Frederick, as well as some accoutrements that have been kept at the Hall over the years.'

What is all that embroidered stuff in a pile on the table? Can't make it out at all. She must mean that.

Stephanie Twyst, nee Timbers, Duchess of Chellingworth, brought all her past experience in public relations work to bear upon the matter in question. She held the assembled group in the palm of her oratorial hands as she told the story of Frederick, son of a mother determined to marry him off, who had a passion for plants, and who became so well respected for his knowledge in that field that he was despatched by Kew Gardens to gather rare species from China, despite a war. She made sure his adventures and challenges there sounded as thrilling, and dangerous, as they had been, and her voice quivered with tenderness when she told the television producer about the young duke ensuring the safety of his own saviors by bringing them back to Wales, when he returned home. She explained the animosity felt by the fourteenth for the thirteenth, and why that had colored his representation of his ancestor.

Barry could tell she was drawing to a close when she said, 'So, you see, the two Chinese brothers were here, then they weren't, and that's where there's a significant difference between what we have discovered to be the *real* truth, and the report Harold had commissioned, which was written by carefully selected, biased, investigators. Clementine – you wanted to speak about the Chinese room, on the third floor, I believe.'

Barry noticed the duke patting his wife's hand when she sat down, which he had to admit was a sweet gesture, then turned his attention to Lady Clementine. As she stood, he couldn't help thinking he'd seen her somewhere before, but he couldn't put his finger on it.

She's going to witter, he thought, so settled in for what he expected might be a confusing speech.

'When Henry and I were young, we'd play dressing up in one of the rooms upstairs, that has a stunning mural of cranes in flight on the walls – they fly right around the room. It's magical. Two things: first, these are the clothes we used to dress up in.'

Lady Clementine stepped toward the table and held up a somewhat threadbare embroidered red silk garment, followed by several others in an array of colors. She finally held up a couple of pairs of shoes.

Lovely, but what of it? thought Barry. 'Exquisite,' he said.

'Indeed,' replied Clementine. 'And secondly – the mural on the wall was signed by the artist. We now know who painted it. Over to you, Christine.'

Barry was puzzled. *Leave me hanging, why don't you!*

Christine thanked Clementine, and said, 'We called upon the expertise of a woman I have recently come to know who herself is a designer and artist, with a comprehensive knowledge of such works, and she was able to confirm for us that the mural on the third floor was the work of a man who became well-respected as an artist in London, during the late nineteenth century. According to the documents we have here, he shares a name with – and we believe he is the same person as – the brother of the Chinese plant expert Stephanie mentioned. The mural upstairs, and many others, for many years thereafter, was painted by Chen Fang, brother of Chen Li. This proves, we believe, that Chen Fang did not die here at Chellingworth at the hands of Frederick, but rather he left Chellingworth and went to live in Limehouse, in London, where he built his reputation. His biography – held at the V & A in London – states that he died of natural causes in 1903, a relatively wealthy man, with an English wife, and three children. We have managed – thanks to Carol's talents – to contact the descendants of one of those children, and she is able to bear testament to her family history, which tallies with Frederick having been saved in China by Chen Feng, and him having come to Wales, then London, as described.'

Barry nodded. 'And the other one? Chen Li – what of him?' He thought it a fair question.

Clementine stood again, still holding the shoes she'd been waving about. 'These are women's shoes, not men's. And those' – she waved her arms – 'are designs for female clothes, not male. Chen Li wasn't a man at all, she was a woman – who wore men's clothes when she was out and about, and was always referred to as a man…because, otherwise, Frederick couldn't possibly have had the woman he loved at his side for years – his mother wouldn't have accepted it. As it was, we believe that the dowager, who outlived her son by some time – and was instrumental in ensuring that the seat continued through Harold and his son – did all she could to hide any Chinese artifacts. Our own Estate Records show that what we call the Chinese Room – the one with the mural – was locked, and the key literally thrown away upon Frederick's death. The same records show that a new lock had to be fitted for that room in the 1950s, when the entire third floor was being assessed for damage after the roof failed over the east wing. And Frederick didn't die by suicide, by the way...we've established that, too. We believe he died of grief. Ta-daa!' Clementine curtsied, with a flourish.

Barry had it: he'd met this woman at a gallery opening in the East End of London, when she'd been drunk, and cavorting about as though she owned the place. But, back then, her hair had been emerald green. They'd continued drinking until the early hours, he vaguely recalled. *So that was Lady Clementine Twyst...gracious!*

Barry gathered his wits, hoped he wasn't blushing, and asked, 'And why do you suggest a romantic relationship between Frederick and Chen Li?' Another pertinent question any viewer would be asking at this point in a programme – and the idea of a woman having to disguise her gender in order to be able to be with her lover was beginning to get Barry thinking.

'Because of this,' said Clementine, holding up what looked like a large rectangle of embroidered fabric, with a long piece of cloth poking from each of its four corners. He watched, bemused, as Clementine pulled the long pieces under her arms and across her body, then tied them, leaving the rectangular panel on her back – like an empty backpack.

'And?' *Oh for heavens' sake, get on with it.*

Clementine glowed. 'It's a *mei tai* or *bei dai* – the original baby carrier. Its invention in Asia hundreds of years ago revolutionized life for women there, because it allowed them to carry their baby on their back, or front, yet still have their hands free to do other jobs. Also, the cranes on the mural in the Chinese room mean monogamy, long-lasting love…and wish long lives to those who sleep beneath them.'

Barry was starting to see the point of all this.

'Then there's the garden – which is so tragic,' said the dowager, taking Barry by complete surprise. 'Can I do my garden thing now?' The woman was vibrating with excitement.

'Please do, Mother,' said the duke, smiling too widely, thought Barry.

The dowager beamed, and stood. 'Well, when you realize that Fred…sorry, Frederick…planted the garden twice – completely ripping out the first design that had been put together when the Chens were here – then it all makes sense. Which is terribly sad. I have a lovely book which explains the Victorian meanings of hundreds of plants, and the plants in the Chellingworth gardens – the plants Frederick put in there when his journals stop talking about the Chens, in any case – are all sad ones.'

'Sad plants?' Barry was starting to feel lost again.

The dowager sat down, grabbed a crumpled piece of paper and read aloud, 'Yellow acacia means "secret love"; amaranthus means "immortality, or unfading love"; andromeda means "self sacrifice"; aspen trees mean "lamentation". He also planted azalea, campanula, red carnation, citrus gum, Coreopsis arkansa, cudweed, cypress, forget me nots, heartsease and pansies, helenium, honey flower, honeysuckle, purple hyacinth, laburnum, love lies bleeding, white periwinkle, pyrethrum, yellow tulips, water lilies, white lilies and weeping willows.' She paused to draw breath, just as Barry thought she was going to pass out. Then she grinned, triumphantly. 'Every single one of them means something like sorrow, or loss, or the loss of love, or of a loved one, or in memorial for someone loved – and then, of course, there's the bunch of cudweed he's grasping in his portrait, which means "never ceasing remembrance". Come on, you look like you're a clever boy, Barry, you know exactly what I mean.'

Barry was taken aback by being addressed as a 'boy', but he decided to let it go; the dowager had to be somewhere in her eighties, so probably older than his own mother. Not only did he give the dowager a pass, but he was starting to feel the sensation at the back of his neck that meant he was getting a good idea.

As his mind went into hyperdrive, he gabbled as fast as his hands flew about. 'So, Frederick married this Chinese gardener girl, or maybe didn't marry her…it would be good if we knew that, but the story works with a few loose ends, nonetheless – always leave 'em wanting more, you know – and she had a baby and…what…they both died?' Barry was realizing this might turn out to be a better story than the one he'd first thought he had. 'And the garden is their memorial? Are they buried there? Is that where the rumors came from?' *It sort of makes sense.*

'Indeed.' The duke was on his feet, looking triumphant. 'There were no murders – there weren't even two Chinese men to be murdered; one was a woman, and one a man we know lived a long and prosperous life. Love found, and lost, that's what we're talking about. But, because of the dreadful way that the Chinese were viewed by society at the time – this being a period of war and animosity – the whole thing was kept quiet. That's what was hushed up – not murder, but forbidden love.'

Barry was already thinking, *Fantastic! History, gardening, racism, the class system at work, the politics of war with China, the villagers versus the duke…and I can see the closing shots now – camera on a drone above the gardens, swooping down to the spot…*

He asked, 'Do you know where they're buried?' *Please say yes, please say yes.*

Mavis stood and said, 'Come here and take a look at this.'

The producer stood to attention and joined her beside the table. Everyone else huddled behind Barry, making him feel a bit claustrophobic.

Mavis pointed at a large sheet of paper that concertinaed out of a massive leather-bound book. It showed the gardens at Chellingworth, and was a bit of a mess – not just because it was dirty, and well-used, but because even the original markings had been fiddled about with. Shrubs and plants were shown as blobs with rounded edges, and each contained a number. The list of plants corresponding to those numbers had many amendments. He could see lots of the names the dowager had reeled off. Mavis was pointing at the center of the hedged garden.

'See that? That's a plain circle of marble. No plants. The hedges surrounding it are not walls, and have no gates. Our research – again, courtesy of Carol – suggests both factors mean the site was designed to be auspicious for a Chinese burial or interment. Originally a tree was planted right there, where the marble dais now stands, but the whole thing was changed between 1850 and 1853, according to these records. The records also show there was a specific deadline for all this major work to take place, at least at the center of the garden – which sounds as though Frederick was aiming for what would be termed an auspicious date for the funeral rites. We know Chen Fang arrived in Limehouse, with enough money to buy a small house there, in 1854. We believe he stayed until his sister's final interment, with her child, was fulfilled. We're continuing to search for what is clearly one volume, or maybe more, of Frederick's journals, covering this specific period. But maybe he was so grief-stricken he kept none. Maybe the garden took all his time, and passion. We also know his mother never set foot in the place – not even after her son's death – and the garden was never an interest for any of the dukes who followed. Indeed, to hear the current head gardener speak, they actively allowed it to be poorly attended to.'

Barry was conjuring scenes in his mind's eye. 'We could bring in a piece of ground-penetrating radar equipment…get that onto it,' he said – aloud, as it happened.

'We shall never allow such a thing,' said Henry forcefully, in a tone that suggested to Barry he was channelling Winston Churchill.

'We could consider it, Henry,' said the duchess, cooing at her husband.

Got him tied around your little finger, haven't you dear, thought Barry. 'I think Her Grace makes a good point,' he said. 'Something for consideration. After all, why wouldn't you want to have one more way to prove that this is the site of a memorial garden marking the interment of two loved ones – rather than where a killer duke got away with murder?' He thought that might carry the day.

Henry rolled on the balls of his feet, his thumbs in his waistcoat pockets. 'Well…perhaps. Yes, we can give it some thought. But, for now, wouldn't you agree we've done away with the idea that Frederick was a cold-blooded killer? Doesn't all this newly discovered information support a completely revised interpretation of the so-called facts? Which obviously weren't facts at all. I believe we've done enough to lay the rumors to rest, once and for all.'

Barry gave the matter some thought. 'It's always best to attract an audience with a proposition that one then unpicks. I could see myself putting together an appealing proposal, entitled "The Case of the Disgraced Duke", then using what you've discovered to undermine that idea. How about that? Maybe you'd allow me access to all the records you've found, and maybe I could even retain the services of one or two of your local detectives to add…color. What do you say?'

'Well, I'm not so sure about that,' said Henry.

'Food for thought, I'd say,' said Stephanie.

Althea hobbled away saying, 'Not sure that Harold, or Frederick's mother, are going to come out of this smelling of roses, no matter what type they might be.'

Edward appeared at the door. 'The…ahem…festivities are due to commence in one hour, Your Graces. People are beginning to congregate.'

'Oh goodie,' exclaimed the dowager. 'Now you must stay on for this, Barry. We're reviving some ancient Celtic traditions to celebrate *Nos Galan Gaeaf* tonight. Are you aware of the observation at all?'

Barry felt his eyes grow round. 'Er, no, I can't say that I am. Is that like Halloween?'

The dowager gripped his elbow and began to steer him toward the door. He grabbed his coat as they passed the chair he'd been sitting on.

'Not really, dear,' said the forceful little woman, 'but I'm sure you'll enjoy it. However, should you run into him, don't listen to anything the Reverend Ebenezer Roberts says about it all – if he bothers to come, that is, which I dare say he might not.'

Barry was out of the room in seconds, and only vaguely aware of a lot of hugging taking place between the group he'd left behind.

CHAPTER FORTY-NINE

It was already dark when the party descended the steps from the Hall to the grounds where the festivities were to take place.

Mavis was surprised to see Ian Cottesloe wandering around carrying a flaming torch, dressed as…well, she wasn't quite sure what he was dressed as, but he seemed to be wearing a black fur rug over his shoulders, which puzzled her a great deal.

She asked Althea, 'What is Ian wearing, and why? Come to that, I could ask the same of you…I haven't seen that coat on you before.'

Althea was taking things steady, watching her footing with great care, as Edward accompanied the dowager and Mavis toward a wooden platform that had been placed at the edge of the ha-ha, beyond the formal gardens.

She answered Mavis quietly, 'Ian did such a good job in the role of *gwadhoddwr* ahead of Henry and Stephanie's wedding, that I thought he could do his thing again tonight. I wanted someone to play the role of a bard, travelling Wales, telling the assembled masses about the traditions of the land. Ian's a good public speaker, and he can talk to the villagers in both English and Welsh, which is handy. The black furry thing is the best we could come up with; it's a rug from somewhere in the Hall, and at a certain point in his talk he's going to rear up, as if out of the flames of that big bonfire, as the vision of *Yr Hwch Ddu Gwta*, a tailless black sow who chases the children to bed – eating the one who remains behind.'

Mavis sounded bemused when she said, 'That'll give them all nightmares, I shouldn't wonder. I dare say their parents won't be thanking you for that.'

Althea laughed, 'Oh, it's just a bit of fun – Ian will show them all it's just him. I do understand that, while children these days seem to be drawn to horrific things, they're essentially sanitized for them, whereas this is all new, and raw – so Ian's agreed to make the whole thing quite jolly…which it never was, of course.'

'Ach, pigs eating children...go on with you. And what about that coat of yours then? Where's that suddenly popped up from? Did you magic that up from one of the rooms in the Hall too? I can't say the pattern is quite you...orange and yellow zigzags, on a coat?'

Althea preened. 'It was in the window of a little charity shop in Brecon. I saw it there a few days ago and it fitted so well that I thought...why not?'

Mavis spluttered, 'A charity shop? I'll no' say anything against them but why you felt the need...ach, well, on your own head be it. But when were you in Brecon, and why?'

Althea took a seat on the wooden platform they'd reached, thanked Edward, and settled down, happily allowing Mavis to fiddle with a blanket for her knees. 'I'm going under the knife next week. It's decided. I met with the specialist in Brecon, and then visited my solicitor. My affairs are all in order, Mavis, and you won't be left high and dry if I don't come out of the hospital, you can be assured of that.'

Mavis stood back and looked down at Althea. 'Ach, my dear, wee woman – you'll be just fine. They do thousands of hip replacements every year – trust your doctors, they'll know what they're about. Of course you'll come home...in fact, don't be surprised if you're out of there in just a few days. But never worry, I'll be at the Dower House to make sure you get all the attention you need during your recuperative period. I'll oversee your physical therapy, and can liaise with all the necessary healthcare professionals to ensure you're back on your feet in time for the arrival of your first grandchild.'

Althea grasped Mavis's hand. 'You are such a good friend, Mavis, and I know you'll understand what I mean when I say I have valued your presence in my life this past year. Friendship is a wonderful thing, my dear, and it works both ways. So thank you for your offer of support; I shall accept it, but know that I'm always here for you too, in whatever way I can be.'

The women hugged.

Mavis said, 'Talking about friendship, that Val Jenkins is close with Stephanie, isn't she? Nice woman. Sound. Did you have a friend like that, from your life before you became a duchess, to help remind you of who you once were?'

Althea looked beyond the bonfire at her son and daughter-in-law, who were both laughing at something Val had said. 'For a little while. But when Henry and Clementine were born, those friends rather drifted away. I should have made more of an effort to keep in touch with them. And you're right, Val's a good woman. I dare say it won't have occurred to Stephanie and Henry, but she might make a wonderful godmother for their child. I'll have a word with them about it.'

Having formed her own opinions about Val's father's affinity for his particular brand of religion earlier in the year, Mavis wondered how that would work out, then was distracted as the children started to squeal at the arrival of Ian beside the bonfire.

'Oh, I hope he does a good job of this,' said Althea.

Ian Cottesloe did a very good job of it indeed. His pleasant voice rang out in the night air, above the crackling of the bonfire, which occasionally sent a shower of sparks flying into the darkness, lending an even more supernatural air to the whole theatrical event. He'd prepared a speech, which he delivered like a story, alternating between English and Welsh as he capered about the bonfire. He entranced and delighted young and old with his talk about how the original traditions of paying off workers at the end of the harvest season, and celebrating the last time of plenty before the shortages of the winter months, had been marked by the supper at the church hall the month before. Then children ran to their parents shrieking happily when he explained that the night before November the first, the first day of the Celtic winter, was an *ysbrydnos* or spirit night, when the veil between the living and the souls of the dead was at its thinnest.

He warned of the *gwrach*, the witches who would be on the lookout for children who strayed too far from their parents – there were lots of cuddles – but he offset the fears of the young by telling them they'd be fine if they just stayed away from crossroads and churches, where the spirits congregated, and, if they found themselves there to always look out for *Y Ladi Wen,* the ghostly figure of a white lady, who would protect them from more dangerous spirits.

When it came time for him to leap about, being the tailless black sow, the children were delighted, not frightened – and he then explained an admittedly sanitized version of the *Coelcerth* tradition of writing names on stones, and announced that a whole pile of stones had been kindly donated by the Hughes family, to allow anyone who wanted to participate to be able to do so, but he made it abundantly clear that only Ivor – who was dressed in a motley outfit – was allowed to place stones into the fire.

He concluded his performance by telling his rapt audience about where they could find baked potatoes, warm drinks, and platters of Welsh Cakes, and the applause and cheers from the crowd were warm and heartfelt.

'I don't see how the Reverend Roberts can possibly think any of this is heathen,' observed Althea happily as the crowd milled about.

'It'll be interesting to hear his sermon next Sunday then, I should think,' replied Mavis.

'Not my problem, dear, I shall be in hospital, or at least not up to attending church,' replied Althea, her cheeks dimpling.

David Hill had brought Albert to meet Carol, and the family had snuggled a safe distance away from the bonfire, enjoying Ian's performance.

'It's great that our boy will grow up with this community around him,' said David. 'And I'm glad he'll get to discover his roots, all the traditions that can mean something to a little Welsh boy, growing up in Wales. And I'm also glad he'll do it all with a mother who is more than capable of dealing with anything life throws at us – because she understands it's throwing it as *us,* not just her.'

Carol hugged her husband and child. 'You're right that traditions are important, David; they've grown over the millennia because communities understand, and codify, the need for mutual support in times when a common fear needs to be addressed – like winter shortages, or death. And, you know what, we're also our own support unit; Albert will grow up knowing we're both going to be with him through whatever he has to face, because he'll see us being there for each other. We'll be the best parents we can be. Oh, and speaking of parenting, here comes Sarah Hughes.'

David leaned in. 'And those are her two boys with her, the ones who stole all those preserves?'

Carol nodded, as she said, 'Hello Sarah – did the boys enjoy that, then?'

Owain and Rhys Hughes didn't make eye contact with Carol when their mother prompted them with: 'So, what have you got to say to Mrs Hill?'

Mumblings of 'Thank you' and 'Sorry' floated up to Carol over the sounds of other children squealing and laughing.

Sarah added, 'Given they're not spending hours every day staring at their computer games, you'll be seeing these two out and about selling the jars of preserves they stole to raise money for the trip they *will* be going on, whether they like it or not…and they'll also be donating all the money they raise with their guy from now until Guy Fawkes' night to the fund as well, won't you boys?'

'Yes, Mam.'

Carol said, 'Very community-spirited. Good for you.'

'Yes, Mrs Hill.'

'Now go and find your father, he's getting you potatoes – but don't eat them if they're too hot.' The boys ran off. Sarah beamed at Carol. 'They're not bad boys, really, but they needed a bit of a wake-up call. And it's my responsibility – well, mine and their father's – to make sure this works. Better to tackle this now, than let it grow. But there – you've got all the best years ahead of you, haven't you, when all his problems will be small…and he'll be too little to answer back. Thanks again, Carol. See you around.'

Sarah Hughes waved as she headed toward the serving area.

'It's a big job, being a parent, isn't it?' David was speaking to his son.

'Biggest there is,' said Carol.

Alexander had arrived about halfway through Ian's shenanigans, so was a bit confused about what was going on, until Christine filled him in. Since their 'misunderstanding' – which was how they'd agreed they'd refer to the episode when Christine had suspected Alexander of wanting to do some permanent damage to Ronnie Right – Christine had driven to London, giving a somewhat subdued Annie a lift. Annie had wanted to spend a couple of days with her parents, while Christine and Alexander had spent a couple of days mainly alone, sorting things out between themselves. Christine had brought a more buoyant Annie back to Wales, and now, finally, Alexander was able to join her.

'So, it's all done then? You and Bill have sorted it all?' Christine hoped they had, because the discussions about their contracts had begun to get her down, much as contracts had back in her City days.

'All done and dusted. It's fifty-one percent his, forty-nine mine. I'm a sort of silent partner now. He and Nat have sorted out how to put the whole thing into the pre-nuptial agreement they're entering into, because it's her money, and the shares will go along the Coggins family line. Their decision. You liked her, didn't you? You two talked all through dinner the other night in London. Heck of a woman – highly talented, and entrepreneurial.'

Christine nodded. 'She was such a big help with the Chen Fang thing. Two seconds it took her to identify his work, from just a snap on my phone – which is amazing in itself. Then she couldn't do enough to help. And it's clear that she and Bill are potty about each other. It's sad, in a way, that they didn't meet twenty years ago, isn't it? Then they could have had so much more time with each other. Bittersweet, and all that.'

Alexander nodded, stuffed a hand into one of his pockets, and stood there, suddenly silent. Christine wondered what was wrong.

He said, 'It's been quite a year, hasn't it? Since we met.' Christine nodded her agreement. 'And I know a year's not a long time in the scheme of things…but I think it's long enough to know…look, I'm devoted to you, Christine. I don't believe there's anyone else out there for me. So what would you think—'

Christine interrupted, 'I agree that a year's a short amount of time, in the scheme of things, Alexander, and you're right that it's been one heck of a year. But can we see how we do over the next little while before we go doing anything we might…regret? I'm…I'm learning to put my trust in someone, for the first time ever, really. Seeing Bill and Nat was…well, it was a revelation. They're both so much older than me, have so much more experience of life than me – yet there they are, just throwing their lives together because they don't want to miss a moment of the time they can possibly share as a couple. Me? I'm not sure I know myself well enough to make life-long decisions yet. Does that make sense to you?'

Alexander stopped fiddling with whatever was in his pocket, cupped Christine's face in both his hands and said, 'Luckily for you, I'm a patient man.'

'And a generous one…the happy couple are going to love that honeymoon in Barbados you gave them as an early wedding gift.'

'It was you telling me about the Timbers going there that inspired me – a great place for a November honeymoon, don't you think?'

Christine smiled. 'As I said, I'm sure Bill and Nat will love it. By the way, any more news from the Costa del Sol? More fireworks at the non-marital home in Marbella, courtesy of Danielle "Right"?'

Alexander chuckled wryly. 'It seems Ronnie thought he could turn his back on his responsibilities in London to revel in a life of luxury with Danielle in Spain, but I have absolutely no doubt that woman's about to make his life hell. It looks as though almost everything's in her name – and she genuinely knew nothing about the five kids. To say she's on the warpath would be understating it.'

'Women can be…hmm…predictably unpredictable?'

'You're telling me.'

Gertie and Rosie all but attacked Annie and Tudor when they realized there was a chance they might get some bits of cheesy baked potato to nibble on. Once Tudor was free of his bouncing pup, he asked, 'Did you have a good couple of days with your parents in London?'

Annie smiled. 'I did. I needed it. Swansea was…well, I'm finding it difficult to come to terms with the emotions I'm feeling because of it, truth be told, Tude, and I needed to talk to Eustelle. She's my mum, she knows me better than anyone. Even better than Carol does.'

Tudor petted Rosie and Gertie as he turned to face Annie. 'You've not been your usual self since you've come back from Swansea, that's for sure, but I didn't think it was my place to keep asking if you were alright. I mean, that alone can drive a person nuts, can't it? So…is there anything I can do to help? Or is it your friends – you know, Carol and that lot – you really need? I don't know what to say or do for the best. Sorry.'

Annie leaned over and kissed Tudor on the cheek. 'You're doing it, Tude. You're being you, and that's just what I need. And an especially big thank you for not saying, "There, there, it'll be alright", because I know it might never be. I've got the contact details of a counsellor in Builth Wells I'm going to go and see.'

Tudor grabbed Annie's hand, and said, 'Good decision.'

Annie took a deep breath and said, 'Thanks. It's his eyes, Tudor. I can't stop seeing them. I…I wasn't ready for it…I didn't scream or nothing, and I did everything I needed to – I even touched him. But I can't help wondering if I could have done more – if I could have said something the night before, when I met Jeanette, that might have made her and her accomplice have second thoughts. That poor man could be alive now, and in some sort of recovery program to help get him off those terrible tablets she was feeding him. Oh Tude, I can't help feeling that I let him down…and his eyes know that, when he stares at me. I need to find out how to deal with it, or live with it – and that means I need professional help. My friends will support me, I know – and I know you will too. Though I don't know yet what sort of support I'll need.'

Tudor kissed Annie tenderly. 'A truly strong woman – which is what you are – knows when to accept help, of the right sort. Another reason why I love you, Annie Parker.'

Annie said, 'You mean *love*, love, don't you?'

'I do.'

Henry turned to his wife, whose head was buried in her pillow. 'What a day! We've managed to salvage the family's reputation, which is so wonderful, and I thought the evening went off very well. I didn't realize Clemmie knew the TV chap, that came as a bit of a surprise: she said they'd rather hit it off, once upon a time, at some sort of event in London. Then she clammed up, which is not untypical. For my sister. Not a bad day, all in all. Wouldn't you agree?'

'I would, Henry. Now let's get some sleep, I'm tired.'

Henry sat up. 'You're feeling quite well? Everything's...alright? You know.'

'Everything's fine. I'm fine. The baby's fine. It's just been a long day.'

Henry lay down again. 'Good. Good. But don't feel you have to join me for that meeting in the morning. That Vince chap Clemmie invited along for the evening seems like a bit of an odd type, but he's promised to show me some of his work in the morning, so maybe he will be the one to capture me in oils, after all. Might even get it done before the baby arrives.'

'Capture you in oils? Oh, Henry, the essence of you is absolutely uncapturable – if that's a word. But maybe he'll be the one who can get close. I've seen some of his stuff online, and it's good. I think you'll like it. But the decision will be yours, of course.'

'Well, if you like his work, then maybe I shall too.'

'Maybe, Henry. Now, goodnight. Sleep well, knowing we've saved the reputation of our family, and that your mother managed to escape being branded a heretic by the local clergy, in public. A good day, indeed.'

'Indeed.'

ACKNOWLEDGEMENTS

My thanks to my mum, sister, and husband, for their unwavering support, which allows me to continue with my writing. My thanks to Anna Harrisson, my editor, and Sue Vincent, my proofer; we've all tried to make this the best possible version of this story. My thanks, too, to every blogger, reviewer, librarian, bookseller, and social media user who might have helped – in any way – to allow this book to find its way into your hands. Finally, thank *you* for choosing to spend time with the women of the WISE Enquiries Agency.

ABOUT THE AUTHOR

CATHY ACE was born and raised in Swansea, Wales, and migrated to British Columbia, Canada aged forty. She is the author of The Cait Morgan Mysteries, The WISE Enquiries Agency Mysteries, the standalone novel of psychological suspense, The Wrong Boy, and collections of short stories and novellas. As well as being passionate about writing crime fiction, she's also a keen gardener.

You can find out more about Cathy and her work at her website: www.cathyace.com

Made in the USA
Las Vegas, NV
23 August 2022

53900676R00144